A Political Pilgrim in Europe

by

Mrs. Philip Snowden

A Political Pilgrim in Europe
by Mrs. Philip Snowden

ISBN: 978-93-67140-19-2

Published by

DOUBLE 9 BOOKS

2/13-B, Ansari Road
Daryaganj, New Delhi – 110002
info@double9books.com
www.double9books.com
Tel. 011-40042856

ABOUT THE AUTHOR

Mrs. Philip Snowden, was a British author and political activist known for her advocacy of social reform and women's rights. Throughout her life, Mrs. Snowden was deeply involved in various social causes and political movements, particularly those related to workers' rights and women's suffrage. Her writing often reflected her commitment to these issues, and she used her platform to address the social inequalities of her time.

Her travelogue, "A Political Pilgrim in Europe," showcases her observations and insights on the political climate in Europe, emphasizing the struggles of ordinary people and the need for political change. Mrs. Snowden's work remains significant for its commentary on social justice and the role of women in the political landscape. Her legacy lives on as a symbol of the intertwined relationship between literature and activism, reminding us of the power of words to challenge societal norms and inspire progress.

CONTENTS

INTRODUCTION

In these days everybody is writing his memories. Disappointed politicians decline to be forgotten. Successful and unsuccessful generals refuse to be neglected. People of all sorts and conditions insist on being heard. The most intimate affairs of a life are laid bare in order to arrest public attention. Intolerable to most is the fear that the world will go past him. Nobody will willingly let himself die. This is the conclusion to which one is driven by the publication during the last two years of a vast mass of autobiography.

I am writing my own memoirs—two years of them. It never would have occurred to me unaided that they could be of the slightest interest to anybody. Friends have listened to my stories with interest, and public meetings on several occasions have, by their silence and attention during the telling, shown a certain pleasure in their recital; but only the insistence of a valued few has induced me to put some of them into a book.

These are not the most interesting experiences of my life. The four years of the war could reveal much more, and better, if it were possible to write about those times. I doubt if I could—fully. The big experiences of life are seldom even spoken about, much less put down in black and white. Things happened during the war which are as sacred as the birth of a child or the death of a lover.

The twelve years of agitation for woman suffrage, during which time I addressed more than two hundred public meetings a year in as many different towns, were packed full of incident, grave and gay, which a little quiet thought might dig out of the recesses of the mind. They were gallant days, full of fine friendships.

But these stories of my wanderings in Europe since the Armistice, with no other purpose in view than to do what one person might do, or at least attempt, to restore good feeling between the nations and the normal course of life as quickly as possible, will interest chiefly those who understood, and those honest folk who wondered at, the position which a few of us adopted during the war.

Those who have been brought up to believe, as I was, that war is alien to the spirit and teaching of Christianity, will scarcely blame me for taking that teaching literally. I believed with all the intensity of conviction that evil could not be wholly destroyed by evil. The application of this belief to war was clear: Militarism could not be destroyed by militarism even though the princes of this world declared that it could.

I had read enough history to prove to myself the mad folly of wars. All of which never clouded my apprehension of the fact that war may be an evil and yet, by reason of vicious policies and pledges over a number of years, become the lesser evil of two wrongs in the eyes of many wise and good men and women. To choose between the evil and the good is simple. To decide which of two evil things is the lesser evil is anything but simple. I believed myself to be intensely right. This never meant that the other person was necessarily wrong. I never tried to influence by so much as a hair's breadth the judgment of the young man called upon to fight. What he did was his business, not mine. If pure-motived, he was entirely honourable whether he chose prison or the front.

I believed from the first hour that the overwhelming majority of those who enlisted for the war and of those who supported the war did so from the best of motives, and from the same idealism which made it impossible for me to believe in its good issue. It was all a matter of method. The young men went to fight for the thing which I believed could not come by fighting. But as a woman, who could not be called upon to go into the trenches, it was peculiarly my business to seek to end the war as soon as possible for the sake of the gallant lads who had no choice consistent with their sense of duty.

During the last year of the war, after Trotsky had proclaimed the terms of a just peace at Brest-Litovsk, after the German Reichstag had embodied the same terms in a resolution passed by an overwhelming majority of its members, after President Wilson in his wonderful speeches and Mr. Lloyd George in his masterly phrases had given the world to understand that these objects were theirs also—self-determination and the rights of small nations, universal disarmament, and the League of Nations for the preservation of peace—I toured the country from Land's End to John o' Groats making speeches in favour of a just and lasting peace by negotiation. A moderate estimate places the number of people I spoke to on this topic at not less than 150,000.

I have re-read those speeches, widely reported in the local Press. I can find no word that I would alter, no principle which I would retract, no position stated from which I would withdraw.

In them I gave my reasons for fearing the effect upon Europe and the world of the policy of the knock-out blow. Every one of those prophecies has come true. They are becoming more dismally true every day.

I made it clear that a negotiated peace might not be successful. It might be proved that the peace honourable to all concerned, which was to justify to the immortal spirits of our dead the sacrifice they had made, and make their dreams come true, was not possible by conference. Very well. The loss of young life was so appalling that it ought to be attempted.

I gave the utmost credit for sincerity and honesty to those who differed from me in their views. I paid my full debt of sincere praise to those who fought and died for the right.

No; there is nothing in those speeches to be regretted. And I do not regret them.

I am still profoundly convinced that the war went on two years too long, and two years more than were necessary. Time will prove me right or wrong. I am content to wait.

But I cannot wait, and no patriot in this country can afford to wait, for the *Peace* to come right. He must begin to make it come right. The imperialists of Europe are poisoning the world. Into the pit which they are digging for one another they are destined to fall themselves, dragging the innocent with them. Russia, Germany, France, England, America—all will go the same way to ruin unless the great awakening comes soon, and men learn that the bonds which unite nations are indissoluble, or are cut by them at their own peril.

It is needful that all should become, if not pilgrims, priests and prophets of peace and good will. It is vital to do so. Communism cannot save mankind if it be imbued, as so far it has been, with the old bad spirit of hate. Capitalism is failing before our eyes. Militarism has failed.

A new conception must be born, or an old vision reborn in the minds and hearts of men. The everlastingness of Love! The indestructibility of Faith! The eternity of Hope!

> "Many waters cannot quench Love,
> Neither can the floods drown it;
> Who shall slay or snare the white dove
> Faith, whose very dreams crown it?
> Gird it round with Grace and Peace
> Deep, warm and pure and soft as sweet sleep.
> Many waters cannot quench Love,
> Neither can the floods drown it."

CHAPTER I
THE SECOND INTERNATIONAL,
JANUARY, 1919

"How infinitely little is the best that we can do, and how infinitely important it is that we should do it!"

To begin a new book with an old quotation is bad; but it must be forgiven because it expresses in a phrase the sentiment upon which the whole of my public life has been built, and it explains in a sentence the object and purpose of those wanderings in many lands of my colleagues and myself about which I have engaged to write.

Nothing less than a clear understanding on the part of the critical observer that they held very strongly the belief, old-fashioned it may be, that "out of the mouths of babes and sucklings" is strength ordained, can save from the charge of madness or of folly the plunge of twelve members of the British Labour Movement, with a bright hope in their hearts, into the maelstrom of Europe and of European politics in January of 1919.

Mr. Arthur Henderson, M.P., Secretary of the National Labour Party, had made strenuous efforts during the later days of the war, and after his return from Russia, to open a door to international understanding and possible reconciliation by trying to obtain from the British Government permission for representatives of British Labour to attend an international Socialist conference at Stockholm, but without success. Time alone will prove the folly of the Government's refusal. It is sufficient here to remind the reader that a deep and widespread desire for some attempt at an honourable peace by understanding had existed in Great Britain for nearly two years before the end of the war came. A working women's organization, the Women's Peace Crusade, collected in a few weeks nearly 60,000 signatures to a petition for a negotiated peace; and at 133 public meetings addressed in less than a year by myself, with an average attendance of 1,000 persons, was carried a resolution on similar lines, with fewer than thirty dissentients in all. These were small things in themselves, but symptomatic.

So great was the anguish and concern at the time of the Stockholm proposal that a great Conservative London newspaper headed one of its daily leaders with the words: "Hands off the Socialists!"

Whatever may have been the reason for the Government's refusal to allow British workmen to meet the workmen of other lands at Stockholm, whether on account of French pressure, which was said, or through fear of impairing the *moral* of the soldiers, which was inferred, they withdrew their opposition after the Armistice, and in January of 1919 we left for Berne and the Second International.

I have the most vivid recollection of that first journey to Europe after the war, probably because it *was* the first. I think that every delegate felt the same, a revival of faith, a renewal of hope, a quickening of life. For months before the sudden end of the war, acute sadness and cruel pessimism had possessed us all. Ten, twenty, thirty years, the best that life held, had been devoted by one or the other to the building of a better humanity, and this destruction of everything we had worked for, this swift rattling back to the beginning of things, and to worse than the beginning in some ways, was at times too tragic to be borne. But before the opening of new opportunities pessimism promised to fly and hope to return and stay.

"Isn't it glorious!" shouted Margaret Bondfield to her colleagues as we shot swiftly into Folkestone station.

"Isn't what glorious?" I asked, thinking she meant our first view of the sea, stretching black and restless beyond the veil of fine rain which dimmed the windows of the railway carriage.

"Why, that we can travel once more, and that we are flying as fast as we can to see the comrades from whom we have been separated so long." And she waved her passport gaily. "I wonder if Clara Zetkin will be at the conference; and Balabanova? It is ages since I saw Angelica."

Margaret's bright face beamed with happiness, and her brown eyes shone like stars as she gathered up her wraps and bags for transport to the boat. She was like a bird set free from the cruel cage that had held her for four tormenting years. She suggested a warm little bird in her looks and manners. Small and brown, with a rich russet colouring of the cheeks, and quick in her movements, there is nothing in the world she resembles so much as the robin with the red breast.

She was one of the delegates representing the Parliamentary Committee of the Trade Union Congress. I was a representative of the political side of the Movement. Miss Sophie Sanger was invited to accompany us as interpreter, and was possibly the most practically useful woman of the party. She speaks four languages with equal fluency. What Miss Sanger does not know about the world's laws regulating labour and labour conditions, especially those affecting women, is said not to be worth knowing; which probably accounts for the fact that she now enjoys an appointment of considerable value and importance in the League of Nations Labour Department.

Mr. Henderson did not travel with us. He had gone ahead several days previously to help M. Huysmans with the final arrangements for the Conference. There had been some slight hitch with the Swiss Government, which at that time was tormented with the fear that we were a body of Bolsheviks out to subvert the loyalty of Swiss citizens. It was necessary to reassure President Ador and his associates on this point. Mr. Henderson was the man to do it. Nobody could look at him, the simple strength and solid respectability of him, and think *him* a Bolshevik! In spite of assurances given by him, every delegate was obliged to sign a statement repudiating the Bolsheviks and all their works before he was permitted to enter Switzerland!

Mr. J. H. Thomas was also one of the delegates; but whether he was attending a special conference with Mr. Barnes at the Hôtel Majestic in Paris, or whether he was busy settling a strike I cannot remember—strikes were epidemic at this time. He came to Berne later in the week.

The short passage across the Channel was quiet and uneventful. We sat in our deck-chairs well covered with warm wraps. A grey mist soon hid the land from our view. A slight rain moistened our hair and faces. We could not read for excitement and the blowing of the wind. We sat watching our fellow-passengers' efforts to control their nerves and the busy sailors engaged upon their various tasks.

I do not know why the sentimental confession should be made here, but ever since I was a child chatting to the fishermen on the beach at Redcar I have felt a peculiar liking for the men of the sea. Perhaps it is an inheritance from a seafaring ancestry. It should be in the blood of every Briton. There is something in the brave, blue eyes of the sailor, his jolly frankness, his courage, his simplicity which goes straight to the heart of one. His unending contact with Nature in all her moods has stamped itself upon his being as plainly and unmistakably as the heated atmosphere of the weaving-shed or the smutty environment of the mine have set their mark upon the workers in these places; but in a pleasanter, more wholesome fashion.

In an hour or so we sighted Boulogne. It was raining hard, and the little French town looked very dreary and very dirty. French, British, and Belgian troops in considerable numbers mingled confusingly, the bearded *poilu* laughingly replying in cockney slang to Tommy's amusing French. Incredible quantities of war material of all sorts met the eye. The railway track which we crossed from boat to train was a swamp. We had waited till our backs were almost broken with fatigue for the examination of our passports in the smoke-room of the steamer. At that time the element of common sense had not entered in the faintest degree into the organization of this business. Several hundreds of people, packed like sardines in a tin, waited their turn in the crowded ship's corridor, and as the war had spoilt everybody's temper and ruined most people's manners, elbows were freely used to jostle out of their rightful places in the queue the timid and the polite.

A similar rushing, pushing, squeezing, tearing of clothes, wounding of ankles with the sharp edges of boxes, which the owners were too mean to give to the porter or too faithless to trust to him, occurred in the *douane*. At this time every box was opened and its contents carefully examined. The fatigue was immense. Women fainted and children screamed. Men swore loudly, unashamed. Unperturbed, the blue-uniformed officials pursued their avocation.

Once again an examination of passports, this time by French officials, and again a swaying mass of people in front of the narrow, wooden door, and a hideous scrimmage to enter every time the little French soldier opened it to admit the two or three persons who were permitted to go through at once!

The delegates lost one another in the general confusion. We made a bee-line for the refreshment room as soon as we got through our business, hats awry, hair blown, cheeks flushed with hot air and suppressed fury. Some had lost their umbrellas in the scramble. One missed a good overcoat which he afterwards found. A moderate recovery of spirits and temper followed the appearance on the scene of hot coffee and flaky rolls, the good-natured waitresses smiling a coquettish welcome as we took our seats at the little square tables. Another wave of feeling threatened to overwhelm us when the bill was presented, but this we conquered, and paid up like lords! After all, there were a *few* food profiteers in England, and it was a little early to complain!

Our indefatigable secretary and comrade, Jim Middleton, had engaged seats for us in the Paris train which left Boulogne two hours after our landing. "Jim," as he is affectionately and familiarly called by his many friends in the Movement, is one of the rarest souls in the British Labour Party. When the history of the Party comes to be written his name will figure in it very importantly if there is any sense of right and proportion in the historian. What the Labour Party owes already to his selfless and unremitting devotion to the work of its organization can never adequately be estimated or expressed. His is the sort of work which is done quietly, out of the public gaze, with no newspaper advertisement and no clamour of praiseful tongues. But it is there. It is done well and without stint. And it is of the very stuff and fabric of the great machine which Labour is slowly but steadily building for its uses in the struggle for its economic and political emancipation.

Jim is slim and fair as a Norseman. His kind eyes are forget-me-not blue. His blond hair has turned to grey, but he is young. His patience and good nature are inexhaustible. He is never too tired to oblige a friend, and he can always find an excuse for an enemy. He is as good as gold and as true as steel.

So are the other young men on the headquarters staff. There is "little Gillies" as he is everywhere called, whose clear brain and Scottish capacity for hard work have contributed big things to the international side of Labour's work; and I know no department of future Labour activity more important than the ideas and schemes the Party may develop for the conduct of international relations. By these, even more than by its domestic policy, will Labour government be judged and justified by public opinion.

There is Will Henderson, already a Parliamentary candidate, who will surely follow in his father's footsteps; Herbert Tracey, excellent writer, full of a fine idealism as well as a practical common sense, who gave rich gifts to the cause until a larger opportunity called him temporarily abroad; Captain Hall, as straight as a die, the Party's financial secretary; Fred Bramley, the brilliant young under-secretary of the Parliamentary Committee (Trades Congress); E. P. Wake, the very able chief organizer of the Party—but it is impossible to mention them all and the conscientious women who assist them. They are young men of whom any Party is entitled to be proud.

The great strength of the Labour Party lies in the amount of devoted, unpaid work which it is able to command from its members. "But the men you have mentioned are paid good salaries. Why so much praise of men who only do what they are paid to do?" says the carping critic. The query is a common one, and pitifully mean. And it embodies a stupid lie. A few hundred pounds a year is no payment for the work done for the Labour Movement by these admirable servants of the Party from Mr. Arthur Henderson downwards. There are things which cannot be paid for in cash.

We arrived in Paris at seven in the evening. There we stayed several days. We wanted, if possible, a preliminary conversation with certain of the French delegates. We hoped to meet the Belgians. Some of us had designs on the Hôtel Crillon and a possible interview with Colonel House. The Crillon was the headquarters of the American section of the Peace Delegation.

Paris, alas! was the ill-chosen seat of the Allies for the Peace Conference. The fate of mankind might have been vastly different had some other centre of discussion been selected.

Paris was likewise a very crowded and uncomfortable city at the time of our visit. Every hotel was full. The enormous staffs of the various national Peace Delegations were a large element in the overcrowding— they, their friends and their visitors. Suppliants to the Conference or to individual members of the Supreme Council were so numerous that hotel accommodation for the ordinary traveller about his simple business scarcely existed; but then the ordinary traveller was not encouraged to travel. A deliberate policy of embarrassment and inconvenience was adopted to persuade him to stay at home; and if he suffered for his wilfulness he had nobody but himself to blame. With a new world in the making, what business abroad had any ordinary person which mattered a tinker's curse? Thus the official view of affairs.

So that when Miss Bondfield, Miss Sanger, and myself found ourselves without beds, and with no quarters suitable for women to go to, nobody in Paris was surprised. A generous fellow-countryman, hearing of our plight, placed at our disposal his own large and elegant bedroom. There were two beds and a comfortable sofa in it. One of us occupied the sofa for two nights, when we were able to take up our quarters in the Hôtel Moderne overlooking the Place de la Revolution.

Paris immediately after the Armistice was a woeful spectacle of neglect and dirt. It was not much better six months ago. In those early days it was like a handsome slut in need of a bath; which in view of its sufferings was not surprising. The paint on the woodwork of houses and shops was almost all peeled away. Shutters hung awry on their broken hinges. Roads were unspeakably filthy, and full of dangerous holes and swampy gutters. The parks and gardens looked ragged and tattered. The Bois de Boulogne and the Champs Elysées were marred with the shreds and patches of war equipment. Dismal weather made everything look a hundred times worse than it really was. We were wise enough not to come to a hasty judgment about Paris. After all, we had a vast gay literature to contradict the sad story written *on* Paris when first we saw it!

The living in the hotels and restaurants was riotous and expensive. In the homes of Paris it was another story, we were told. Foods were strictly rationed, but of some kinds it was difficult to get even the meagre portion allowed. The strain was heavy upon the city housewife of the humbler classes. Prices were ruinously high. Wages scarcely kept pace with them.

Strikes were frequent and menacing, apt to hold up one or another of the public services at any time, as in England.

But in the public cafés, the dance-halls, and the hotels, nothing dimmed the joyousness of the Parisians, set free at last from the haunting fear of the German invasion. Day and night, and night after night, a lively, exuberant, passionate crowd in each of these public places abandoned itself to an ecstasy of song and dance and play, in utter and unrestrained intoxication.

M. Jean Longuet, the grandson of Karl Marx, and at that time a Deputy in the French Chamber, invited Mr. Macdonald and myself to lunch with him at a little Italian café near his business quarters. We called for him at the office of his newspaper, *Le Populaire*. On our way all together he took us past the restaurant where Jaurès was shot. He pointed to the window at which Jaurès was sitting at the time of his murder. If I understood him rightly Longuet was present when the awful thing occurred; particularly awful in view of the certainty that the issue of affairs for France might have been infinitely happier, and for Europe infinitely less sorrowful, if this great man had lived during the war.

One of the great scandals of history will be the acquittal of the murderer of Jaurès. He was one of the giant political characters of France. The squalid politicians who govern the affairs of Europe at the present time could never have been where they are if there had not been removed either by force or fraud, or by the ordinary process of nature, death, so many of the great men entitled by intellect or character, sometimes both, to occupy the seats of power. Jaurès was murdered by a common assassin, and official France has seemed to rejoice. But I recall the impressive fact that the most arresting picture in the Chamber of Deputies is the immense canvas of Jaurès addressing the chamber from the tribune. They may have hated him, but they insist on his being remembered!

Jean Longuet was born in London, and speaks excellent English. He is tall and dark, with curly hair and brown eyes. He has a rich voice, and is a very eloquent speaker, full of passion when moved. Friends of his assure me that I may trust his sense of humour, and, in order to present a quick picture of the physical man to an English reader, I may say that when Longuet makes a public oration and warms to his subject he assumes an attitude and appearance which irresistibly remind one of a genius of another sort, Charlie Chaplin. Given Charlie's creased trousers and big feet, the picture would be complete!

But Longuet is no comic figure in international politics. He is a sincere idealist and a most engaging personality. There are those who would regard this statement as less of a compliment than a comparison with the artist whose amazing gift makes honest fun for millions. This, they say, is much better, and much safer for mankind, than to be the advocate of ideals too lofty for statesmen and people to achieve because too great for them to comprehend; ideals so high that they mean crucifixion for the few who live up to them, and greater degradation for the many who deliberately elect to live below the best they have heard and seen.

The tiny Italian café I sought again on the return trip, but never found it. One delicious dish of macaroni, prepared as only the Italians know how to prepare it, was more pleasing to the taste than all the accumulated delicacies of the best Parisian *table d'hôte*; for those rich hotel meals were impossible to eat without a thought of the millions who were reputed dead or dying, in fields and ditches, and on roadsides, in their houses, in hospitals, in prison camps, for the lack of a crust of bread or a glass of pure water. Our friend and host of the café we learnt afterwards was a Socialist, and a member of the Party; a fact we had rather inferred from the whispered asides with Longuet during the smoking of cigarettes and the drinking of the wine and coffee.

Our chief business in Paris was to try to persuade the Belgian Socialists to come with us to Berne. They were sitting in conference at Brussels at the time. They had there decided not to attend the Berne Conference, and had sent delegates to Paris to explain the reason why. We met them at the headquarters of the French Socialist Party. All our pleading with them was of no avail. Their conference had so decided, and though they would personally have liked to go, if only for the fellowship of the thing, Party discipline must be maintained. Camille Huysmans would be there as secretary of the International, but they could not go.

Their great difficulty was their unwillingness to meet the German Majority Socialists, who had supported the war and who had not protested against the invasion of Belgium. How could they take part with such men in the building anew of the International? What sort of internationalists had these men proved themselves to be? The German Majority must first express its contrition. Then would be the time to forgive. They could never forget.

"Why do you not come to Berne and say all this to the Germans themselves?" I asked in my speech. "Come and say all you feel about this, where not only the German Majority but the whole world can hear you say it." I reminded them of the brave and splendid gesture of the Belgian women who came to the International Conference of Women at the Hague while the war was still raging, and who, seated on the right of Miss Jane Addams, with the German women on the left, resolved with them and with the women of all nations represented there to do all in their power to make wars impossible in the future.

"Surely," I said, "so far as the plain citizens of every country are concerned, we are all in the same boat. We are all far more the victims of circumstance than its architects. We have all been deceived, cheated, lied to. In the clash of various loyalties mistakes are made and cruel things are done and acquiesced in. But is there one of you who, in his heart of hearts, blames any man for taking the part of his country in an international quarrel? Is anyone amongst us quite sure that in the same circumstances we would act otherwise? I refuse to believe that any German Socialist rejoiced over the invasion of Belgium. In any case, is it not better to get face to face and talk it all out, where no false newspaper can come between, and no misunderstanding blind and paralyse, instead of brooding alone over wrongs for which the wrongdoers may be only too ready to atone? Come!"

We left without them. The first meeting of the Second International included no official Belgians. But I left the meeting in Paris with the feeling that the time of complete reunion would come very soon. Eighteen months later in Geneva the Belgians were present, and no more international note was struck in that gathering than the speech of Emile Vandervelde, the Belgian Minister of Justice.

We were obliged to travel from Paris to Berne in two parties, and even then were unable to enjoy sleeping compartments. The trains were packed in every available corner, and many of the passengers were obliged to spend the night in the corridor. There had been an immensity of passport business in Paris, but the burden of all this had been borne by the secretary. He could not save us from the individual examination at the Gare de Lyon, nor the ever-recurring nuisance at intervals along the whole route.

Belgarde is the French frontier town, and here we were hauled out of the train for further torture by passport and Customs officers. It was the outrageous imperturbability of these fellows that made me sick. They seemed devoid of all human feeling. At Belgarde we were roughly questioned about our money. Had we any gold? Had we more than £40 in any kind of currency? More than this sum was not allowed to be taken across the frontier. Later no silver was permitted to be transported. My bags were diligently searched by a woman official, but not one cigarette did she find for her pains, nor wine, nor spirits, nor jewels, nor perfumes, nor any one of the half a hundred things they appeared to be on the prowl to discover.

These performances were repeated at Geneva in the Swiss interests; and half a dozen times between Belgarde and Geneva Swiss police examined our unfortunate passports, which were rapidly assuming a limp and dog'seared appearance with so much handling. I never inquired, but I imagine these people were the officials of the various cantons through which the train passed. Any other theory would establish the Swiss Government as insane with fear and suspicion. But finally, through sheer weariness of flesh and spirit, I ceased to question the doings of these minions of the law, but quietly submitted to any number of exasperating formalities.

The Paris train arrived in Geneva at 9 in the morning. The connexion for Berne left at 4.10 in the afternoon. We had ample time to see this famous old city, beautifully placed at one end of the great crescent lake of the same name. Mr. Macdonald, like a true and faithful Scot, left us to visit John Knox's church. Some lingered over the ample breakfast in the comfortable café. The fascinating lake drew the attention of the rest. It was along the side of this lake that my friend—well, I will not disclose his name—was walking, gaily swinging his stout English walking-stick. He knew two words of French, *oui* and *merci*. Humming a gay tune and twirling that stick, he struck a man in the face. "Ah, merci!" he cried, meaning "I beg your pardon." The man stared in blank astonishment, and then said in good, plain English: "I think it is I who ought to cry 'Mercy,' young man."

Snow lay hard and frozen upon the ground, and capped and covered the mountains in the distance. The vast masses of Mont Blanc were visible in the clear, crisp air. Delivered from the cramped and poisonous conditions of a filthy railway carriage, super-heated, we enjoyed blissfully the bright beauty and clean orderliness of this Puritan capital of French Switzerland. And in the evening, when the last rays of the sun had changed into a glowing pink the white of the Alpine snows, we entered upon the last stage of our long and tiresome journey, to begin our labour of reconciliation.

We were met at the Berne railway station by an odd assortment of European Socialists.

"Willkommen, kameraden," said a little man with a profusion of long sandy hair and an abundant beard. "Es macht uns Vergnügen die Englischen kameraden wieder zu sehen." (Welcome, comrades. It is a great pleasure to us to see the English comrades once more.)

I gazed fearfully at this amazing group of people, who looked for all the world like a committee of anarchists ripe for an expedition! They were, in fact, the gentlest of human beings and as pacific as Quakers! The man who welcomed us was Kurt Eisner, President of the Bavarian Republic, who was afterwards murdered in the streets of Munich, in part for the attitude he adopted in this Conference. But in his large-brimmed hat and conspirator's cloak nothing could have saved him from the suspicion of a raw Englishwoman, unused to the manner of dress and style of speech of so many Socialists in European lands. And those who met us were all alike.

"Comment allez vous, camarades," exclaimed a French-speaking delegate, and I found myself shaking hands with an even more terrifying apostle of the gospel of Karl Marx, whose brilliant red tie would have served for a railway signal!

I recall a conversation I had with M. Renaudel, at that time the editor of *L'Humanité*, when we travelled together in Georgia eighteen months later.

"Why do you English Socialists never use the word 'comrade' in speaking to each other? In France it is always 'comrade,' never 'monsieur,' except to the bourgeoisie."

"The word comrade is often used in England also," I replied. "I rarely use the word myself, and if you want to know why, my reason is very simple. It is a very beautiful word, but it has been frightfully misused and has lost a good deal of its value. I have heard it so often in the mouths of people who have no more comradely feeling for me than a nest of mosquitoes, that it is now no guarantee to me of real friendship. On the contrary, I am suspicious of those who use it most. It is like that even more beautiful word 'love,' which has been cheapened and vulgarized by its misuse until now it means exactly nothing on the lips of most. What value would you attach to the love of somebody who in the same breath expressed the same fervent devotion to a jam tart? 'Comrade' means nothing. It is a mere form of expression, a hackneyed formulary. I keep this word for those I know to be truly my friends."

I told Renaudel of an acquaintance of mine, a Trade Union leader who received a post card from an angry fellow unionist, with a skull and cross-bones at the head. "Dear *Comrade*," it began, "What do you mean by selling out like you did? You are getting something good for yourself out of this. You are a liar and a scoundrel! You ought to be shot! Just you wait till I catch you out by yourself! Look out for your dirty hide! You filthy dog! Yours *fraternally*, B. S."

It was nearly midnight, and we were worn out with the long journey and sleepless night. Soon we were fast asleep between the spotless white sheets of those exquisite beds, happy in the thought of the morrow's meeting and its possibilities.

CHAPTER II
THE SECOND INTERNATIONAL (*continued*)

The secretariat of the Conference had its headquarters at the Belle Vue Hotel. The Conference itself was held in the Volkshaus, the headquarters of the Socialists. This fine building in the heavy German style comprised within itself an hotel, a theatre, a restaurant, a lecture-hall, and any number of Trade Union committee rooms. The funds for its building were supplied by the members of the Party and the Municipality jointly. If this were the only building of its kind in Switzerland it would be remarkable; but I very much doubt if there are a dozen cities of any size in the whole of Central Europe which have not a similar Labour Temple. Some of these buildings are very fine indeed, and can lay claim to a certain architectural distinction. Their numbers put to shame the British Labour Movement, which has not a single building set apart for the social uses of all its members.

Similarly with their newspapers: The *Daily Herald* is the only daily newspaper in Great Britain which can claim to represent organized Labour in the slightest degree, and the *Daily Herald* is not the property of the Labour Party, which has no right to dictate its policy nor control in any way its activities. In Germany alone, before the war, there were more than sixty Socialist dailies.

The necessity of frequent meeting obliged all the British delegates to remove from the charming *pension*, to which some of their number had gone, to the Belle Vue Hotel. This public palace could tell strange tales if its walls could speak. Some day a writer will appear who will tell the true story of this modern Babel; but he will have to wait until this generation is dead and gone before he publishes it, or else commit suicide when it appears! It housed the most extraordinary medley of princes and peasants, dukes and dockers, ex-kings and Socialist presidents ever collected in one building since the Great War turned the world upside down! In the wake of these illustrious or dangerous personalities crept that indigenous growth of the centre of diplomatic life and political activity, the political agent or spy.

Unaccustomed to the society of this individual I never sought him. Unaware of his existence before the war I never recognized him. He may have spoken to me. It is possible he extracted enough information from me to fill several sheets of a report and earn his squalid wages; but the fear of him never obsessed me. It was painful to observe how suspicious everybody was of everybody else. Nobody dared to speak freely. You realized that your companion, whoever he might be, was making reservations and preparing an escape when he was talking to you. Nervousness showed itself in every gesture, fear in every glance.

To be an object of suspicion oneself is not pleasant. To have to be frightened of everybody else is disgusting. I refused to do it. I would avoid nobody. I would speak to everybody who wanted to speak to me on serious business. I wouldn't pay any attention to his nationality beyond the inquiry necessary for an intelligent appreciation of his conversation. So far as I was concerned there was nothing to hide. What I felt and thought about the political situation I was prepared to say from a public platform, and did so, not only in this Conference, but later in Zurich, at the Women's Conference held there in June. I had come to Switzerland on a mission of reconciliation, and it was obvious from the first hour that the personal touch and warm human sympathy were more needed and would be more warmly appreciated than any number of Conference resolutions.

A friend—one of those well-known friends possessed by everybody, who always hasten to tell one the unpleasant things—told me that I was in the reports of the spies of every Legation in the city. "Splendid!" I said. "It will give them something to think about, and will keep them all guessing."

I made four separate journeys from London to Berne between January and July of 1919. On various occasions during that period I heard a great deal about myself that I had never known before! I was a dangerous Bolshevik! I was a spy of Clemenceau's! I was a British agent! I was an active pro-German! I was an anti-German pretending to sympathize with Germany! I was aiding and abetting the royalists of the ex-enemy states! I was an anarchist in disguise! I was in the American Secret Service! I was a pro-Turk! I was a friend of Karolyi's! I was a secret Communist posing as a moderate! I was a pacifist!

Of all these stories only the last was true. And in these days, when I hear pacifists defend the methods of Bolshevism, I want to have a definition of *that* word before I desire to be classed under it.

Poor little spies! They have to earn their salaries, so this is the sort of thing they say. A chance phrase in their hearing, and you are promptly labelled. You take tea with a charming princess who speaks a little English, and wants to practise on you, and you are in some Royalist plot! You talk to a polished French diplomat with a Scottish ancestry, as I talked with

Lieutenant Gilles of the French Embassy, and you must be in the pay of the French! You entertain a sweet English lady who is the very lonely wife of a German attaché and you are a pro-German! You seek knowledge from some authoritative person on one of the thousand questions in which you are interested, not knowing that he is the agent of one Government, and the spy of another Government reports you his confederate!

During our Conference the Swiss police picked up in the streets of Berne a packet of papers in a language which they did not understand— English. Seeing the name of Mr. Arthur Henderson in the context they sent the papers to him. They purported to be a detailed report of one of our private meetings, a tissue of lies from beginning to end, with a pathetic note at the end asking for more money! Mr. Henderson was at first annoyed, as anyone would be who took such things seriously; but he preserved enough of the ironic sense to send the papers with his compliments to the address for which they were intended, the British Legation!

It took my breath away to learn that the staff of every Legation and Embassy in Berne contained scores, even hundreds, of men and women agents, at any rate, before the war when money was not so scarce. In any sphere of life other than those of politics and diplomacy such activities would wear an ugly name. By a general consensus of opinion in diplomatic circles such a system is necessary. So much the worse for a society which requires lying and trickery for its preservation. It is admitted that ninety-nine out of every hundred reports are entirely worthless, often misleading. It is for the hundredth valuable discovery that all this costly machinery is maintained. With the system goes an enormous amount of corruption. Bribes are freely given and taken by surprising people in the most unexpected places.

A young girl from Bohemia came to see me in the Belle Vue Hotel. I invited her to my room where we could talk quietly. Ostensibly she had come about child relief, in which she knew me to be actively interested. But her talk was all of the ex-Emperor Charles, whom she had seen; whose secretary, with the assistance of a British officer whose letter she showed me, had helped her to get into Switzerland. I was distinctly puzzled. What was her game? Was she soliciting British interest in unfortunate ex-royalty? Incredible! Was she trying to make me say something which would result in my being sent out of Switzerland? To this hour I have not the faintest idea. I never saw her again. She was young and very pretty, with brown eyes and fair hair, an English type. If she really were a spy she was an artist in her work, for when I spoke in the clear English which fifteen years of public speaking have developed into a habit, she held up a deprecating hand, answered in a whisper, and looked fearfully round.

"We are quite alone. What is troubling you?" I inquired. "Say anything you wish to say. Nobody will hear you. Nobody knows you are here."

"It is not so sure," she said anxiously. "In some of ze bedrooms is ze machine and ze speak is heard. Zey listen to us. *Il faut que nous parlons doucement.*"

The general conduct of Conferences in Europe differs very greatly from the method in England. Delegates from the four corners of the earth come to an International Conference, and owing to the exigencies of travel, it is quite impossible to assemble them all at exactly one time. They arrive in batches during the two or three days preceding the Conference. But it is equally impossible to waste these days waiting for the late-comers, so the method pursued is to have a preliminary discussion of the questions set down in the agenda. The general feeling of the delegates on a particular topic, the broad divisions of opinion among them are known beforehand in this way, and the form of the final resolutions on the subject made easier of design. The fresh arrivals who join the group take up the discussion where they find it.

When the Conference proper assembles the first thing done after the speech of the chairman and the announcements of the secretary is the division of the delegates into Commissions. Each important subject is delivered over to a Commission, whose duty it is to report in the form of a resolution when a unanimous decision has been reached. Each country represented in the Conference is entitled to be represented on each Commission. The Commissions adjourn each to a separate room, elect a chairman (at this time a neutral), and begin business. The full Conference begins its deliberations with the presentation of the first Commission report.

These Commissions are not committees, as might very well be supposed. They are the Conference in miniature. The speeches are as long and as fervid as if delivered to the full Conference. I was a member of the League of Nations Commission of the Second International, and well remember a speech of great eloquence upon the subject delivered by a Frenchman which lasted for an hour and a half! Then followed two translations, English and German. I never expected to reach the report stage during that week or the next! And there were only twelve members of this Commission.

Delegates may not rise and speak when they wish. It is not the man with the loudest voice or the most aggressive manner, nor the one who is lucky enough to catch the chairman's eye, who speaks. The would-be orators are taken strictly in their turn. Names are sent up to the chairman, who calls upon each in order, and all are expected to speak from the platform.

Disorderly interruptions are frequent, and sometimes quite terrifying. On this occasion the French and German Majoritaires raged at each other across the heads of the delegates. But then so did the French Majoritaires and their Minoritaires. These last were just as bitter and violent as the first two sections. Similarly with the German and Austrian Majorities and Minorities. When feeling ran high the hall became a veritable bear garden. The one astonishing thing to those of us who expected every minute an ink-bottle or a book to come hurtling across our heads at one or another of the combatants, was that these furious men never came to blows. Infuriate rage and cheerful good humour followed each other with the suddenness and regularity of sunshine and rain in an English April.

But it was all very tiresome to those of us who were more concerned with the future than the past. Just when we were about to settle down, as we thought, to something really constructive, up would jump Albert Thomas, bursting with rage and quivering like a jelly, shaking his long hair and roaring like a mad bull; or Renaudel shrieking in a high-pitched voice like the enraged tenor at Covent Garden when he sees his lady-love in the arms of the villain; provoking the plethoric Wels to an apoplectic fit of frenzy, and the angry Müller to an ironic reply shouted above the heads of the lesser partisans on either side, whose fearful and monotonous yells: "You are guilty! They are guilty! We are not guilty! We are right! You are wrong!" almost made the tops of our heads come off!

Then the English delegate Stuart Bunning stepped quietly up to the platform. He made no brilliant speech. There was no attempt at eloquence. He was just as tired of that as the rest of us. He spoke in an even, level voice, making a few quiet, common-sense observations about the object of our Conference and the need for getting to work. The effect was magical! The storms ceased raging. The Conference quietened down. From that moment the idiotic charges and counter-charges ceased to be made. It was one of the two noteworthy and outstanding events of the Conference.

But the British delegation was the most harmonious in the room. It was not that we had no differences of opinion. We had many differences; and some of them were so deep that several of the delegates preferred not to travel with the rest. But when we got to Berne we kept these differences for the privacy of our own committee room, and endeavoured to present a united front in the conference hall. Only once did something bellicose threaten to develop amongst the Britons. It was when two gallant miners, who had borne with marvellous patience the interminable speeches they couldn't understand, saw a jolly fight about to begin between two sections of the French. It was too much for them. They would be in at that; and, anyhow, they were sick and tired. Why not have some fun and set the whole Conference going again. "Come on, fellows!" said one of them, leaping to his feet, his ruddy face glowing with pleasure. "Come on, chaps! Let's have a b— —y row!"

A foreign conference is certainly no picnic. It means very hard work for a conscientious delegate. Both commissions and conference sit irregular and interminable hours. There is no stopping at 5 to resume at 10 the next morning as in England. The delegates go on until they finish or as long as they can keep their eyes open. At Berne we were sometimes debating at 2 in the morning. On the other hand unpunctuality is the besetting sin of the Continental. With him 10 o'clock means 11, 1 o'clock, 2 or even 3. To the British this is a maddening vice; but I fear familiarity with it resulted in our embracing it ourselves.

Our first meeting with the Germans took place in the Belle Vue Hotel three days before the Conference proper began. I had anticipated this meeting with curious and painful interest. I knew that some at least of the men we were to meet had opposed the war from the beginning, even voting against the war credits; but it is curious how the separation of two nations by war can affect the consciousness of the individual national. All such feeling of hesitation and reluctance on both sides vanished at the sight of one another, men and women bound by a common aim in indissoluble bonds.

The little group which we approached in the vestibule of the hotel included Herr Kautsky and his wife, and several Austrians I met here for the first time. The physical appearance of all was very touching. Kautsky who was at all times frail and delicate, is now an old man with a fringe of white hair round his smooth and well-developed head. His wife is a clever, dashing woman, full of energy, the antithesis of her less dominating spouse. Both showed in a marked manner the effects of terrible underfeeding. The eyes were red rimmed, and the skin dry and of a yellowish cast. Their faces lit up with pleasure as we greeted them. We asked about their journey, and found that for two days they had travelled in an ice-cold train, with broken windows and tattered upholstery, and with no opportunity of eating warm food. Such was the general condition of transport in the countries of Central Europe at this time. Naturally the strain of the journey had added to their appearance of suffering; but I never heard them complain about themselves. Their instant concern was for the sufferings of their children, the German children, innocent of the war, and dying like flies from diseases which were the result of under-nourishment. And we were only too painfully aware that the blockade of Germany and the embargoes against Austria were our share, the British share, in the responsibility for this unnecessary torture of little children. We felt shamed in the presence of men who had never wavered in their opposition to their Government's policy, that our Government should be using the very weapon most conspicuous in the defeat of Germany three months after it was decided to lay down arms!

Kautsky is the greatest living exponent of the philosophy of Karl Marx. He is at the moment the great philosophic antagonist of the Bolsheviks and supporter of Social Democracy in Europe. He is hated with a deadly hatred in every part of the world by the Communists, and is denounced as a "social traitor" by the slavish adherents of Zinoviev and Radek, the two most extreme Bolsheviks in Russia. A lifetime of self-sacrificing devotion to the cause of Socialism has not saved this distinguished writer and his able wife and collaborator from the unmerited scorn of the extremists. But the extremists in every land have always had more hatred for the colleagues from whom they differed in method than for the capitalist enemy, separated from themselves by oceans of difference in principle. On this the capitalist and his allies count to defer the day of their doom.

Herr Seitz, who was one of the group in the hotel, was then President of the new Austrian Republic. I am quite sure from his sad expression of face and the tone of his conversation that he had found more pain and anxiety than honour and glory in his new position. He is a tall and strikingly handsome man of perhaps fifty years of age. He spoke no English, but Mr. Charles Roden Buxton, our gifted English interpreter, translated his talk for us. Again it was of the children, this time of the Austrian children who, if one half of what he told us was true, were enduring things which were a disgrace not only to the conquering nations but to civilization itself.

I determined then and there to go to Austria to satisfy myself by the sight of my own eyes if such things could be true. Here was a matter engaging the honour of every Briton, for the reasons I have already given; and things must be bad, I felt at a later stage, when even the neutral Swiss took occasion to point out to some of us very earnestly the real loss of prestige the Allied cause was suffering from what appeared to be the wanton destruction by famine of the helpless and innocent children of the ex-enemy states. "Eight hundred thousand children in Germany have died of starvation during the war" was a statement made by one of the German delegates during the Conference, a statement which made for a moment even the most belligerent delegate speechless with pity. The man who made it became afterwards the Chancellor of Germany, and one of the unhappy men compelled by superior force to sign a treaty at Versailles which no sane man either in Germany or in England, having thought about it, believed for one moment that Germany could carry out.

The Socialist Governments of Europe—Austria, Bavaria, Germany, Russia—entered upon their responsibilities at a time very unfortunate for themselves. The terrible war had left everything in ruins. The difficulties of restoration were so appalling that the old governing classes had everywhere fled, not only from the anger of their peoples, but from the wellnigh insuperable difficulties of government. The people were everywhere hungry. They lacked clothing. They were without fuel. They were full of disease and had neither medicines nor disinfectants with which to deal with it. Transport had wholly or partially broken down. Money had woefully depreciated. Trade had entirely stopped as in Russia, or seriously diminished by reason of blockades and embargoes. Prices were incredibly high. There were the hard conditions of the Armistice to be fulfilled. In addition to all this, revolution and counter-revolution, Red rioters and White Guards, brewed special troubles for their unhappy rulers, and kept their countries in a constant state of terror and unrest. Into this indescribable mess and muddle were tossed the Socialists by a newly-born will of the entire people. Who else was there to take the responsibility, the old rulers having fled? And was it not possible that the Socialists, whose programme was magnificent, and who had not been tried, might restore them to the prosperity that had been destroyed by the rulers who *had* been tried and found wanting?

But it was precisely because they had not been tried that it was unfortunate for the Socialists. They had to make the biggest of experiments in the circumstances least favourable for them. They had to please their parties, which expected certain things of them, and satisfy their constituents who demanded certain others. They made mistakes. They were bound to make mistakes. No Government of any kind could have avoided making mistakes. I doubt if any alternative Government in any of these countries would have made fewer; but the mistakes made by the Socialists were those most likely to provoke the reaction which has already so disastrously set in, the mistake of putting the party programme before the general interest in the face of the conquerors ready to smite; and that of adopting the militarism of the Governments they had overthrown.

Less than any of the Socialist Governments of Europe had the Austrian Government offended, largely on account of the firmness and moderation of its leaders, of whom I shall have something to say later, and of the discipline of the party, which is perhaps the best organized and best-disciplined Socialist Party in Europe.

But a growing knowledge of all the circumstances of Europe made it increasingly clear why no Socialist Minister I have met in Europe looks happy; unless it is Lenin. And I am inclined to think that even Lenin's merry, red eyes must be frequently shadowed in these days, as he sees his great experiment gradually withering away in the atmosphere of realism created by hungry workmen and angry peasants.

The great test of a system, any system, the Communist system amongst others, is its power to produce healthy, happy men and women and keep them so. If it fails in that it is condemned in all.

The German Majority Socialists did not arrive in Berne until some time after their comrades of the Minority. They had supported their Government after a fashion, but not by any means in the uncritical manner of the British Labour Movement during the first two years of the war. And this in spite of the fact that the Labour Party held a meeting in Trafalgar Square on the Saturday preceding the declaration of war in which it had called for non-intervention! The quarrel between the nationals of Germany and France was, as I have said, of the greatest bitterness. The German Majoritaires kept strictly to themselves during the whole of the Conference, probably shrinking from the harsh judgment which they knew would surely be passed upon them by their comrades from the enemy countries. To my mind they showed great courage in coming to Berne; and the restraint and moderation of their ultimate actions made for a greater measure of unity than had been expected by the most sanguine.

This small group of men were the most pathetic in the Conference. The last time I saw Müller he was a big, broad-shouldered, stalwart man, six feet or more in height, and straight as a ramrod, with a fat, jolly face. Here he appeared stooping and shrunken, a shadow of his former self, his skin grey, and his lips bloodless. Wels looked a little better, for he is a dark man, and his complexion is naturally ruddy; but his manner was nervous and apprehensive, and his eyes were restless and unhappy. Mölkenbuhr, who, the year before the war, had attended a Labour Conference in England, a happy, jovial fellow, was old and feeble beyond recovery.

Edouard Bernstein, the best-known figure in England of the pre-war Socialist Movement in Germany, an opponent of his Government's war policy, was another ghost of himself. He shuffled about the Conference room in soft slippers, his hands shaking nervously, his short-sighted eyes peering out of his strongly Jewish face as if looking for something he had lost. But he was looking for the faces of old friends, and exhibited an almost childish delight whenever he discovered one, wringing the hand of his friend vigorously and beginning to chat volubly, unmindful of the speeches which were being delivered or the votes which were being taken.

"I have a son and daughter in England. They have been there during the war. I hope to see them in a few days," said the old man to me whisperingly, as he passed to where Mr. Macdonald was sitting. His amiable wife followed him about, making good his defects of memory. The step was very feeble, and the crisp black hair had grown grey. I knew when I heard the rumour that his colleagues would send Bernstein as Ambassador to England that it was but a rumour. He would never recover enough of vigour and health for that.

The able lawyer Haase, attached to the pacifist minority, made an excellent impression upon the British delegates. His manner was less deprecating than that of the others, and he had a merry twinkle in his blue eye that went straight to the heart. He is dead now. He was shot on his way from the Reichstag by an assassin and died after a few days' illness.

When the full Conference assembled on January 26 it was found that twenty-seven countries had sent delegates, including the principal antagonists in the Great War—Germany, France, Russia and Great Britain. The neutrals included Holland, Sweden, and Spain. The secretary was Camille Huysmans of Belgium, who, with M. Branting and Mr. Arthur Henderson, made an Executive Committee of three persons. A Council and a Committee of Action were formed from the Conference, which were to meet when important decisions had to be made for which it was impossible to call the full Conference. And so was created the simple machinery for the work of rebuilding the Workers' International.

Of the two dramatic figures who appeared at the International one I have already mentioned, the weird, arresting personality who met us at the railway station, who paid with his life for his simple and courageous speech, the Bavarian Prime Minister, Kurt Eisner. Of him I shall write at length on another occasion. Here I would paint at some length another picture on an even larger canvas.

We were somewhat listlessly pursuing our debates when suddenly there appeared on the platform a short square figure of a man with broad humped-up shoulders and a shock of fair wavy hair. He still wore his travelling coat. His short-sighted eyes peered through a pair of large spectacles. His nervous hands fidgeted with his coat. He began to speak, quietly and distinctly, with a slight pleasant drawl.

It was Friedrich Adler, "the man who killed Count Sturgh," who made this dramatic appearance towards the end of the Conference. We were told he was on his way some days before. Then we heard he had been detained on the Austrian frontier by the Swiss police, who refused to permit him to enter Switzerland on account of his political crime. Curious, that the men who applaud William Tell and teach their children with pride the story of the tyrant Gessler and the apple, objected to the Austrian version of their national story. Moreover, the Emperor Charles had pardoned Adler.

Knowing the dilatoriness of officials all hope of seeing him at the Conference in time to take part in the debates had fled.

At the sight and sound of him the delegates sprang to their feet electrified. "Adler! Adler!" they shouted. For several minutes they cheered without intermission. Wave after wave of genuinely passionate pleasure was expressed in shouted greetings and thunderous applause. It was remarkable; the most astonishing thing that happened at the Conference! To see the French and German antagonists, and the Majoritaires and Minoritaires of the various countries allied in a moment to render tribute to this one man was as delightful as it was puzzling to the simple soul whose quarrels are not so easily set aside.

But the explanation was really very simple. It was not what it looked like, a company of pacifists illogically applauding a murderer. It was the spontaneous tribute of his comrades of all lands to a man whose consistency to his ideals called for their devotion. Very few men in that gathering had remained true during the war to the central idea of the International. Henderson had been a member of the British War Cabinet; Branting had taken the side of the Allies; Müller had supported Germany; Thomas had been a French "patriot"—all, or almost all, had taken sides and had forgotten their International obligations and their peace ideals in the overwhelming disaster of the war. Adler had stood firm. From the first to the last hour he had never faltered in his allegiance. From the first he had denounced the war as a crime against the peoples. And he had carried his party with him. The Austrian Party was the only Socialist Party in Europe which had denounced the war and defied the war-makers from the beginning to the end. This was one of the reasons why the Austrian Government did not dare to assemble Parliament upon the declaration of war. For more than two years of the war the Constitution of Austria was in abeyance. The Socialists and Nationalists clamoured in vain for the rights of the people. Force ruled. Adler decided that only force could upset that rule. If the man who represented the autocratic system were killed, it would be a symbolic act that would be understood by the people. The head of the tyrannical Government dead, the system would follow. So this gentle dreamer and man of letters, who had never before had a revolver in his hand in his life, went into a restaurant and shot the Austrian Prime Minister dead in his chair!

His trial became famous. His speech of defence lasted for more than seven hours. It was full of devastating accusations against the Government of Count Sturgh. The speech has become one of the greatest political documents in existence, and is, as I am informed, one of the masterpieces of German prose. Reading it and knowing Adler, one comes to understand why this kind and gentle man came to kill; and one understands how it was that in spite of that every man in the International rose to applaud him.

He was sentenced to death, but the sentence was commuted to one of twenty years' imprisonment; and just before the Austrian Revolution he was pardoned by the young Emperor Charles. This treatment by the Austrian Government of Adler is in painful contrast to the British Government's treatment of Roger Casement.

There is a certain quality of poetic justice in the last chapter of this interesting story. A few months ago the ex-Emperor Charles made an attempt to recover the throne of Hungary. He left his place of asylum in Switzerland and appeared unexpectedly in Hungary. The inevitable happened. The armies of Czecho-Slovakia and Rumania were about to be set in motion. Hungary was menaced from all sides. The Entente expressed its official disapproval. The Hungarians threatened to revolt against the Government. Charles was obliged to leave the country. At a little railway station in Styria the royal train was held up. Eight hundred enraged workers threatened to capture the ex-emperor and his suite. Bloodshed was imminent. The man sent to appease the workers and save the unfortunate prince from the effects of his folly was Friedrich Adler. So, he paid the price of his pardon of three years before. So, the ex-monarch learnt by practical demonstration the value of generosity in government.

Let no thoughtless reader imagine that Dr. Adler, eminent scholar and scientist, the gentlest of men in private life, liked doing the thing he did. He hated it; but this man, Count Sturgh, stood for every tyranny. Adler removed him, and the long-delayed Austrian Parliament was called together immediately after.

Adler's work since he was set free has been to save his country from the Bolshevism menacing it from Hungary. The wild men of his party would probably have preferred the Adler of the smoking revolver. Once an extremist always an extremist is their creed. A noble inconsistency is not for them. Hate is the fundamental of their gospel. He was falsely charged with running away from his principles. But, in spite of everything, he maintained a moderate attitude, had the courage to be a coward in the estimation of the vulgar, and saved his suffering country from the tyranny of the Red, which is invariably followed by the tyranny of the White, both disastrous in the appalling circumstances of Austria's menaced existence.

Adler is the foremost figure in the enterprise which aims at bringing together the two Internationals on the basis of honourable compromise. A

Conference of what is universally spoken of as "the 2½ International" was recently held in Vienna. I admire the optimism of these people, but have little faith in the issue of their work. So far the compromise has the appearance of being that of the lion and the lamb. They will lie down together—the lamb inside the lion!

Many of the spectators at the Conference, and even more newspaper men expressed to me deep and bitter disappointment that the Conference had done so little; but what did they expect? Did they hope that a few Socialists from several countries could accomplish what President Wilson, backed by the idealism of the world, had failed to achieve? Before the echo of the cannon had died away, did they expect this small group of people could have cleared the debris from the field and buried all the corpses? It was a mad thought. The utmost that ought to have been expected was a *beginning* with the reconstruction of the great world-organization of workers, which is destined some day to make itself a terror to evil-doing Governments all the world over. And that we did.

The main achievement of the Second International was the bringing face to face after years of agonizing strife men and women severed from one another, not only by the compulsion of circumstances, but by wounded and outraged national feelings. It was a delicate and difficult task. But it was done. The ice was broken. Men breathed more freely who before had felt a tightening of the heart. For the future common action would be easier, unless the Russian Bolsheviks pursued the disruptive tactics of the militarists and capitalists of the European bourgeoisie; and if they did so it could be only for a time.

The Conference devoted itself to two outstanding pronouncements, although very much more was discussed. It recognized as imperative that the German Majority should make clear its position, both in relation to its past attitude and future conduct, if the French were to be appeased; and on this subject a resolution satisfying to both sections was eventually carried.

In view of the amazing events taking place in Russia at this time, and of the reported Red Terror, the great body of the Conference felt it highly important to put the International unequivocally on the side of democracy as opposed to the dictatorship of Lenin and Trotsky, which it did in an ample resolution that did not neglect to congratulate Russia on the overthrow of the hated regime of the Czars.

Friedrich Adler and Jean Longuet ventured to submit a second resolution, in which they sought a middle way, one they believed would be less offensive to the Bolsheviks. They did not want us to shut the door of the International in the faces of the Russian extremists who, they hoped, would one day return to the fold. They declared that too little was known about the Government of Lenin and Trotsky to warrant an out-and-out condemnation of it. Their resolution is recorded in the minutes. But I venture to think they must now be feeling that they wasted their efforts. The Russians have never done denouncing Longuet and those who think with him. And they have established their own International in Moscow, commonly called the Third International, an International governed from Russia, where all individuality, whether of person or nation, must be ruthlessly suppressed at the dictates of the governing brain in Moscow. All attempts at an honourable compromise with the arbitrary Russians is doomed to failure. It is impossible to reconcile the irreconcilable. The haughty and bigoted doctrinaires of revolutionary Russia will continue their violent and destructive work of poisoning and dividing the working-class movement of the world, unless the age of miracles revives.

A marked feature of the International was the immense number of newspaper men who attended. I am convinced there were more reporters than delegates in the hall. They were there from every land, representing every sort of newspaper. There were as interesting personalities at the Press table as on the floor of the conference hall. Oswald Garrison Villard, Editor of the American *Nation*, Simeon Strunsky, of the New York *Evening Post*, and Norman Angell, representing *The Times* newspaper, were amongst the ornaments of their profession present. Dr. Guttmann, who was the representative of the *Frankfurter Zeitung* in England before the war, was amongst the ablest and most sympathetic of the journalists who attended; and Herr Rudolf Kommer, of the *Neue Freie Presse*.

I may be quite wrong, but I formed the opinion as the result of careful observation and subsequent inquiry, and of a close acquaintance which has ripened into friendship with very many conspicuously able journalists abroad, that a higher standard of culture is required of journalists on the Continent than is expected of those of a similar status in this country. Perhaps I ought to put it a little differently. The leading lights of British and American journalism are of the first degree both in general culture and in literary attainments. But there appear to be two very separate and distinct classes of journalist in England and America: the one thoroughly educated, the other entirely uneducated. I saw no such wide difference in the various ranks of journalism abroad. I doubt very much if there were one European reporter at the Conference whose standard of education was below that of a good university. Would this be so in England? It certainly would not in America. In America a "good story" is wanted. In Europe a good argument or a witty satire is more in favour. I know very few journalists in Europe, though doubtless they exist, who would consider it serviceable to their journals deliberately to misinterpret a speech or misreport a conference. They may make a little fun, employ a little irony, caricature a speaker; but very few would deliberately mislead their readers on matters of fact. Courage in facing realities is commoner in some countries than in England. Our prowess is in the field, whether with the hunt or in the battle.

CHAPTER III
THE SECOND INTERNATIONAL (*concluded*)

The International had an audience, a very large and interested one. It sat at the back of the room, glad of an experience which relieved for a while the tedium of life in Berne. Amongst the listeners of every nationality I observed Indians with turbans and Turks wearing the fez. There was a beautiful dark-eyed Jewess sporting three vast links of matchless pearls. A handsome American woman, full of vivacity, wearing a large picture hat, sat next to her husband, a tall, good-looking Hungarian with a clean-shaven face and an American accent to his excellent English. There was the faded but vivacious mistress of a notorious ex-king; two red-haired Greek ladies of extreme beauty; several ambassadors; a whole medley of chief secretaries; a gang of spies of both sexes, and a group of well-known pacifists engaged on preparations for their own conference, which was timed to follow the International. There was Mr. William Bullitt of the American Peace Delegation in Paris; Mr. George Lansbury, and Mr. John de Kay, famous for mystical millions! Last but not least there was a sharp little woman unknown to any of us who sprang upon Mr. Macdonald like a tiger-cat. "How dare you come to this conference to talk to the enemies of your country!" she demanded. "Aren't you ashamed of yourself, you and Mrs. Snowden and all the others?" Mr. Macdonald was white with anger, but he behaved like a gentleman. If the lady had said it to me I should have told her that it took far less courage to come and talk to an ex-enemy than to marry one and produce four or five little enemies. The spiteful lady was an Englishwoman, and is the wife of an Austrian and the sister of a notorious English suffragette. She has several fine Austrian children!

There was something very interesting about those rabid anti-enemy people. Examine them closely and you found that those who hated most often did it because they were implicated either by birth or marriage in enemy associations, and felt it necessary to protest their loyalty as loudly and as frequently as possible. I believe that language also had a great deal to do with war affinities. People took the French or German side according to the language they had mastered! The knowledge of a foreign language is a distinguished accomplishment in a Briton! Protesting too much is always a mistake. I do not believe it has ever done the protestant one ounce of good. Often it has done positive harm by raising suspicion. I have a distinguished friend in England, German by birth, English by sympathies. From the beginning of the war he has taken the side of the Allies. His writings prove that unmistakably. The English authorities have treated him outrageously. It is a long and painful story. They refuse to allow him to stay in the country, although before the war he lived here for more than twenty years, owns property here, and his daughter was born here. He has abundant credentials from important people. He wants to adopt English citizenship. Nothing that is done to him can alter his devotion to this country; and yet the Home Office is inexorable. There are violent pan-Germans in this country who are suffering less than he—gentlemen on whom the Peace Treaty has bestowed a new nationality!

One particularly tiresome day, when the air of the Conference hall was thick and close with human breath and stale tobacco smoke, and when the lions raged more loudly than usual, pounding the table with their fists as they consigned to perdition their various antagonists, there walked into the room an interesting figure of a man whom nobody could forget who had seen him once. He was dressed in a grey suit, which matched his silvery hair, and showed in a marked way the exceptional breadth of his powerful shoulders set upon a short and sinewy frame. He walked the whole length of the room with all the dignity and solemnity of a reigning prince come to review his loyal troops; his head thrown back and his slightly swaying body vibrant with a self-importance and a quality of proprietorship more arresting than displeasing. A closer acquaintance with him as the Conference proceeded confirmed in everybody the judgment formed at the first casual glance, that the lines round his mouth and at the corners of his bright grey-blue eyes betokened a keen sense of humour.

His immense blue necktie fluttered shoulder-wards and marked him, in conjunction with a clean-shaven face, the American citizen, although it was alleged he was born in the East End of London. But where else in the world, unless in the Quartier Latin, would you find so much good cloth wasted on neckties as in America? Like big butterflies these enormous bows repose upon the breasts of their wearers, as serviceable as the Stars and Stripes in designating the home and habitation of their owners.

Mr. John de Kay was the mystery man of the Second International. Nobody knew whence he came nor whither he was going. His business in life was a secret never revealed. He was a mystery to a great many more than the delegates at the Socialist Conference. He had a castle in Switzerland and another in France. He had an estate in Mexico, and was *persona grata* with several revolutionary governments. His bust had been sculptured by Rodin.

Sarah Bernhardt had appeared in one of his plays. He had written books on social science. He composed poems. He was a multi-millionaire, sprinkling his millions on the altar of good causes like talcum powder after a bath. He kept a marvellous suite of rooms at the Bernerhof, and ordered his dinner with the pompousness of a Napoleon commanding the advance of an army. All these things and a thousand others were said of this extraordinary man; but the mystery remained a mystery to the end.

He was anxious to finance the publicity work of the Second International, and actually contributed large sums to this side of the work both in Berne and in Lucerne. But his larger scheme never materialized. It was discovered later that he had a habit of offering millions for this cause or that, to the International, to the German Socialist Government, to the famine children of Austria, to Turkey, to Hungary; but never have I been able to discover that those millions were forthcoming. There was always some hitch in the business somewhere, some fantastic condition attached to the gift, or some impossible preliminary to carry through satisfactorily.

He was dreadfully impatient of what he called the "blue-sky politics" of some Socialists. He hated equally the politics of the White Guard reactionaries. Strange, queer, haunting character, with the lion head and the despot manner; time alone will tell us who you are and what your place in the scheme of things; but that you meant to help and not to hinder the work of the International I am profoundly convinced.

Mr. de Kay lost his favourite daughter a few months ago. She was drowned in Lake Michigan while on a visit to America. The mystery of her death, like the mystery of her father's life, is still unsolved. She lies still and cold in her grave. But her father flits fitfully in and out of the game of international politics, too arresting a personality to be ignored, too mysterious a being to be acclaimed.

Seated in that part of the hall reserved for visitors was a dark-skinned Jewish lady wearing an enormous picture hat. It was not she of the ropes of pearls, but another and an older woman. She was dressed in a smart black dress and wore over it a valuable sealskin coat. She followed the debate with a certain amount of interest, but her black eyes roved restlessly around the room in search of somebody in particular. I did not flatter myself that I was the person she was seeking, but presently a little pasteboard card was passed along the line to me, and looking first at the card and then at the visitor, I caught the smile of the picture hat lady and recognized an old acquaintance. She was Frau Rosika Schwimmer, the first woman Minister.

The then Premier of Hungary, Count Karolyi, had signalized his term of office by several acts of a radical character, notably amongst them the appointment of a woman Minister to Switzerland. It was a bold thing to do, at such a time and in such a country, and of such a woman. I wish now that I had accepted the invitation to be the guest of Count Karolyi, extended to me in his name by his secretary and friend Herr Paul von Auer. Courage of this sort, which associates a man with feminism, is extremely rare. It would have been interesting to meet the man possessed of it. The conservatism of the Swiss is well known. They share with the Latin countries the dishonour of an unenfranchised womankind. To send to such a country the first woman Minister, and that woman a Jewess, was to challenge too violently the prejudices of the Swiss. The experiment was bound to fail.

Frau Schwimmer's business with me was to ask my help with the organization of a women's conference. Of course, the proposal interested me; but my mind travelled back to my previous association with Rosika and the occasion of my first meeting with her.

It was at the Conference of the International Woman Suffrage Alliance of which Mrs. C. Chapman Catt is the President, held in London about ten years ago. Rosika (as everybody called her) was one of the most eloquent speakers in the Conference. Her style was ironic. She provoked shouts of laughter amongst the women by her pungent attacks on male mankind, and her wit and humour made of her a general favourite as a speaker. She and I were thought to be as great contrasts in our style of speaking as in our physical appearance, and a favourite design of organizers was to send the two of us to address the same meeting. This happened two years later at the Opera House in Stockholm, when the grave and the gay of the woman's question were divided between the black and the blonde.

But I never really knew Frau Schwimmer till after our several meetings in America. The first occasion was a meeting in the theatre in Lexington, Kentucky, where we discoursed on women and peace to a fashionable audience. It says a great deal for Rosika's power as a public speaker, that she was able by her eloquence to overcome amongst those critical American women a plainly expressed distaste for her peculiar style of dress. She affected at that time the loose, flowing robe more suggestive of the boudoir than the public platform. Black harmonized with our mood as well as hers, for the war was at its height; but the ill-fitting black gloves she persisted in wearing during her speech robbed her otherwise expressive hands of all their eloquence.

It was to the unauthorized activity of Rosika that I owed my meeting with President Wilson. A propaganda in favour of the calling by America of a conference of neutral nations for continuous mediation amongst the belligerents was being conducted all over the United States, with which I found myself in full sympathy. America was not then in the war, and the greater part of her citizens appeared to be hostile to the idea of entering. Their distaste for the war did not go the length of an all-round strict neutrality, economic as well as political; but there was a very genuine desire in 1915 on the part of vast numbers of American citizens to avoid active participation in the war, for reasons, for the most part, entirely honourable to themselves and the country.

One afternoon in November of that year I had already risen to address a great theatre full of business men in Milwaukee on the importance of their giving the vote to Wisconsin women when a telegram was handed to me: "President Wilson will receive us at the White House on November 23rd. Please return at once.—Schwimmer."

I had not the faintest conception of what it was about. I looked at the message and read it twice. I was unable to believe my eyes. I had never sought an interview with the President. I had no business of sufficient importance to warrant my seeking his presence. I have always had too much respect for the time of busy men in high office to seek to use it on matters of other than the gravest consequence. I was filled with annoyance at having been placed, without my knowledge or consent, in the position of an intrusive and self-important busybody. But there was the invitation. The arrangement had been made. And my one consolation lay in the thought that the approachableness and well-known courtesy of the "First Gentleman of America" had made the thing possible and would make it delightful. But my indignation against the "meddlesome Matties" who had so outrageously interfered did not cool and is alive at this hour.

I had several important public engagements in Wisconsin and Illinois to fulfil, which I could not cancel without causing a vast amount of inconvenience and expense to organizers, so I wired that it would be a pleasure to attend at the White House if the meeting could be arranged for November 27.

I travelled a day and a night from Chicago to New York, tried there to find out what it was all about, heard a few vague stories sufficient to let me know that it had to do with the peace propaganda, and left the next morning for Washington. I arrived in Washington at 3 p.m. and was taken in a large automobile to one of the theatres where a big meeting was in full swing. Rosika rose to speak after I had taken my place on the platform. Her speech froze me to my chair with its passionate exaggerations: "Millions and millions of people are dying on the battlefields and in the homes of Europe," she said, which since that time has become only too true. "Millions and millions of men are praying for peace," which was totally untrue. If "millions and millions" of men in Europe had wanted peace they could have had it. "The soldiers of Europe are looking to you to deliver them — —" and so on.

I had had no part in calling the meeting. I could only guess its purpose. I had no idea under whose auspices it was being held nor who was finding the money for it. My peace sympathies were unquestionable, but when I rose to speak I felt myself under a real obligation in the interests of truth to neutralize the impression made upon the minds of the audience by Rosika's burning words.

"Alas!" I said, although these may not have been the exact words, "I am not able to say out of my own experience that the men of Great Britain are praying for peace. On the contrary they are voluntarily enlisting in millions for what they believe to be the most righteous cause they have ever served. The appeal I make to you is not to act in the belief that you are thereby saving millions of unwilling men forced by cruel tyrants to enter a war which they hate, but by conferring with other neutral nations to discover some terms, honourable to all concerned, which shall save from *what they believe to be the absolute necessity of killing and being killed*, the gallant young manhood of every nation which is in this fight."

The meeting over, we drove to the White House through a great concourse of people. Frau Schwimmer and myself were received by the President with the dignity of a *grand seigneur* joined to the simplicity of a plain American citizen. I liked him. I believed in him. When years later men in Europe laughed at his idealism, I recalled my impression of him and felt he was sincere. When he failed, after the first awful shock of the failure, I believed he had failed where no man could succeed. During our conversation with him his hatred of the war was clear. His desire to maintain the peace in America and restore it, if possible, to Europe was unequivocal. He expressed very warmly his sympathy with the idea of a neutral conference. But the thought of practical difficulties oppressed him. Would China and the South American Republics be invited to such a conference? What should be the basis of representation? Would such an effort be looked upon with favour by the fighting Powers? Could anything be done except through the ordinary diplomatic channels? He welcomed Lord Courtney's brave speech in the House of Lords and hoped it might be symptomatic. He looked for signs of a growing peace sentiment amongst the belligerents but found few. I agreed with him on this last point and remained silent. Rosika grew voluble, bitter, insulting. She hinted at America's munition profiteering. The President flushed a little and looked annoyed.

"Surely," he said warmly, "there are such profiteers in other countries?"

We talked for half an hour or more. The great crowd of men and women outside stood in silent prayer for the success of our effort. They were mostly members of religious organizations; and it was so arranged. Numbers of reporters with pencils and notebooks in hand surrounded us and pursued us in automobiles to the hotel where we had taken up our quarters. Here the secret spring of it all was revealed!

In a sumptuous suite of apartments at the Great Washington Hotel sat the great man. And in another equally sumptuous sat Rosika, with her army of secretaries. Her rooms were filled with costly flowers. Her meals were served privately by waiters specially chosen for the work. Messengers whose sole business appeared to be to attend to Frau Schwimmer's every wish ran in and out in a constant stream. Newspaper men waited in the ante-room for such crumbs of news as she was disposed to scatter. Well-dressed and important-looking men and women left their cards. Busy, intense, energetic life thrilled through the whole of the hotel. Something more than the usual was afoot. What could it be?

It sprang from a source which kept itself hidden, except when at one dramatic moment in the theatre a thin, clean-shaven man with a keen, sensitive face leapt to his feet and declared in a loud, drawling voice: "I never made a speech before in my life. All I want to say is this: We'll have those boys out of the trenches by Christmas."

It was Henry Ford, the great manufacturer of automobiles. He meant every word he said and really believed it possible to do what he wished.

It was this generous, warm-hearted man who was finding the money for Rosika's lavish expenditure. It was he who secured us the talk with President Wilson. It was he who had even then been involved by the dominating Rosika in the idea of the peace ship—the wonderful ship full of peacemakers which should sail to every neutral land in Europe and invite their Governments to persuade the warriors to make the peace.

As an advertisement for the peace idea the scheme had some value; but knowing something of the temperamental Rosika and her lack of staying power as well as of her extravagance, as anything more serious than that the plan was bound to fail. I felt an enormous pity for Mr. Ford, whom I failed to see after the meeting; but I doubt if at that time anyone could have convinced him that an ambitious woman was using him and his dollars in the most foolish and reckless enterprise that was instigated through the Great War.

I refused to have anything to do with it. I feared what actually happened, that the peace movement would be smothered in ridicule from one end of the world to the other, and that the reputation of sincere and able pacifists would be cheapened and vulgarized by this mad expedition to the ends of the earth of a company of individuals whose motives were mixed and whose abilities were in most cases mediocre.

What was my annoyance and astonishment when I boarded the ship for Liverpool the next morning to hear from a reporter of the *New York Times* who came to see me before sailing, that I had telephoned from Washington a full column of eulogy of the Ford peace ship in the form of an interview! I had done nothing of the sort. I had never had the telephone to my lips all the time I was in Washington. I had, moreover, travelled all night from Washington to be in time for my steamer the next morning. Someone had telephoned in my name!

Like the dove from the ark the gallant ship set sail with flying pennant; but in a little while crept back to port with drooping wing, dragging in her wake broken spirits and bedraggled reputations. Mr. Ford left before the end of the tour. The domineering Rosika became too much for him. The greatest discontent amongst the passengers throughout the tour was felt owing to the inaccessibility of Mr. Ford, who could never be reached without a permit from Frau Schwimmer. "Whenever we tried to reach him," said one woeful and malicious pressman, "we found him entirely surrounded by Rosika!"

With the memory of this experience surging up I grew thoughtful as I looked at the little card in my hand. I made a cautious response to the smiles of the Hungarian woman Minister. Of course, I talked to her. Her new position interested us all. I asked her how she liked being a diplomat. She told us a sorry tale of treachery and espionage. The drawers of her bureau had been rifled, her telegrams opened before they reached her or altered when she sent them out. Everything had been done to make her position impossible. We were sorry and indignant till we heard that she had appointed these scoundrels herself and had made the mistake of having recalled many of the old Hungarian officials who had possessed a genuine desire to help her.

Some of these men had declined to go, and *their* side of the story was of shameless expenditure, unbridled personal extravagance at the cost of a poverty-stricken little state, mangled by the war and the peace, and suffering incredible penury. They spoke, it may be with malice, of an expensive automobile, costly furs, cut flowers and extravagant rooms, all paid for by her unhappy Government, bankrupt and despairing. The Bolshevik Revolution occurred a few days later.

She was recalled after a few weeks of office, having committed a number of political indiscretions involving the reputation with the Allies of at least one innocent and unsuspecting tool. This unfortunate lady was ignominiously returned to her native country.

Frau Schwimmer is of middle age and middle height, with masses of crisp wavy black hair slightly tinged with grey. She wears large gold-rimmed spectacles, and has a hard, aggressive manner and a loud, dominating voice. In speaking she uses her hands a great deal, the forefinger of the right hand playing a conspicuous part in the enforcing of her points. She has a quick intelligence with a brilliant surface cleverness, is sarcastic and voluble, good natured and easy going. She has temperament, but is without stability. She is cruel in her thoughtlessness, but, like her race, has a deep sense of loyalty to her family. She is genuinely devoted to the cause of feminism.

Another visitor to the International I feel constrained to do more than mention was Mr. Oswald Garrison Villard, editor of the New York *Nation* and a lifelong friend of President Wilson. Mr. Villard has a rich inheritance from each side of his family. He is the descendant on the father's side of one of the famous German revolutionaries who fled to America in 1848. His mother is the daughter of William Lloyd Garrison of anti-slavery fame.

During the visit to America, to which I have already referred, I met Mr. Villard and Mr. George Foster Peabody in the lobby of the House of Representatives in Albany. They apologized for not being able to attend the meeting of the State Legislators I was to address, as they were engaged on business connected importantly with the propaganda for keeping America out of the war. "Mr. Villard has just seen President Wilson—they are lifelong and intimate friends, you know—and he has the impression that enormous pressure is being put upon the President by a section interested in dragging this country into the war. We are very unhappy about it," said Mr. Peabody.

This does not mean that when the war broke out Mr. Villard took neither side. His sympathies were pro-Ally and anti-German; but he hated the whole bad business of the war and desired to end it quickly. The severe terms of the Armistice and the startling conduct of the Paris Conference caused him to react favourably towards the Bolshevik Government. But from various reactions, he has come to the settled conviction of the need for the revision of the Peace Treaties, and for the establishment of some kind of international political organization like the League of Nations for the securing of permanent peace on the earth.

Mr. Villard is not unlike Mr. A. G. Gardiner, the popular one-time editor of the *Daily News*. Both men are tall and fair, both fresh complexioned and blue eyed. Both have the same political ideals; though I imagine a distinction inoffensive to both men might be made in expressing the view that Mr. Villard's passionate hatred of the wrong causes him to swing more violently to the right or to the left and back again whenever he delivers himself up to the dominion of his warm-hearted and generous emotions.

I met Mr. Villard in the Hôtel Continental in Paris first, and persuaded him to come to Berne. There we dined together at the Vienna Café.

Berne is the famous capital of Switzerland. It is a lovely old city with quaint fountains and coloured houses. It is beautifully situated on a ridge of hills, with snow-covered Alpine ranges in the distance, the Jungfrau, handsome and conspicuous, in the middle. The swift river girdles the town, gleaming blue and green in the valley below.

There are stately new buildings in Berne, and a fine market square. There is the monument of the International Postal Union, a globe encircled by female figures clasping hands, representing the various races; and there is the bear pit with its fascinating shaggy inhabitants; but place all the attractions of Berne in one scale and the Wiener Café in the other, and the balance will sink in favour of the café, at least for those unhappy human beings compelled by the misfortunes of their country or the tragic circumstances of the Great War to spend their enforced exile in the restricting circumstances of a small Swiss city.

To the Wiener Café daily went these men and women to eat the food so renowned for its cooking. Where was such delicious coffee to be found in Berne? Where was there a greater variety of well-cooked and properly seasoned dishes? The wine was a glory. The Hungarian gipsy band played bewitching music, and brought home near enough for tears to those who came from the lands of the East.

But the Wiener Café drew men and women from the four corners of the earth for something more than its good food and glowing wines. They came for talk, to meet fellow exiles and entertain interesting strangers; to discuss the terrible march of events; to debate political theories; to escape loneliness; to hear gay music, and forget their sorrows in congenial fellowship.

Mr. Rinner of the Wiener Café radiated a welcome from his whole portly person. The waiters, always smiling and efficient, served you as if it were their great privilege to do so and not, as in so many English cafés, as though they were conferring a favour upon you. You never felt constrained to eat so fast that you choked in an effort to get out of the place as quickly as possible. You stayed hours if you desired to read or to play cards or chess. A second portion of every dish could be had if wanted without any further charge. All sorts of delightful odd corners, softly cushioned and conveniently partitioned, furthered conversation, and supplied a certain amount of privacy, contrasting favourably with the square horse-box appearance of so many eating houses in other places. And this is a typical good-class European restaurant.

I made my first acquaintance with the Wiener Café as the guest of Mr. Rudolf Kommer. Mr. Norman Angell and Mr. J. R. Macdonald were of the party. We talked for hours of the day's happenings at the Conference, and reviewed the prospects of an early peace now rapidly vanishing into thin air. All the time there came through the glass partition the tantalizing strains of the 'cello and violin playing Hungarian dances. I had hoped to see as well as hear these gipsy musicians. And so it happened. The door opened and in they came to give us a private performance.

Smiling, bowing, they drew near to the table, almost bending over it, playing softly, sweetly, merrily, the expression of their faces interpreting the song. They had never studied a note of music. They played solely by ear. Yet they had caught the magic spirit of music, the soul and the rhythm of it. Their bodies swayed in time with the song. Their intimate black eyes invited to the dance. Our feet tapped time to their swaying forms. It was utterly joyous, abandoned, divine! I hear it now:

"Nimm Zigeuner deine Geige, lass sehn was du kannst."

Our host crowned the evening's enjoyment with stories of the old café's famous habitués. At the very table where we were seated Lenin in exile had discussed his political philosophy with admirers and doubters through a summer's night. In the chair I occupied the volatile and relentless Trotsky had lounged and gossiped. The charming, exuberant Prince Windischgraetz and his beautiful wife had frequently supped there. Crownless kings and exiled grand dukes had played their less dangerous game at the bridge-table in the corner. Poets and philosophers, journalists of all nations, destroyers of old states and architects of new, propagandists of the old order and spies of the new, lovely women of scandalous reputation, virtuous and sober citizens of Berne, delegates to international conferences, travellers to Paris held up on the way, connoisseurs of good beer—all found their way to this famous house of good cheer and joyous fellowship, and have helped Herr Rinner and the Gipsy Primas to make of it to thousands a memory of rich delight or of the haunting sorrow which is akin to joy.

When shall I see the Wiener Café again? I ask myself. And I know that I shall never see it as it was in those days of the war and the peace. All the old friends are gone. Even the gipsy band has fled. Perhaps there remain a few political exiles in Berne who find their way to the café occasionally. It may be that Dr. Ludwig Bauer, that amiable giant who eats at a sitting enough for four ordinary men and washes it down with incredible quantities of beer, calls occasionally to play a game of cards with a fellow-journalist, or to write his daily article in the little back room reserved for honoured and familiar guests. I do not know. All I know is that I have but to close my eyes and listen, and through the windows are wafted softly the strains from the gipsy band:

> "*Nimm Zigeuner deine Geige, lass sehn was du kannst,*
> *Schwarzer Teufel spiel und zeige wie dein Bogen tanzt.*"

CHAPTER IV
THE LEAGUE OF NATIONS
CONFERENCE (MARCH 1919)

I have written a great deal about the annoyance and discomfort to which the traveller abroad was put in the days immediately following the Armistice; I have said nothing about the performance which had to be gone through before the journey could actually be begun. Some day sanity will be restored to the government of these affairs; but as a matter of purely historic interest a record of this business will be very amusing.

The Executive Committee of the Union of Democratic Control (of Foreign Politics) was holding its weekly meeting, when a letter arrived from Dr. de Jong van Beek en Donk, the secretary of the Dutch Peace Society, inviting the Union to send delegates to the League of Nations Conference which it was proposed to hold in Berne early in March, 1919. It was strongly felt that no opportunity of forming international connexions should be missed. One member after another was pressed to go. Nobody but myself appeared to be free to do so. I had only just returned from Switzerland and the International. The journey home had been full of discouragement and fatigue. I was asked if I would very much mind the trouble and weariness of a second long journey soon. I said I had not the slightest objection to the journey, but that the thought of the passport business was rather daunting. It was agreed that someone in the office should do all that for me, and on that understanding I agreed to go.

But the condition was not fulfilled. It could not be. Passport formalities are personal matters and only in the rarest circumstances can they be gone through by proxy. I had immediately to set about the task myself, and a terrific task it was. The date was already February 27. The Conference was timed to begin on March 3. Two days of that time I knew would be consumed in the journey itself. That left two for the business of preparation. I knew no human being at that time who had accomplished this in less than a week. Generally three weeks was looked upon as a fairly satisfactory minimum of time for this work.

The following was the routine for a would-be traveller to Switzerland in the early days of 1919.

To get a passport you filled in a long form requiring answers to all sorts of impertinent questions about yourself and your immediate ancestors, including offensive queries about your personal appearance! You had to attach to the form a photograph of a particular sort and size. This had to be endorsed, and your passport signed by a magistrate or some other worthy person who knew you, and who would guarantee your character and the truthfulness of your replies. Two other persons of recognized social position and personal rectitude had to permit the use of their names as guarantors. You handed the completed passport form to the clerk at the passport office, and were generally told to call again in three or four days. The urgency of my case inspired me to enclose a letter to the chief passport officer in the fond hope of considerate treatment; which to my surprise was granted to me. I remember that my appeal fell into the hands of an extremely considerate and courteous official.

If you were prepared to wait on the chance that your business would come soon, you were given a number which was called out in its turn. By sitting incredible hours without food, unless you were wise enough to bring sandwiches, it was just possible that your number might be called unexpectedly and your business gone through quickly. Most people grew impatient, or could spare only an hour or two and left. They had to take a new number and a similar chance next day; with probably similar ill-luck. It was of the first importance to "stick it out." Then when the magic number you held was called, you paid your fee of five shillings and went your way.

After you received your passport you proceeded to the Swiss Legation for a visum. You had to fill in two forms here and attach a photograph to each of them. You were required to sign a paper stating you were not a Bolshevik, and had no dealings with them. You were obliged to provide a letter from the organization on whose business you were travelling. On the occasion of my third application I had to bring a certificate of health and a banker's letter stating that I was a person of substance not likely to become a charge on the Swiss Exchequer! Another five shillings and the visum became yours.

The next business was a British Military permit. This, I think, you had for nothing. But you filled in two more forms, attached two more photographs and waited long, weary hours for the calling of your number before you got it. I waited five hours on this occasion, and stood the whole of the time!

Lastly there was the Military Permit from the French to be obtained by suffering the same ghastly torments. For this eight shillings was the market price!

I regard it as one of the exploits of my life that I got through all this disgusting business in two days. I could not have done it but for the good fortune that threw me into the hands of considerate officials and for my own British pertinacity. As it was I came out of the French office in Bedford Square only five minutes before the office closed!

So I started by the usual early morning train to Folkestone, tired but triumphant, and feeling that the nuisances ahead of me, calculated to ruin more tempers and create more racial antagonisms than half a century of war, were light by comparison with that whirling rush from photographer to guarantor, from guarantor to passport office, from passport office to doctor, from doctor to banker, from banker to Legation, from Legation to Permit offices, with the endless filling of forms and the interminable aching hours of waiting which I had endured before the journey could begin.

It was a madwoman's rush across sea and land. The Paris train was nearly two hours late. The Gare du Nord and the Gare de Lyon are on opposite sides of Paris. The wildest scrimmage for taxis took place. My lucky star being still in the ascendant, I secured one, hurled myself across Paris like a lunatic and, like a maniac, tossed myself and my bag into the Belgarde portion of the Geneva express as the train was actually signalled to leave!

There was no empty seat in the whole of the train. I had a first-class ticket, but I passed the night in the corridor sitting on the end of my suitcase. French trains are always super-heated. There had been no time for food in Paris. Hunger, thirst and sleeplessness made that night memorable to me. And as I have already shown, Geneva was not the end. There was the long wait in the city and the seven hours' journey to Berne to follow the sleepless night from Paris to Belgarde. But it is marvellous what can be done and endured if one is only determined enough. I drove up to the Belle Vue Hotel at 11 o'clock on the evening of March 2; and the Conference was due to begin the following morning. My two fellow delegates of the Peace Council were still in London, although they began the passport business days before I knew that I was to be a delegate; but they yielded to the fatal temptation to leave after waiting for a short time, returning at intervals to the office, instead of seeing the thing through.

I had been in my room just long enough to turn the key in the lock when the telephone bell rang vigorously: "Hallo, Mrs. Snowden!" came the cheerful voice of a friend. "I have just seen your name in the hotel register. But this is wonderful! Come and have coffee at the Vienna Café."

"Thank you, no," I replied. "I'm almost dead with fatigue. If anybody tries to keep me out of bed for five minutes, I'll denounce him to the police as a Bolshevik spy! I'll see you in the morning. Good night." Swiss beds are soft and white and very comfortable. In ten minutes I was snugly curled up in one of the best of them, for the first and only time in my life grateful for the Continental habit of unpunctuality. "That Conference is timed to begin at ten, but I am quite sure it will be eleven," was the last muttered thought as I fell soundly asleep.

The sun was streaming in at the window when I awoke the next morning. I sprang out of bed and pulled back the curtain. Thick snow lay on the ground and reflected dazzlingly the light from the sun. The sky was a bright blue and without a cloud. Again the telephone bell rang. "There are two young ladies to see you, madam. Shall I ask them to wait?" asked the hotel clerk. "No, send them up—and the coffee," I said, scrambling back into bed and wondering who on earth it could be. Two minutes later there followed the waiter into the room two pale girls about twenty years of age with soft, shy manners.

"We have come to give you a welcome to the Conference and to ask you if you will be good enough to speak at the opening session. Dear Mrs. Snowden, we know how tired you must be, but it is so wonderful that you are here. Do please come and say a few words of greeting to us. It will make us so happy and we are very miserable." They were starved girls from Munich.

"Of course," I said. "If you will leave me now, I will be with you in half an hour." And they left looking very pleased.

This Conference was not so large as the International. There were several of the Socialists present; but, generally speaking, the Congress was different in its personnel and in the character of those present. It was more bourgeois in appearance. I do not say that with the intention of reflecting upon its quality in any offensive way. I have not the hatred of the bourgeois *because he is a bourgeois,* which animates some Socialists. I am not sure, indeed, what the word means precisely in the mouths of some people I know. As used by many it appears to mean a man who wears a clean collar and cuts his hair short; or a woman who speaks in a soft voice and wears a pretty dress. With such persons, educated manners, courtesy in debate, destroy a Socialist's *bona fides;* whilst well-cut finger nails and a pair of white cuffs positively mark him down as a "social traitor." I am not joking. I am stating a literal fact. With these solemn idiots the bourgeois is a man who keeps his family respectable and goes to church on Sunday. He is a man who retains some affection for the old-fashioned virtues of industry and thrift. There is, for them, a bourgeois morality, a bourgeois mentality, a bourgeois faith. Radek writes of the necessity of destroying the bourgeois institutions of religion, the family and private property. Lenin jeers at the bourgeois idea of liberty. To be middle-class is to be bourgeois, even if you have to work hard for a living. To take a pride in clean table-linen is bourgeois. To delight in a daily bath is bourgeois. And to be bourgeois is to be condemned by this class of "superior" person in Socialist circles. It is all so very silly—and so very young!

The delegates to the League of Nations Conference were in the main professional people, lawyers, professors, doctors, teachers, journalists. One or two were aristocratically connected—Count Max Montgelas, for instance—and there were two or three generals. But the same features marked this Conference as the other. The German and the Austrian delegates looked hungry and ill-nourished. All that I have said of the German Socialists—the dry grey skin stretched tightly over the bones, the bloodshot eyes, the pale lips, the thin nervous hands—was true of the men and women who confronted me as I spoke on that glorious March morning. It was a very pitiful sight and told eloquently of what the German people had had to endure up to the time their rulers fled before the indignant revolutionaries.

I was very happy to have arrived in time to give the greetings from the two organizations I represented, the National Peace Council and the Union of Democratic Control, and to be able to promise them the presence in a few days of my two colleagues, Miss Joan Fry and Mrs. Charles Roden Buxton.

Miss Joan Fry is one of the daughters of the late Sir Edward Fry. She is an active member of the Society of Friends. She came to the Conference to testify to her foreign friends of the same religious persuasion as herself the solidarity with themselves of the like-minded women and men of Great Britain. She made several speeches of deep spiritual power which were well received by the delegates.

Mrs. Charles Roden Buxton, the daughter of the late Professor Jebb, is also a Quaker. She has two very lovely children whom she adores, and the knowledge of Europe's suffering children moved her to come to Berne, not only to attend the Conference, but to see what might be done immediately to send aid to the little sufferers in Vienna. During the weeks we were in Switzerland, she and I (but chiefly she) did what we could to start an international organization for child relief. It was a difficult piece of work. The Swiss were apt to be afraid of doing anything which would seem to violate the principle of neutrality, although I am sure they never faltered in their desire to help. The Austrians were incapable, through suffering, of very energetic co-operation. The French were *intransigeant* at the time. Also, it was very difficult to avoid falling into the hands of the selfish and unscrupulous, never deterred from their habit of exploitation by the thought of the poor people they were robbing. We were warned of this man and that woman. This man was buying in a certain expensive market for reasons of his own; that woman was taking a fat commission for securing contracts for goods to be bought with our funds!

The Vienna children were dying for lack of fats. Mrs. Buxton determined to send them a truck load of cod-liver oil at once, preserved milk and milk chocolate to follow. She pledged the greater part of her private fortune in order that its going might be expedited. It is almost inconceivable how many difficulties were placed in the way of its going by the authorities, in spite of the generous act of Mrs. Buxton which satisfied the business interests. Endless delays for no obvious reason; endless calls on dilatory officials; endless pleadings with suspicious legations; endless regulations to be subscribed to, and finally the probability that it would never arrive at its destination. A military guard had to be provided to go with the train. Incredible though it may seem, at that time, and even now, not only goods travelling by train but whole trucks, down to the wheels and the buffers, have entirely vanished during transit, and not a rivet or a plank has been traced. How it is done is a matter of wild conjecture. But no valuable stores were ever sent by train in that part of Europe without a strong military guard.

Out of Mrs. Buxton's noble efforts in Switzerland and those of her devoted sister in England, Miss Eglantyne Jebb, has evolved the Save the Children Fund, the British branch of which alone under the chairmanship of Lord Weardale has, since its inception, raised nearly one million pounds of English money for the relief of child-life in the famine areas of Europe. The fund does not itself administer, but allots to Relief Organizations already in existence if satisfied with their work and their workers. Its great hope and desire is to continue in existence after the pressing needs created by the war have been met; to unite, not only in this country but all over the world, so as to prevent waste and overlapping and to get the maximum of efficiency out of the workers, the organizations of all kinds connected with the nurture and protection of children in all lands. I am neither a prophet nor the child of a prophet, but I venture to think that when the history of these times comes to be written, the work of the Save the Children Fund will be regarded as one of the redeeming features of a situation otherwise black and wellnigh hopeless.

The other bright gleam on the dark sky-line of European politics in these years will be the Society of Friends. The Quakers have done infinite things for the relief of distress in Europe. A gallant young soldier told me of the strength he received whenever he saw set up on a hut somewhere in France, "Société des Amis." In every big city and in countless little villages of Europe their work has been quietly and persistently carried on, without noise and self-advertisement, with no looking for praise, and no expectation of reward. It began with the war. It has been carried on during the peace. Many workers have died of their labours, poisoned with typhus germs or collapsed from overwork. Hundreds of thousands of sufferers will live to bless them, who would have died but for their work. Countless little children have been saved alive or preserved from stunted manhood or womanhood through them. Their selfless devotion has softened the cruel impressions made by the war. Their presence amongst the defeated has saved from utter hate and despair many of those who pictured the foe to themselves as wholly given up to revenge. To the Friends must be given the credit for the preservation of such little faith and idealism as may still be left in Europe.

The purpose of this Conference as of the other was the creation of machinery which should aid in the preservation of international peace. It was met to give support in particular to the League of Nations idea. It sought to suggest such points for the Charter issued from Paris as would make of the League of Nations a real and vital thing. Without going into the discussions at great length it may be briefly stated that the Conference recommended the inclusion of all nations within the League, all-round disarmament consistent with the preservation of internal order, and a thoroughly democratic organization. The Peace had not yet been concluded, so that the delegates were not influenced in their conclusions by the astounding deviations from the Fourteen Points which that peace was so soon to reveal. They were in the mood of wishing to join all nations in an effort to put together the pieces of a broken and suffering Europe. And they believed in President Wilson.

One of the most interesting personalities at this Conference was Professor Brentano of Munich, the famous political economist. I was coming down the stairs leading from the conference hall to the street when a handsome old man with white hair and a keen face stopped and addressed me. He had a nervous and slightly deprecating manner, stooped a little, and showed pitiful signs of under-nourishment in his pale face and rather tearful red eyes. He found it difficult to speak without emotion of the condition of things in Bavaria, and his voice trembled as he told of the nerve-strain under which the population lived, partly through anxiety about food and partly through fear of revolutionary disorders. His very obviously democratic sympathies did not reach quite so far as the Communist regime and the amiable but incompetent President Eisner. He told me that nobody who had food in the house, however small in amount or poor in quality, went to bed without feeling that his throat might be cut in the night by men mad with hunger, who knew about the little store. He showed me a scientific chart exhibiting in figures and curved lines the appalling tragedy of starving and dying children in his city, the city of soft church bells and beautiful pictures, of glorious music and fine dramatic art. It was a Munich girl of eighteen who told me her painful story of an elderly and unscrupulous admirer, who endeavoured to buy her with food, a common experience in the stricken lands.

"I will give you two fresh eggs every day if you will be my 'friend'," he said (it was the first time I had heard the word "friend" used in such a sense). "I did not know that it was possible to be tempted to so dreadful a thing by anything in the world," said this poor thing, her pale cheeks flushing as she spoke, "but we are all so hungry and my mother is a sick woman. The eggs would have been very good for her. And an egg costs many, many marks with us." Her lip quivered and she played nervously with the edge of her shawl. "But my Socialist faith kept me pure. I could never have borne all the misery and hunger; I should have drowned myself but for my belief that Socialism would do away with war and bring a better day for us all."

The young Socialist Toller, who spoke out bravely for the young people in the Movement at the International, talked to me with the same bright hope in his shining eyes. Two or three months later he was sentenced to four years' detention in a fortress for leading the Red Guards in a revolt against the Whites. I had talked with him long about the need for peacemakers in our Movement, and then he was a sincere and unqualified pacifist. His Red Guard exploit puzzled me; but it was explained to me that he had hoped to restrain the Red troops from committing excesses if he went with them, and that he did not actively provoke a violent attack. His release should be imminent—if he is not already free.

One of the most distinguished of German pacifists who attended this Conference was Professor A. W. Förster. Dr. Förster published a letter or manifesto during the war which made some of us wonder if he were the only Christian left in Europe, so brave and strong and unequivocal was it! He was for some years professor at the University of Munich; but during the war his pacifist attitude enraged the nationalist students and members of the Faculty. His lectures were continually interrupted by the demonstrations of these students, and the atmosphere of study made utterly impossible. He was therefore induced to take a year's holiday on full pay, and retired to Switzerland to continue his pacifist activities there. One cannot help contrasting this treatment of its distinguished pacifist citizen by Bavaria with the treatment accorded to the Hon. Bertrand Russell by the British Government. Six months in prison for one of the greatest intellects that ever a country possessed for a sentence in a magazine article which offended them! It was an act which invited and excited the derision of the whole world of letters.

After the Bavarian Revolution, Professor Förster was made Minister to Switzerland under Kurt Eisner. His relations with his chief were very peculiar. These two men were equally firm and uncompromising in their pacifism, but in their political policy they differed. Eisner, like most Germans, favoured the union of Austria with Germany provided the Austrians themselves desired it. Förster was opposed to such a union. In articles, interviews and speeches he fought against the idea, and the people of Switzerland enjoyed the peculiar spectacle of the Prime Minister of a German State and his Minister taking opposite sides on one of the most important issues of foreign policy then exciting the interest of nations! Any other Prime Minister would have recalled Professor Förster. Any other Minister would have resigned. In spite of many remonstrances received, Eisner declined to dismiss his Minister. His worship of free speech was so great that he forgot all about the common sense of politics, which requires that the representative in a foreign country of any state should either support the policy of his Government or be deposed. Malicious critics saw nothing but duplicity in the extraordinary situation. They loudly and cynically averred that the two men were marching along two different roads to the same end; that there was a good deal of pretence about the business intended to deceive the general public and conceal their real design; that they were secretly hand in glove with one another. But it was not so. It was sincere comedy sincerely played by players who did not mean to be funny. It was one more demonstration of the effect of the supersession of government by the debating society, and of action by talk. I have the evidence of my own eyes and ears of the enthralling power of Dr. Förster's eloquence upon the young men of Berne and of the captivating charm of Kurt Eisner's theorizing oratory upon the delegates of a great Conference; but theories do not quell mutinies and dogmas do not deter the oppressor; and if ever there were a time when Bavaria (and Europe) stood in need of practical common-sense politics it was during the years succeeding the war and the revolutions.

I made one other friend from the city of Munich. There stepped into the lift in the Belle Vue Hotel one day, a tall, slender woman dressed in deep black who thanked me for something, I don't know what, and began then and there a friendship I very deeply prize. Annette Kolb is said to have in her veins the blood of Bavarian kings. I know nothing about that. I only know there are few women of my acquaintance who have so much charm of personality as Miss Kolb. She is kind and tactful and of an extraordinary wit. In a dreary wilderness of men and women without humour she shot sparks of the divine fire and kept us from the deadly peril of unutterable boredom on many a weary occasion.

Annette is the child of a French mother and a German father. She is the perfect type of "one between the races." To say that her soul is torn is no flippant use of serious language. It is written in her face. Her emotions ebb and flow. When France was down she was pro-French; now that Germany is out, she is probably pro-German. She wants a union in friendship of the two. She speaks continually of this. It is the great theme of her writings. She had rough treatment in Dresden when making a protest in public against the malignant lying of a certain section of the Press. Her book, "Briefe einer Deutsch-Französin" (Letters of a German-French), created a great stir in France and for a time was prohibited in Germany. She is a woman of most brilliant gifts. The intimate friend of Busoni, she is a first-rate musician herself. The friend also of the German poet Schickele she has a just appreciation of good verse, and writes well. She speaks several languages with the fluency of her native tongue, and her English is a model for many an Englishman.

There was one name on the list of delegates which attracted my special interest, Andreas Latzko, the author of the book which caused such a world-wide sensation, "Men in Battle."

"What is Latzko like?" I asked a friend.

"Latzko is a pacifist monkey of Hungarian birth," replied this complimentary individual. Latzko is small and dark and vain. He makes fiery speeches with nothing much in them except emotion. I should say his experiences in the trenches have seriously impaired his constitution and his nerve. He gives the impression of being neurotic and erratic. He is very self-absorbed. I must tell of a curious experience which befel, illustrative of Latzko's temperament and character. A friend and I were supping at the hotel where he lodged. Presently came a message from Latzko's son begging that we would call and see his father. He was seriously ill in bed. "Will you go?" asked my friend. "By all means when he is so ill. He must have something very serious to say," was my reply. My companion smiled sardonically, but sent the boy with a message to say we would come up in half an hour. When we arrived we found the poor little man sitting up in bed, propped with pillows and making a great moan in a weak, strained voice. He thanked us effusively for coming, gasping as he spoke. I thought he must be dying. He spoke of his wife as of one who would soon be left to struggle with the wicked world alone. He showed us her photograph. She was away in Hungary. He was longing to see her. Then he came to the real business of the occasion. Would I call and see his publisher in England and find out why the royalties were not forthcoming. My companion grinned again.

"Why are you laughing?" I asked, rather puzzled, as we descended the stairs. "I am laughing at an amusing farce just played," he said. "At supper you sat with your back to the hotel entry. I saw Latzko enter during our meal, look in at the glass door furtively, recognize us, and rush upstairs to prepare for his part. The rest you know."

"Then he is not ill," I said disgustedly, thinking of the pillow I had smoothed, and the tenderness I had wasted.

"Oh yes, he is ill, very ill; but not in the way you think," was the slow reply. "He is sick of self-love."

One more interesting delegate at this Conference comes to my remembrance, Professor Nicolai, a slight, fair man with hair pushed back over a large forehead, and a thin, small chin. He presented rather a limp appearance, doubtless due in part to under-feeding, but a little also to the radical idealist's too-frequent inattention to matters of the toilet. His collar had a greyish look and his cuffs were not there!

Dr. Nicolai enjoys the distinction of being the first person to establish the war against war on a scientific basis. His "Biology of War" is an arresting and most valuable contribution to the literature of the movement. During the war he was constantly coming into collision with the German authorities for his pacifist utterances. He was several times tried for his offences, sentenced to prison, retried and tried again. The Government never actually imprisoned him. Such cases as his and Dr. Förster's are worthy of note for two reasons. There are many people in England who believe that no voice was raised against the war and the war policy of the German Government by Germans in Germany during the war. This is demonstrated untrue. Then the comparatively mild treatment by the German authorities of their pacifist professors is interesting in view of the reputed intolerance of the German war-lords for those not of their own political breed. In 1918 Dr. Nicolai escaped to Denmark in an aeroplane, but is now back in his chair at the University of Berlin. There he is the centre of vicious attacks by reactionary professors, who pit against his new, their old, hoping the turn of the wheel will bring back the old order to the Fatherland.

The Conference and its several Commissions sat for three weeks. There were many occasions for social intercourse between the various sessions. The hotel was packed with interesting personalities. In view of his elevated position as Prime Minister of Hungary, I recall with interest my meeting with Count Teleki. He was presented to me as a moderate Socialist. It all depends upon definition. At that time the Bolsheviks were in power in Hungary. By comparison with Bela Kun I imagine Count Teleki sincerely believed himself a moderate Socialist. Or perhaps I took seriously what was intended for a joke. Perhaps it was one of those insincerities of speech, uttered to please and without the slightest regard to the truth, I found so common in the nationals of Latin and Balkan countries. Count Teleki's present behaviour suggests the aristocratic reactionary rather than the Socialist. He is said to have aided Kaiser Karl in his ill-timed escapade. But in the Hôtel Belle Vue at the brilliant dinner table he was the charming, cynical, cultivated friend of political saint and sinner alike; a scientist in exile; a professor without a chair; a patriot without a country; a good fellow and a jolly companion. He is a man of moderate height, with thin features and a clean-shaven face. He is not unlike Mr. Bertrand Russell in appearance, and is probably not more than forty years of age. From my conversation with him I cannot imagine for a moment that he is in sympathy with the action of the Hungarian extremists, who have instituted a "White Terror" worse than the Red since the fall of Bela Kun and his associates. And I think it only fair in this connexion to say that every Hungarian with whom I spoke in Berne agreed that Bela Kun himself was no sympathizer with the behaviour of his own extremists. He suffered the common fate of rulers tossed up by violent revolutions—the poisonous association of worse and stronger men than himself.

There was presented to me one day in the lobby of the hotel a tall thin man with laughing eyes and an engaging boyish manner, who had just challenged Fate by dashing at break-neck speed from Geneva to Berne in a powerful motor-car. His English was halting but perfectly intelligible, and he had a way of insinuating himself into the regard of a stranger which reminded one of the wiles of the "White-headed Boy." It was Prince Ludwig Windischgraetz, the Winston Churchill of Hungary; the gay, irresponsible hero of a thousand romances, military, political and human. He is only thirty-eight years of age, but he has had a very full life, and has held positions of great responsibility in his country's public life. At the time of the Conference in Budapest of the National Union of Women's Suffrage Societies he was one of the distinguished champions of votes for women. He was very much concerned that I should understand that he was a sincere democrat. I remember with some amusement at a lunch, where he and his wife, Mr. Rudolf Kommer and myself formed the party, taking his side most heartily in a hot discussion on the relative value of autocracy and democracy. He, the kinsman of kings, was all for democracy. Who was against it must be inferred. But the Prince was very much in earnest.

His memoirs, which are to be published in English very soon, will be interesting reading if they are anything like complete, for the adventures of this temperamental romanticist, this gallant and not too discreet patriot, this reckless and warm-hearted young aristocrat have been many and varied. Recklessness in politics is a dangerous thing; but Prince Windischgraetz has the personality which reminds one how mean a thing discretion can be. I have not the slightest doubt in my own mind that Prince Ludwig Windischgraetz was the prime instigator and organizer of the Kaiser Karl exploit.

But the Prince's greatest romance is surely his wife. Princess Maria Windischgraetz is one of the loveliest women I have ever seen. Her beauty is of the English type: fair skin, golden hair and blue eyes. She is one of the few women outside feminist and Socialist circles I met on the Continent whose gaze is frank, and who leaves the impression of a decent attitude towards men. I wearied of it almost before I understood the sex-game as it is played in the cosmopolitan cities of Europe (doubtless of this country also). The insolent, sidelong look, the provocative dress, the tasteless conversation and gross manners of the women habituées of fashionable cafés and big continental hotels are a weariness of the flesh to the self-respecting. A relief it was after the hectic atmosphere of the hotel reception-rooms to meet this sweet Hungarian mother of five beautiful children who looks like a girl, and hear her unaffected talk about her home and her country. She very modestly claimed no understanding of politics; but had she had the power she knew enough and felt rightly enough to have saved her country from the pit into which politicians with more experience but less common sense had let it fall.

We met several times, each occasion happier than the last. From entirely different worlds, I think she would agree that we understood each other and held many ideas in common. I remember one meeting with peculiar tenderness. We were the guests of Mr. Rudolf Kommer on the Gurten-külm. After dinner we walked through the trees to see the moonlight on the Bernese Alps. I tried to comfort her with prophecies that all would be well with Hungary one day if Hungary did not lose faith in herself. "And when that day comes, do not, I beg of you, copy the methods you deplore in the Bolsheviks, establishing a White Terror instead of a Red. Someone has got to take a stand against the iniquities and cruelties of terrorism. Let those to whom more has been given do that, the educated, the rich, the aristocratic."

I do not know what part, if any, Princess Maria has played in the recent politics of Hungary. Her estates have been restored to her; her country is hers once more. Whether or not she approved of the insane policy which has treated simple Trade Unionists and Co-operators as Bolsheviks, and still strikes discriminating blows at the poor Jews, I am not able to say. Probably not. But she said to me when I begged her to take up the cause of women in Hungary: "I have five children to care for and a husband to look after. I have little time for politics."

Princess Maritza von Liechtenstein is another beautiful blonde who was living in Berne at the time of the Conference. She is stronger looking than Princess Windischgraetz, and more vigorous and active. Her English is amazingly perfect. She is the daughter of Count Geza Andrassy, the Hungarian patriot, and the mother of five or six handsome boys. She bitterly blamed Count Karolyi for having let loose the flood of Bolshevism upon Hungary, especially criticizing his land policy and the break up of the big estates. She evinced considerable interest in English politics. So did her distinguished uncle. Both confessed to a real liking for England which I believe was quite genuine. Count Andrassy appeared much broken by his country's afflictions. In appearance he struck me as a refined edition of Thomas Carlyle in his later years. He has grey hair with touches of white, a square forehead, shaggy eyebrows, clear-cut features, a slightly stooping figure. A striking resemblance to my own father attracted me. He walked about the hotel full, as one could see, of grave preoccupation: not too occupied to save a woman from a mistake! I was taking tea with him and one other when the concierge brought to me a note from a man who claimed a mutual friendship with a highly respected friend of my own. This man in his wife's name invited me to his home. I had never heard of the man. I read the name aloud. Count Andrassy suggested that I would be wise to decline the invitation, which I did. I afterwards discovered how right he was!

Prince Johann von Liechtenstein, the father of the six splendid boys, is a tall, grave, elegant man with blue eyes, black-fringed, and a reserved and earnest manner. Soft and slow of speech, without a trace of self-assertiveness, he made a friend of all with whom he came into contact.

Before leaving Berne I paid a visit of investigation to a camp for hungry Austrian children at Frutigen, on the invitation of Baroness von Einam, who ran the camp. This extraordinary woman collected incredible sums of money and organized this camp whilst other people were busy thinking about it. There in the Swiss mountains for seven weeks each, five or six hundred starving little Austrians lived. They were housed in the smaller hotels. Their teachers came with them. The villagers told us in answer to our questions that when the children first came nobody knew they were there, they crept about so languidly and quietly. The second week they began to sing and run about. The third week they tore the air with their happy yells. When we saw them they were about to go home. They looked rosy and brown and jolly. They had played in the fields all the morning. For us they were going to sing and dance. Their costumes were of paper, but very prettily made. And they went through their exercises with great grace and beauty. One incident only marred the day's proceedings. A little girl had written to Vienna complaining that her teacher ate all her food. She was brought before Baroness Einam. The teacher, a red-faced girl of over-fed appearance, feeling herself wronged, rushed at the pale child as if to strangle her. The girl was stubborn and refused to make amends. What was done to the little Bolshevik I don't know. But it was gratifying to the organizers of the scheme, and very interesting to us to discover that the kindly Swiss peasants grew so attached to the little Austrians that when the time came for them to go home they offered to keep them all until the next Austrian harvest.

We drove home through the lovely Swiss scenery in the cool evening air. But what obtrudes on the mind to spoil the memory of that drive? The six luckless idiots, with vacant faces and staring eyes, the disfiguring goitre thickening their poor throats, we counted on the roadside before we were out of sight of the little mountain town.

CHAPTER V
THE CONFERENCE OF WOMEN
AT ZURICH (JUNE, 1919)

The Women's International League for Permanent Peace came into existence during the war. It was founded by that section of the National Union of Women's Suffrage Societies which withdrew from the parent organization because it felt that the attitude of the Union to the war was compromising too seriously the reputation of its members for clear and calm thinking and constructive enterprise. Neutrality for an individual on questions related to the war was very difficult; for an organization it proved impossible. The educated women of the great women's Union were quite unable to agree to differ on such matters as the causes and conduct and remedy for this and all wars. Some had to resign. The pacifists did so and formed their own organization. They included many of the best and most devoted workers for women's causes in the country, such as Councillor Margaret Ashton and Miss Maude Royden. The broad line of division between these two sets of equally able women, now happily friends again, was nationalistic. "My country, right or wrong," and "Let us get down to root causes," are probably the phrases that represented fairly the different lines of action. Although in the Women's International League there were many who believed with the others that right in this conflict lay wholly with this country, they differed in believing that the war should not be pursued to the knock-out blow, but should be ended as speedily as possible by the peaceful method of negotiation, if that were possible. But it is only fair to say that in their ultimate hopes and desires for permanent peace the two organizations do not differ by so much as a hair's breadth.

The Women's International League held its first Conference at the Hague in April of 1915. Immense difficulties blocked the way to the holding of this Conference. The British Government obstinately withheld passports till the last moment. These were finally granted with extreme reluctance, and more than a hundred women from Great Britain prepared to attend. Many of them actually reached Tilbury, bag in hand, ready to step on board, when the news came that the Channel had been closed and the ship would not sail. Many women to this hour are convinced that the closing of the Channel was a deliberate act on the part of the Government to prevent those women attending the Conference. I am inclined to think that the reason given was the correct one, that there were naval engagements actually begun or feared, which absolutely necessitated the stoppage of ordinary traffic. It would be altogether too encouraging to believe that the activities of a few women had such power to determine the conduct of the Government at such a time; and too flattering to imagine that our influence was of such consequence that this indirect method of achieving its will must in wisdom be adopted by the Government.

Only two British women were present at the Conference, the two who had gone to the Hague some weeks before to help with the organization. Forty American women, including the chairman, Miss Jane Addams, crossed the Atlantic to attend. Both German and Belgian women were present, and women from several other European countries contrived to attend in spite of the difficulties of travel which beset them. The Conference accomplished nothing of a material character, but it gave moral courage to those who were there, and directed the thought and activity of thousands of women throughout the world at a time when most people were feeling too intensely to be able to think clearly.

Miss Jane Addams, the President of the Women's International League, is a very remarkable international figure. She is a tiny woman of sweet Quaker aspect, with her hair parted in the middle and brushed smoothly back from her ears. She has large sad eyes which look as though the pain of living were too great to be borne, so acutely does her sensitive spirit react to the suffering and injustice in the world. Her dress is simple. Her manner is calm and dignified, but tender to the young and needy, inviting confidence but not frivolity. She is, notwithstanding the general seriousness of her manner, full of humour, and can laugh with the best at a piece of genuine fun. The first time I visited America I sought her at Hull House, Chicago, the chief monument to her life's labours. "You must go and see the greatest man in America," said John Burns to me just before I sailed. "You mean President Roosevelt?" I queried. "I mean Jane Addams," he replied. "The greatest man in America is a woman." There are those who think they pay the highest compliment to a woman who speak of her greatness as of that of a man. My friend Dr. Anna Shaw told me that she was once introduced to an audience as a "very great woman—a woman with the brain of a man." The Rev. Anna rose with a mischievous smile twitching the corners of her mouth, and in a drawling voice began: "Before I can take that as a compliment, Mr. Chairman, I want to *see* the man whose brain I've got!"

Jane Addams is indeed great with her own woman's greatness, great with the greatness of pure goodness and intense and loving sympathies joined to more than ordinary powers of organization. Hull House was the first great Settlement House in Chicago. It was meant primarily to minister to the social and intellectual needs of the crowds of immigrant citizens flowing continually into the city. It comprises club houses for both sexes and all ages, a restaurant, a hospital, a gymnasium, baths, workrooms, library—everything, in short, which is necessary to make life tolerable in a dreary neighbourhood devoid of any of the amenities and most of the decencies of ordinary civilization.

The district round Hull House is filled with Greeks, Italians, Bulgarians, Czechs, Poles, Russians, Lithuanians—a little Europe. Most of these people speak no English when they arrive. The young ones learn it quickly; the old ones slowly, or not at all. The young ones adopt American clothes, American manners, American slang; the old folk, particularly the women, keep as long as they can to their picturesque native dress. The young people turn up their noses at the old folk; the old people are lonely and miserable. Family life becomes threatened in many a home. Miss Addams noticed this. She established a workroom with primitive spinning wheels and weaving frames. She gathered the old people into this room to work at their native craft. She praised their work. She sold it for good prices. She brought rich citizens of Chicago to look at the work and admire it. The old people recovered their self-respect. The young people became subdued. Good feeling was restored and many a family made happy again. By such simple devices did Jane Addams make herself beloved of the poor and her international work of real account.

Miss Addams is, I am told, of Quaker ancestry, highly educated, and the friend of the élite of America. During the war she shared with others the pain of misunderstanding and abuse. I caught a glimpse of her suffering at the Kingsway Hall when she told of her work in Chicago in the early days of the war—five hundred bright Italian boys marching past Hull House to entrain for the war, followed by an equal number of young Bulgarians on the same errand, friends and brothers of the Settlement, soon to fall before one another's fire in a war for which they were in no way responsible, and for reasons which they could not understand. Jane Addams's mission of peace to many of the Courts of Europe was the outcome of a deep compassion for the young victims of war based upon experiences like this.

Her association with the peace ship was unfortunate, and her general attitude to the war caused her to suffer the unpopularity which all nonconformists must endure. But history will right her and them.

It was felt desirable after the Armistice to hold a second conference of the League in order to gather up the broken strands of international friendship and activity. During the League of Nations Conference in Berne a joint meeting of the women delegates and the officers of the Swiss branch of the Women's International League was held to discuss the possibility of holding the Conference in Switzerland. The Swiss women were willing if the Swiss authorities would permit it and if help could be given them with the organization. I wired to Mrs. Swanwick, the British President, and satisfactory promises of help having been received, it was agreed that the Conference should be held in Zurich in June of 1919. All Europe was despairing of the Peace Treaty not yet published, and the delays were felt increasingly to be full of bad omen. Our Conference opened in brilliant sunshine amidst the gloomiest of fears.

Zurich is, like all Swiss cities, a model of bright cleanliness, its streets filled with flowers in the summer, its surroundings of wood and mountains a physical glory and a spiritual delight. And to add to it all there is the wonderful lake—truly a city for inspiration, if inspiration is anywhere to be felt in times like these.

I travelled in advance of my fellow-delegates, having preliminary business in Berne. During the previous Conference many lonely people, unable to reach their friends, had given me commissions in Paris and London, and I felt obliged to return to report the results. For example: I was writing a letter in the lounge of the Belle Vue Hotel when a beautiful little girl of twelve, with long fair hair and pink cheeks, came and spoke to me in perfect English. I was informed that she was a German child and that she enjoyed a distinguished name—von Kleist. I discovered later that she had a beautiful American mother, which accounted for her English, and that her father, Major von Kleist, was a prisoner of war in England. In reply to a wistful question I offered to see the father and convey greetings from the mother and child. The British authorities at home were as reasonable and generous as I have usually found them in all personal relationships, and I received permission to visit Major von Kleist in Skipton internment camp. He was glad to see someone who had so recently seen his wife and daughter, and who could testify from sight to their health and well-being.

On another occasion came two cultivated Jews from Czernowitz who had a mission to the Jewish Commissioners to the Paris Peace Conference. They could not get their visa and were in great trouble. The Zionist case would suffer if its supporters could not be heard. Would I help them by conveying their written statement to Paris? I knew Rabbi Wise, the Chief Commissioner, and engaged to take these papers to him. On reaching Paris I discovered that Rabbi Wise had returned to America, but delivered the document to his able substitute.

Then there were those who were working for the Siberian prisoners. Terrible stories were told of the sufferings of these wretched men—become nobody's concern with the withdrawal of Russia from the war and the anarchy consequent upon the Revolution there. No fewer than a quarter of a million, chiefly Austrians and Hungarians, were left to starve and die in internment camps in conditions which beggar description. Some joined the Bolsheviks. Some escaped and died on the way home. Some were told to go, and fought, begged, stole their way to the Polish frontier, only to be told they could go no farther. A few, of a stronger breed, reached home in rags, to tell harrowing stories of incredible suffering. The Allies were petitioned to help with money and ships. They were begged to intercede with the Poles to allow the wretched men under proper control to cross the frontier. It was sought to get ships at Vladivostock to take them round the other way. The Hungarian Red Cross had a petition for President Wilson. Would I take it? I agreed to do so, and placed it in the hands of Colonel House. The men left alive have since been repatriated by the League of Nations, through the efforts of Dr. Nansen.

There were other and less important matters to report: The delivery of letters from Baron Szilassy and his sister to their friends in Huddersfield. Baron Szilassy was the newly appointed Hungarian Minister in Berne, and his sister is a fresh, good-natured girl, English in type. Both spoke excellent English.

So I travelled by Berne *en route* for Zurich, happy to be the bearer of many kind messages to lonely and miserable people. When I arrived in Zurich most of the British delegates had not arrived owing to passport troubles; but they appeared before the Conference began.

Mrs. Swanwick, the President of the British branch of the Women's International League, is one of the most commanding personalities of the women's movement. She is slender and fair, with a delightful boyish mop of pale gold hair which curls up at the ends, and sky blue eyes. She is a person of quite extraordinary intellectual power, a little lacking in tenderness to those of lesser calibre. She finds it extremely difficult to obey the scriptural injunction to "suffer fools gladly." She is apt to take strong prejudices against people, which is annoying to herself, since it is inconsistent with her own standard of intellect and the conduct she demands of other people; but she has very good judgment in most affairs, and I should not be surprised to discover that in her prejudices she is generally right. Her courage, both physical and moral, is of the very first order and beyond all praise. She is very delicate and yet contrives to do the work of three people. And like many another, she staked everything except her self-respect when she took a public stand against the ignorant hatreds of the war. She is full of artistic appreciation, hates cant and humbug, and is devoted to practical things and persons. She is a very consistent and intrepid feminist, but happily devoid of the anti-man bias which is the mark of the feminist fool!

At the first session of the Conference, tender-hearted Isabella Ford flitted from one woman to another, busying herself in particular with the frail and underfed women from the ex-enemy lands, saying here and there the comforting helpful word to lonely souls inclined to a half-bitterness. There was one pathetic little creature from Vienna, since dead from privation, whose poor hands and face were a mass of festering sores left by the cold and under-nourishment of the previous winter. She was so happy to be there, and, like a little bird, hopped cheerily about the room, revelling in her reunion with old friends; but I heard privately that even in Switzerland, where food abounded, she was not getting enough to eat. The exchange told so heavily against her that practically all her money went to pay for her room and the morning coffee, and she was sitting all day without food. I engaged the interest of some of the more prosperous women, and believe that they were able by the exercise of tact to improve the circumstances of this brave little woman.

Isabella came to me the second morning with her eyes full of tears. "Dear Isabella, what is the matter?" I inquired. She showed me a telegram just received by her German neighbour announcing the death of her only daughter. "She is heart-broken," said my friend. "She was an only child. And it was through hunger that the decline set in. She cannot speak to us this morning. And I do not wonder."

Two ladies from Munich were the most vigorous speakers on the German side, and were immensely popular. One was Dr. Anita Augspurg, the other Fräulein L. G. Hyman. They live together in Munich, and were as inseparable at the Conference as the Siamese twins. Dr. Augspurg suggests a Franciscan monk in appearance. She wears her grey hair short. Her strong pleasant face has the expression of the religious fanatic whose conviction is founded upon reason, a rare phenomenon in any country, but a type frequently met in the Russian Socialist Movement. In addition, to help the illusion, she wears a severe and loose style of dress suggestive of the robe of a priest. She is kind austerity embodied, simple and dignified. Her intimate friend is more emotional, full of quick passion and, I should imagine, quicker prejudices. Like Dr. Augspurg she is a pacifist and an excellent advocate. Her voice is of masculine timbre, and she has a vigorous and compelling gesture. Both these ladies are extravagant anti-Prussians eager to secure for Bavaria its independence of Berlin. Their account of the revolution in Bavaria was intensely interesting and amusing, and perhaps a few words may be told here quite appropriately.

I have already mentioned Kurt Eisner, the long-haired delegate who met us at Berne railway station on our way to the International. Kurt Eisner was the leader of the Bavarian Revolution, and until his assassination was President-Prime Minister of the Bavarian Republic. For many years this very able Prussian Jew had been the dramatic critic of the German Socialist newspaper *Vorwärts*. He was a witty and brilliant writer, and was considered by æsthetic Berlin one of her greatest living authorities. Up to the time of the outbreak of war he had barely touched practical politics. His Socialism was the idealistic theorizing of the café habitué, or at best the philosophic conclusion of the amiable and able dreamer of dreams which ought to come true, but do not in a lifetime. When the war broke out he violently opposed the war policy of the German Government. His articles were censored; he was thrown into prison. He was living in Munich at this time. The downfall of the military power in Germany set him free. Having suffered for his faith, he was acclaimed by the leaderless Socialist Movement of Munich one of the martyrs of militarism and the predestined chief of the pacifist Socialist Movement of Bavaria.

The young intellectuals of Munich were yelling all the time "Down with militarism," but nobody quite knew how it was to be "downed." The idea occurred to Eisner to march to the palace with a dozen men and demand the abdication of the king. They carried with them a strongly worded manifesto expressing in beautiful language their fine ideals, and marched up to the door of the palace in truculent mood prepared for the worst, hoping for the best. The best was realized. The royal forces offered no resistance. All they asked was that the king might retire unmolested. This was granted. Eisner was set up in the king's place, head of the new Republic. In a quarter of an hour, without the firing of a shot, the dynasty which had ruled for centuries was suspended, and a member of the despised race, a Jew, and a hated Prussian, was elevated in its stead.

It was a revolution made inevitable by the defeat of the militarists of Germany; but it might have been lasting if the militarists of the Allies had gone the same way. As it is, the peace has made that impossible. The present reaction in Bavaria, the general restoration in Central Europe of a belief in the power of the sword, is due to the revelation of the fact contained in the various Peace Treaties that the power of the sword is the power in which the Allies also trust. It would have been better for the revolution in Bavaria if Kurt Eisner had declined to be the symbol of the new order, for a Prime Minister of the race of the Jews was intolerable to aristocrat and peasant alike.

Kurt Eisner was not a politician, as I have already said. He was an artist in words. He was a Bohemian in habits. He loved to frequent the cafés. He could not in his new office drop at once the habits and interests of a lifetime. Infinitely illuminating of the man's tastes and political judgment is his first act after taking office. It was the reorganization of the theatre of Munich! He was not able to keep separate the two sides of his life, the social and the political, as wiser men would have done. He mixed the beer and tobacco and gossip of the café with the work, organization and government of the council chamber. Many of his followers and helpers copied his ways. The young men who served him ought to have been allowed to continue playing billiards in the Café Stéfanie. Most of them were unfit for the great responsibilities so suddenly thrust upon them. Similar to the experience of Lenin and of most of the other Socialist leaders who had power suddenly thrust upon them was that of Kurt Eisner, who became the prey of revolution-profiteers, place-hunters, adventurers, insincere men and women who professed the new political creed as eagerly as they held the old. "This sort of thing," said the great Lincoln solemnly, "will ultimately test the strength of our democratic institutions." It has tainted their reputation already.

At the International Kurt Eisner was prime favourite with the French delegates because he was so bitter and unsparing in his attacks on Imperial Germany. He was not a great orator, but he impressed his audience with the passionate sincerity of every word he spoke. It was one of his speeches in Berne which was said to have determined his murderer, the young Count Arco, to kill him. It concerned the German prisoners of war who were then, four months after the war, still held back in France. Eisner tried to explain the French point of view in the matter. He was represented in Germany as having approved of it. It was felt to be intolerable. He was shot dead. And the shot made a martyr of a man, amiable, kind, gifted, slovenly in dress and habit, who had already outlived his usefulness to the Revolution and was about to resign, and who might have retired to some café and talked and smoked his life away to its happy and unimportant end. For me he is an interesting memory; but I have to confess to the faint lingering of a feeling of resentment, the feeling I have always been unable to conquer for that type of pacifist, to be found in every country, who tries to absorb for his own government the entire responsibility for the war.

It is impossible to name all the brilliant and capable women who attended this Conference. Amongst them was Miss Crystal Macmillan, tall and "bonny" and Scottish, the lawyer of the Conference, born to confound the illogical male; Mrs. Pethick Lawrence, vivacious, eloquent and warm; Frau Herzka of the mischievous smile and the everlasting cigarette; Mademoiselle Gobat, the gifted daughter of the renowned Swiss pacifist; Mademoiselle Melan from France, whose wonderful speech electrified the assembly and melted to tears the hardest pro-Ally and to softness the bitterest pro-German; and a host of others from the four corners of the earth, women whose names are household words in their respective countries. It was a good Conference, and gave direction to the thoughts and impulses of many who would otherwise have struggled in vain against the national psychology, and beaten their idealism to death against the almost indestructible barbed wires of national hates and prejudices.

During the sitting of the women's Conference the Treaty of Versailles was published. The outrage upon the conscience of mankind which it revealed, and the stain upon the reputation of the Allies which it was, pledged to build upon fourteen fundamentals, every one of which was violated or ignored, stunned and stung the Conference into misery first and indignant protest afterwards. On the morning after the publication of the Treaty a unanimous declaration was made, proposed by myself, against the Treaty of Versailles. Lest the cynic should smile at the speed with which the Conference arrived at its conclusion on a matter which had occupied the Conference in Paris for seven months, I should like to point out two things. First, we had a clear idea in our minds of the essentials which the peace should contain. President Wilson and the British Prime Minister had helped us there. As for the elaborate clauses and fine details of the Treaty: more than one of the delegates had spent the best part of a day and the whole of a summer night digesting these for the morrow's debate. As a matter of historic interest I insert the first public declaration against the Treaty by any body of people in the world.

"This International Congress of Women expresses its deep regret that the terms of peace proposed at Versailles should so seriously violate the principles upon which alone a just and lasting peace can be secured and which the democracies of the world had come to accept.

"By guaranteeing the fruits of the secret treaties to the conquerors, the terms of peace tacitly sanction secret diplomacy, deny the principle of self-determination, recognize the right of the victors to the spoils of war, and create all over Europe discords and animosities which can only lead to future wars.

"By the demand for the disarmament of one set of belligerents only the principle of justice is violated, and the rule of force is continued. By the financial and economic proposals a hundred million people of this generation in the heart of Europe are condemned to poverty, disease and despair which must result in the spread of hatred and anarchy within each nation.

"With a deep sense of responsibility this Congress strongly urges the Allied and Associated Governments to accept such amendments of the terms as shall bring the Peace into harmony with the principles first enumerated by President Wilson, upon the faithful carrying out of which the honour of the Allied peoples depends."

I left the Conference that day in the company of one of the most brilliant of living Germans. He had never been optimistic about the Peace. He was more than half in sympathy with the militarist point of view although a sincere internationalist. It was not any fighting proclivity which had shaped his opinion. He hated violence for the vulgar, futile thing it is. But an inherited capacity for facing realities, and a cultivated habit of looking squarely at facts, led him to severe criticism of those he contemptuously spoke of as idealists. He was an idealist himself after a fashion; but his ideal was not of the complexion of that exemplified in the conference of women. He had no use for democracy. He spoke openly of the stupid, ignorant thing which, he alleged, most people really believe it to be if they were honest with themselves and the rest of the world. He differed from those who acknowledge frankly the weaknesses of democracy, but who, recognizing its inevitability, hope that with education and organization it need not to all eternity be the victim of the cunning and the corrupt. He believed democracy to be the predestined victim of power till the end of time. His ideal was the domination of mankind by a few great empires, commonwealths, call them what you will, British, German, Russian and American. The small nationalities he regarded as a nuisance. He was bitterly hostile to those British delegates who contemplated complacently the break-up of the British Empire. He would have applauded the dissertations of Dean Inge on "the squalid anarchy of democracy," laughed to scorn the idea of an entirely independent India, Egypt, Ireland, and through all his pain at the destruction of the German Empire, pleaded for the preservation of that of Great Britain.

For the "strong men" of England he had the warmest admiration. To my astonishment, before I knew him properly, he expressed an equal regard for M. Clemenceau. "What!" I exclaimed, "the man who is doing his best to ruin Germany? Or, at least, to benefit France in such a way that only the ruin of Germany can result? You astonish me!"

"But why not?" he replied. "In Clemenceau there is a man who knows what he wants and means to get it; who looks for the attainable and means to attain it. When did you read from Clemenceau a speech full of delightful and impossible pledges and promises? Has Clemenceau disguised the real objects of this war under a cover of fine and deceptive phrases? All he cares about is France. He would stop at nothing to advance the interests of France. One can understand a point of view like that. It is cruel. It hurts Germany. Very well. That is sad for Germany; but, at least, with such a man we know where we are and what to expect. If that is nothing, it is better to expect nothing and get it than to expect much and be disappointed. Clemenceau knows that in strangling Germany he will satisfy the immediate demands of France. That is all he cares about. This is the present. The future is far away, indefinite. New events will shape and govern that. For the present it is France, only France, all the time France; and for the rest? *N'importe!* It is an intelligible point of view."

There was a long pause during which I marvelled for the hundredth time at the amazing facility for languages of the cultivated European.

"It is not the Clemenceaus and the Ludendorffs of the world, but your Wilsons, your Lloyd Georges, your idiotic idealists who are bringing it to ruin." He glanced at me to see if I were offended. "Please go on," I murmured. "You interest me deeply."

"Your idealists have promised the people impossible things, Wilson's Fourteen Points, for instance, Lloyd George's wonderful phrases, Asquith's war-time speeches, the Russian manifestoes, numberless ministers of religion with no more knowledge of international politics than the Bibles they thump. They have told the stupid masses that this is a holy war; that the peace will be based upon justice: that nothing but good is intended the German people, if they will only get rid of their blood-stained Kaiser. The same sort of amiable idiots in Germany believe this sort of thing. All Germans, with the exception of a few so-called pan-Germans, are intoxicating themselves with the thought that liberty is born anew; that militarism is dead for ever; that with the new German democracy the Allied democracies will make a fair and democratic peace. Pathetically relying on the Fourteen Points, they are pre-figuring a glorious future for free Germany, its place in the sun assured according to plan, a member of the great Society of Nations which shall maintain the peace of the world. Poor deluded wretches! What an awakening there will be!"

All this was in Berne during the International.

We left the Zurich conference hall together and discovered a little café famous for its good tea and delicious pastries. Not a word did we speak for many minutes. I was filled with awe at the spectacle of his misery. The ordinarily smiling brown eyes were black with pain, the pain of a suffering dumb animal. He lit a cigarette. The silence continued. I felt like an intruder gazing in at the windows of a man's stricken soul; but to retire would have been unsympathetic. So I stayed and poured out the tea and waited in silence for the speech that I hoped might come.

"How can you sit there looking so fresh and beautiful? How can the sun go on shining and the birds continue to sing when the world is really dark and black and sunk in rottenness?" was the beginning.

"You feel it more than you expected?" I asked, reminding him of the Berne conversation.

"It is so much worse than I expected. I did not expect much, God knows. But this thing—it means famine, anarchy, war in Europe for twenty, thirty, forty years!" I waited patiently.

"Germany is to pay the uttermost farthing for the damage she did to civilians, which is not unreasonable; an enormous amount of the war damage, of which I do not complain; but also incalculable sums for the mischief for which she is not responsible, or only in part, which is wrong. At the same time practically all the means by which she is to make the money are to be taken from her—ships, minerals, colonies. She is to be disarmed and her deadly enemy is to remain fully armed. Any fool can see where that will lead. And the worst is not told. The slow starvation of Germany, the lynch-pin of European civilization, will mean incredible moral decline and spiritual degradation. Millions of people will think food, talk food, dream food, steal food, lie for food, bribe, corrupt and even murder for food. What man would see his wife and children die of hunger whilst food was to be had? Masses of disbanded soldiers, for whom there will be no work, will enlist for adventures, will quarrel, fight and kill, either for subsistence or in the service of the enemies of their country, having no choice, if they are to live. The new states will be insolent, ambitious, tyrannical, unscrupulous. Instead of one big war there will be twenty little ones—war never ceasing, war for crude material things. Art, music, literature, the drama—these will decay. First class artists will go to America where they can be paid. Grass will grow in decayed cities and ignorant peasants will instal themselves in the seats of power. We shall have restored the age of bigotry and superstition. Central Europe will not merely be Balkanized; it will be atomized. Our horizon will decline to the level of each man's immediate family, if he has a conscience. He will have no horizon but himself if he has none. And as for your ideals"—here he paused—"the failure of Wilson has made faith in them impossible to revive for decades, if ever again. Faith in the pledged word of public men, faith in idealism, faith in religion—this is dying or dead. And our idealists have killed it, not the men who never professed more than the crudest material objectives in this war. Wilson and Lloyd George between them have damaged the world's moral currency infinitely more than the Treaty of Peace has damaged the financial currency of Germany; and the world is poorer by the loss of the one than of the other, grave though that is."

As the passionate words fell from his lips I felt humiliated to the very dust for the failure that I felt myself to embody. Weeping in a public place is not a habit of mine or I might have wept. But if my friend saw no tears, he must have felt the sympathy, for as we rose to go to the University he said:

"But justice and sanity owe much to you. I am grateful for your speech of this morning. It will have no effect. It will accomplish nothing. But it is good to know there are some with the courage to speak what they believe even when it is on behalf of a beaten foe. And the German women will be grateful for your protest against the blockade."

One of the most interesting of the public meetings in connexion with this Conference was held in an immense church, like a great cathedral for size and proportions. One of the speakers on this occasion was a mulatto woman who addressed the gathering in excellent German. Very suitably she pleaded the cause of her race and the importance of a world at peace for the development along right lines of the black man and woman.

At the foot of the pulpit from which we spoke was an invalid chair in which was seated a pale, scholarly looking man with a refined and earnest face. He listened with the keenest attention to the speeches and obviously understood all the languages employed on this occasion. Nobody could fail to be arrested by the personality of this intense listener. The question as to who he was flew from one to another. He was Prince Alexander Hohenlohe, often spoken of as the "Red Prince" on account of his radical views on many subjects. The next day I received a complimentary letter from him and an invitation to tea, which I accepted. I found him seated under the trees in his chair in the garden of the Hôtel Baur au Lac, and we had an interesting talk on the condition of European politics at the time. He spoke in the friendliest way of England. Amongst his dreams for the future is that of a real friendship between France and Germany. His father was for some years German Ambassador to France. His uncle was the German Chancellor. He himself lived in Paris for years. And this close acquaintance with the French people had evidently had a happy result. His invalidism restricts his physical activities; but he is a prolific and able writer, whose writings invariably aim at the establishment of pacific relations amongst the nations of the world.

A speaker who proved most acceptable at the public meetings was Mrs. Despard. Not only was her speaking liked, but she made an extraordinary impression upon the Swiss people by the immense dignity, I might almost say majesty, of her appearance. A walk with Mrs. Despard along the main street of Zurich stands out in my memory. She was entirely unaware of the sensation she made; but it is a simple fact that this beautiful old lady with her aristocratic bearing and fine features, her snowy hair tucked under a black Spanish lace mantilla, her old-fashioned long dress and sandalled feet caused everybody who passed her to stop and stare and stop and stare again, wonder all over his face. There was respect in every look; no vulgar curiosity. Some men, entirely unknown to either of us, raised their hats as they passed us, saluting her as if she were a queen.

Mrs. Despard is more than seventy years of age, yet she shames us all by the strenuousness of her life. She is Irish, with an Irishwoman's quick imagination and warm heart. When visiting an English town to make a speech, she is usually advertised as the sister of Viscount (now Earl) French. Whether this is done to attract an audience by taking the edge off her Socialism through her connexion with titled folk, or whether it is thought that otherwise she would interest nobody because unknown to most, I cannot say; but Mrs. Despard can stand entirely on her own feet for the richness of her personality and the quality and variety of her work, always on behalf of the poor and the oppressed. The only value to be attached to the advertised connexion with Lord French lies in its demonstration of the possibility of there being varied opinions without alienated affections in one family. Lord French and his sister differ as far as the poles in political opinions. She is a democrat, a Socialist, a pacifist. Nobody knows his politics. She is in favour of self-determination for Ireland. He has been Ireland's Governor-General under the Terror. Yet I understand there exists a very tender affection the one for the other; and nothing could shake Mrs. Despard's belief that, in all his actions, whether as a soldier or a statesman, her beloved brother has been actuated by the finest motives that can govern any man in a position of grave responsibility for the lives and welfare of the people in his charge. In England we have christened her the "grandmother of the revolution," because when many of us were babes in arms, Mrs. Despard was carrying the flag of freedom in the cause which we hope will ultimately secure the material happiness of mankind. But in spirit she is the youngest of us all.

CHAPTER VI
THE INTERNATIONAL AT
LUCERNE (JULY, 1919)

It was not the full International, but the special Council appointed by it which met at Lucerne in July of 1919. This time my position was that of a representative of the Press, and not a delegate. I had an honorary commission from a London daily newspaper to report the proceedings of the Conference. I am afraid my report was not too sympathetic. Everybody felt the same thing in some degree. Far too much time was wasted on petty national squabbles. The old fight on responsibility for the war was taken up with renewed lustiness. French and Germans yelled at one another, like children in a street squabble, with the old vituperativeness. Meantime the crime of Paris had been committed, and the world was shrieking from its gaping and undoctored wounds. A problem presented itself to me: How to make a genuine International out of men so filled with national hates and envies that they were at one another's throats for the slightest word! Of course, I am sure they said a great deal more than they meant. They always do at Socialist conferences. Nobody could stay for five minutes in any Socialist Party I know, if he believed that all the abuse and violence of language used by members against one another were intended to be taken at their face value. But it seemed pitiful that the old vice of talking and saying nothing should have possessed the International at such a tragic time in the world's history. Apart from the awfulness of the Peace, the persecution of the Jews and the Hungarian counter-revolution should have absorbed the attention of any body of enlightened Socialists sitting in conference.

Lucerne is not a good place for a congress. It is too beautiful. The delegates wanted to be out amongst the mountains or to be dipping their hands into the lake as they rowed lazily on its still surface. The most inveterate lover of eloquence could not get up any enthusiasm for such indoor sport when he saw the bright sun on the dancing waves and mopped his moist brow on his cool handkerchief.

I arrived at the Conference late on account of special difficulties about my passport. On the way I had a curious experience. It happened at Berne. I had broken my journey there and taken the evening train. Into the carriage stepped a dark-haired girl who evidently knew me, as she called me by my name, and asked if I would mind her smoking "one little cigarette," a very mild one. When she had lit it she settled herself in a corner; and then began a conversation which I speedily discovered was designed to elicit information. She appeared particularly interested in Mr. J. R. Macdonald. I evaded all her questions about Mr. Macdonald, but to silence her on the subject said she should have an introduction to Mr. Macdonald the next day at the Conference. Her story of herself was interesting. She had married an Englishman and divorced him. She had one delicate little son. She had married again, a Hungarian, a Socialist who had accepted a position in the Hungarian Social-Democratic Government. She was going to join him soon. She had been in England, the guest of Miss Hobhouse. She was extradited from England as a pacifist. I recalled some story about Miss Hobhouse having entertained unawares a foreign Government agent. Was this the woman? I introduced her next day to Mr. Macdonald, having previously cautioned him. He was quite convinced she was pursuing her avocation. But what was that? *Was* she a spy?

Some of our delegates were rather apt to imagine everybody was a spy. One of them was taken to see a certain Austrian diplomat, and all the time the taxi was rattling there he was looking out of the little window at the back, quite, *quite* certain that the cab was being followed by he didn't know whom—but somebody!

The personnel of the International gathering in Lucerne was very largely the same as at Berne. Bernstein was there looking very much better in health than in Berne. He is generally regarded as the patriarch of German Socialism. He was one of the victims of Bismarck's anti-Socialist legislation, and lived in exile in Switzerland and England for some years. He is known for his personal kindness and toleration. His revisionist proclivities would place him beyond the pale with Lenin and Trotsky. Although a man of immovable faith he was not fond of blinding himself with illusions. He expected less of mankind than Eisner or Keir Hardie. His adversaries described him variously, some as an Anglomaniac, others a Frankophile, the pan-Germans as a "damned Jew." His friends knew him to be a true Internationalist, a good European. He published a book of reminiscences in 1917, in which he expressed all his really tender love for England. This contains fascinating pictures of famous English men and women he had known. The years in England were the happiest years of his life. This book, published in Germany in 1917, had a considerable success there. (Remember, the war was still raging.) An English edition of it has only just (1921) been produced!

After Versailles, many of his friends thought that he, and only he, would be the right person to represent the new Germany at the Court of St. James. How little they knew the mentality of Downing Street! The reactionary Foreign Office officials of Berlin knew a great deal better than that. They sent a patrician from the Hansa. German Socialists were good enough to help break Imperial Germany, but British junkerdom would scarcely find them tolerable as ambassadors. Even a Socialist Government would be well advised to send a reactionary to London. The wheels would go round more smoothly. When, a few months later, Edouard Bernstein wanted to come to London to attend a conference, in spite of his pro-English record he was refused a visum. Public opinion abroad is steadfastly of the opinion that England does not know her enemies. It is manifest she does not know her friends. I have watched carefully and have come to the conclusion that those aliens who never failed in their friendship for England during the war are having a worse fate at the hands of our Foreign Office than those who hate her most. I know of at least three cases of almost outrageous German pro-Britons who have received treatment from the British Government which ought to make them contemptuous of this country till the end of their days. But it will not. I know them too well to believe that it will make the slightest difference.

I was interested to see Dr. Smeral and Dr. Nemec at Lucerne. They had impressed me at Berne. They were the two Czecho-Slovak delegates. They used to be called "the Inseparables." Now they are the bitterest enemies. Smeral is the leader of the Czech Communists; Nemec the leader of the Majority Socialists. Smeral is an enormously fat man with clear eyes, and is usually as silent as a statue of Buddha. He did not speak at either of the conferences. Nemec on the other hand startled the Conference at Berne with a fighting speech of the first order, though nobody knew what it was all about! Czecho-Slovakia was one of the very few winners in the war, and yet he spoke full of hatred, passion, aggressiveness. He is a sprightly little man, with a red nose and a perpetual twinkle in his eye. Part of the Conference laughed good-humouredly at the tirade; others, not understanding, were bored to tears. Finally Dr. Nemec was stopped by the chairman, and he receded from the platform firing shots as he went, at the chairman, at the Conference, at the Allies, protesting, protesting, protesting!

It was explained afterwards that the whole performance was due to mere force of habit. Having been for ten or twenty years one of the most virulent leaders of the Czech Opposition in the Austrian Parliament, Dr. Nemec mistook the Berne Conference for the Vienna Parliament!

Dr. Smeral is supposed to be one of the strongest and clearest intellects in continental Socialism. Without being reticent he is not exactly talkative.

He was in Moscow shortly before I went there, and came back with the exactly opposite opinion. I do not know what he saw there, what he was told, or what was the point of view from which he examined things. I am sure his opinion was honestly formed. I hope he believes that mine was the same. Lenin has thought fit to change! Smeral may do so also.

After his return to Prague the split in the Socialist Movement, which has happened in almost every country, took place. Smeral's followers took violent possession of the Socialist headquarters, printing-press, etc., and ejected Nemec and his group. For weeks no attempt was made by the Czech Government to restore law and order. Finally the Communist minority had to give way. Smeral's part in all these petty adventures is not clear; but he is certainly the silent and menacing figure on the horizon of Czecho-Slovakia's political future.

His demonstration of how it was possible to grow rich by spending money amused me. He came to Switzerland from Prague, stayed several weeks in a good hotel, returned to Prague, and had more crowns in his pocket on his return than when he left! What is the answer to the riddle? A fallen exchange.

I was having tea in the hotel one day when an extraordinary figure of a man appeared at the door. He had a curly black beard and long wavy hair! He wore a big red tie and a dirty flannel shirt. In his hand was a black slouch hat, and on his feet a pair of sandals. He was carrying a packet of pamphlets written by himself and asked me to accept one. He also invited me to come to a meeting at the Volkshaus to be held that evening. I promised I would do my best, and he appeared satisfied and shambled out of the room a little abashed by something. Nobody knew who he was, but later in the evening the rumour was afloat that an eccentric American millionaire Socialist was trying to get up a Bolshevik agitation, and was canvassing the delegates for support. I heard afterwards that his meeting was a failure.

A character I met of a different sort, and anything but a Socialist, was a Russian diplomat of the *ancien régime*. He was at one time Russia's Chargé d'Affaires at Berne. The sight of him swinging his cane along the Lucerne boulevard reminded me of his interesting career. He had the reputation of being the most intelligent diplomat in Switzerland; of his private character the most merciless stories were openly told. It was taken for granted that even before the Revolution he had been in the pay of the Austrians, but as an excellent Russian patriot he took the Austrian money and gave them Tartar news! He was elegant, amiable, and amazingly frank. Contrary to many of his colleagues, he did not pretend in the least to have any liking for democracy. He was a thorough reactionary, not only in feeling but in ideas. He did not merely abuse the Bolsheviks. He studied and analysed them. He was extremely cynical but clear thinking. He had marvellous powers of conversation, and could describe things with a fullness of language that made them stand out in the imagination of the listener. Under the spell of his voice the old Russia stood clear as the new.

During the Peace Conference he pretended to be Clemenceau's chosen instrument against Bolshevism. Many people in Berne who were waiting to be admitted to the holy precincts of the city of Peace paid him large sums of money to procure them a French visum. Some of them are said to have succeeded in getting one. Others gave up their money, their hopes and their Peace Conference!

In those days his funds ran low. With the assistance of his beautiful wife he established a gambling *salon* at his flat, where a number of young diplomats, and very many of the aristocratic refugees from the Central Empires, were thoroughly plucked. Berne being rather a dull place, and the waiting for visa rather tedious, this establishment became an invaluable social convenience.

Continuing to live at the very height of extravagant luxury he could not avoid his financial collapse. His costly furniture was sold, and one day his orders—Russian, Austrian, Italian, German, English—some of which were of solid gold, were passed on a beautiful plate round the cafés of Berne for sale.

Whatever the truth about his character, it was a fact that most of the diplomats of Berne on both sides would have nothing to do with him. During his last few months in Switzerland he divorced his wife, on which occasion it was revealed that his wedding a dozen years before was attended by the cream of the Russian aristocracy and that he owned vast estates in Russia. He is rumoured to have left Berne for South America in the company of the beautiful blonde manicurist of the Belle Vue Hotel! *Sic transit gloria mundi.*

Miss Catherine Marshall appeared at the Lucerne Conference. She is one of the ablest of the feminists of Great Britain. For some years she had been very ill, the victim of overwork and overstrain. It was feared she might not return to public life. Her appearance in Lucerne gave everybody pleasure. She was lately returned from Germany, whither she had gone in defiance of prohibitions, and had a strange, sad story to tell. Reckless of her own delicate health she had lived as the people live, and showed marks in herself of the poverty of that living. The restlessness of her mind and body were evidence of continued ill-health, and I strongly pressed her to go home and take a quiet time in the country somewhere. The most pitiful thing in creation is the nervous woman unable to rest. The deliberate waste of great powers by their ill-regulated use robs the gift of them of half its worth. Together we walked in the woods and on the hill slopes of Lucerne, and I talked to her, with the cruel candour of a friend, of the need for "going slow" if she wished to do more good work for the cause of women.

At the end of four days I returned to Berne to prepare for a longer journey than I had hitherto taken. I would make an effort to go to Vienna.

CHAPTER VII
DYING AUSTRIA (AUGUST-SEPTEMBER, 1919)

After spending two weeks at the mountain hotel in Berne I succeeded in getting a passport for Vienna in August, 1919; but it was an Austrian passport. A certain relaxation of the rules of the British Foreign Office in favour of the representatives of the Press wishing to travel in Austria was made in July of that year. For the future such people were not required to have a British visum for a journey to Vienna. So I was informed by several returned newspaper men who had taken no trouble of this sort. Twice previously my earnest plea for the necessary visum had been rejected, though Mr. Savery of the British Legation had met me with the greatest civility and had made, I am sure, sincere efforts on my behalf. I heartily rejoiced in the withdrawal of the regulation and made my plans. I had a commission from a London newspaper to report the Lucerne International, and secured a letter from the editor authorizing me to proceed to Vienna on his behalf. Armed with this I proceeded to the Austrian Legation to see what could be done.

Baron Haupt, the Austrian Minister, was exceedingly helpful. The passport was at once prepared by his secretary. A permit from the Swiss police to leave the country by a different frontier from the one by which I entered was all I needed in addition, and this was granted with the cordiality which the Swiss have invariably shown me whenever I have made a request. I was very happy to be equipped at last for the journey I had tried so often to take. I wanted intensely to discover for myself if the painful stories of Vienna's misery were really true. I hoped I might find them grossly exaggerated.

It became rumoured in Berne that I was going to Vienna. Within half an hour half a dozen people unknown to me came and begged me to take parcels of food to their starving relations. The Swiss allowed a maximum of only 8 kilos (about 20 lb.) of food to be taken out of Switzerland by each traveller. It was necessary to protect their own people from the famine which would have ensued if unlimited quantities of food could have been carried away in this fashion. It was manifestly impossible to oblige all those poor people. I took 8 kilos of food for one family of whom I had heard and whose necessity was great. Several times *en route* attempts were made to relieve me of that box of food, but I would allow nobody to touch it. I almost literally sat on it by day and slept on it by night, and so contrived to bring it safely to its destination. I picture now the grateful look of the man who took the box from me with the air of receiving its weight in pure gold. It was my first glimpse at the reality of life in Vienna.

But there were troubles in Berne before I got away. I wanted to travel by the Entente express which touched at Basle on a particular date. To my astonishment I learnt that it was necessary to get permission from the French to board that train. Baron Haupt had received from Dr. Renner in Paris a telegram to say that the Foreign Minister was touching Basle on his way to Vienna with the Treaty of St. Germains in his pocket on a particular date, and that there would be five empty available places in his coach. The Austrian Minister offered me one of these places. But I must first ask leave of the French! It seemed utterly preposterous. The Austrians paid for the carriage. I was prepared to pay for my ticket. The seats were unoccupied. What had the French to do with it, if the Austrian Foreign Minister did not object to me as a fellow-traveller?

However, this was the rule, and must be obeyed. I hied me to the French Embassy feeling anything but pleased. I asked to see the First Secretary. I saw three men in succession, not one of whom knew a word of English, and told my story separately to each. I wanted to go to Vienna to investigate the condition of the people, and in particular the needs of the children, with a view to organizing relief. Where was the harm in that?

Three grave men solemnly debated the matter with shrugs of the shoulder and nods of the head, and finally decided to refuse permission. They excused the discourtesy by saying that only soldiers and diplomats travelled by that train, a statement which I knew to be untrue. Incredible numbers of French traders seeking to sell soaps and scents to the starving Viennese travelled regularly by the Entente trains. The stories I heard in Vienna of the abuse of this quick service would fill a book with scandalous tales. The result of this refusal was unpleasant for me. I was obliged to take the slow train. Instead of the twenty hours which the journey with the fast train would have occupied, I was four days and three nights travelling from Berne to Vienna. The horror of that journey is a recurring nightmare to this day!

It was not so much the physical discomfort I minded. I was prepared for that in a measure. I had brought with me cheese and chocolate for the journey. I dressed with the idea of having to curl up uncomfortably for two nights in the train. I plaited my hair in two severe bands, which I pinned tightly across my head, to present as neat an appearance as might be in the complete absence of toilet facilities. I took with me only a light suit-case, which I could carry with one hand, and the box of food with the other. The masses of flowers which were the farewell gift of the Hungarians had wilted in the heat before I reached Buchs. I left them in the train. I anticipated, as I thought, every trouble. But it was worse, far worse than my imagination had conceived.

The beginning was not so bad, although the inn at Buchs was far below the standard of Swiss inns. My room was small and dirty, and at the top of the building. The food was poor and badly served. Not till noon of the day following did the laggard train move out of Buchs for Feldkirch, the Austrian frontier town. There began the screaming and quarrelling and pushing and swearing I was familiar with on other frontiers, the stupid passport and Customs business which had delayed us at Buchs.

There were about three hundred passengers for the journey. I observed two women at the passport office, but I saw only one of them again. She was a beautiful Viennese prostitute. She succeeded in getting herself attached to a Spaniard who was travelling, a handsome, boisterous boy, with a very fine tenor voice. The other was an elderly Englishwoman married to an Austrian.

"Pardon me, madam," I heard a thin voice say, as we struggled to get into the passport office. "I see you have an English passport, and I heard you say your name was Snowden. Do you by any chance know a Mr. Philip Snowden, who lives in England?"

"I know him very well," I said, smiling at her eager old face. "He is my husband."

Then followed warm handshaking and praiseful words about Mr. Philip Snowden from this lonely old lady, whom the prick of poisoned war pens had caused deeply to suffer. She loved her good Austrian husband; had been very happy in Vienna; liked the merry, kind-hearted people, and was very indignant over the extravagant falsehoods of the sensational Press. She left as soon as she recovered her passport, and I never saw her again. My name had not yet been called. A shrill scream from a railway engine, a clatter of moving wheels, and the last half-dozen of us saw the train move out without us, patiently waiting, still empty handed.

I was the very last to be served, and, as a matter of fact, was never called. Was there some mistake, I wondered? I grew cold as I thought of the possible loss of my English passport. Only later did I realize that only the Austrian one need have been handed in. I pushed past the young Austrian soldier resting upon his rifle, and walked through the Customs House into a tiny office. Nobody was there, but my open passport lay upon the table. I folded it and walked out with it. Nobody hindered me. I inquired for the next train. There was nothing till 8 o'clock. It was then 3 in the afternoon—five hours to wait! I made my way to the hotel garden and took a late lunch under the trees, sharing my Swiss cheese with a Polish musician, who divided his tinned chicken with me. We discussed the various operas in a droll mixture of French and English. He had played often in Paris, and conducted at Covent Garden, and was even then planning a return to London in the following spring. He wished greatly to improve his English, which was really very bad. "Your Engleesh it is très difficile. It have many meanings, one word. I speek never"; and he flung out both arms with a despairing gesture which nearly upset the slender garden chair on which he was sitting. He was intensely poetical, emotional, sentimental. "Ah, madame," he exclaimed effusively, "a scene like this, the blue skies of Italy, soft music, and you—Mignon—pairfect!" And he hummed a strain from the old opera of Thomas, alternately singing and sighing until the going down of the sun, and the slow incoming of our shabby little train.

Picture a long length of incredibly dingy railway carriages with most of the windows broken, the leather straps cut away, the stuffing protruding from the torn cushions, the plumbing out of order, no lighting and no heating. Contemplate massed numbers of people of all nationalities, dirty, tired, quarrelsome, packing the carriages and crowding the corridors, filling the air with oaths and odours of unimaginable filthiness. Think of our being turned out of these carriages twice in one night, and groping our way along the railway lines in the pitch black darkness to find other carriages equally repulsive in other trains equally disreputable; a screaming babel of tongues with not a word of English deafening the ears; dragging heavy suit-cases and thrusting and elbowing with the rest of the unruly throng in the mad rush for a seat!

Eight of us found our way into one first-class carriage. It was dark, and we could not discover our companions. One man produced a piece of candle which he stuck on the table with a little melted wax. This supplied us with a dim light for several hours. After that we sat in the dark, the men roaring out comic songs to help keep up their spirits and while away the long tedious hours. The company this time included the Spaniard and his newly attached lady, two Poles, one Czech, one Hungarian, and a Frenchman, besides myself. French was the language used by all.

During two full days and nights we suffered every conceivable torture from dirt and discomfort. Offensive small creatures bit our arms and legs. We could not wash except by running out of the train when it stopped and dipping our hands in the water from the station fountain. Three hundred persons moved with the same desire would have reduced almost to zero the chances of any one. We were afraid to miss the train or lose our places, and stayed where we were. In addition to all this, the women found it wiser to stay awake during the night to save themselves from the unwelcome attentions of amorous men, unable to conceive that any business other than one could take a woman alone to Vienna in such circumstances and at such a time. This particularly disagreeable experience I do not forget I owe to the wanton discourtesy of French officials.

A curious incident took place when we were within a few miles of Vienna. The train stopped and a number of soldiers fully armed entered the train and insisted on examining the baggage of all those passengers who had not come from beyond the frontier. I observed a similar opening of bags whenever afterwards I was in the Vienna railway station. These were the soldiers of the Volkswehr attempting in this extra-constitutional way to stop profiteering in food. Thousands of people, unable to live on the ration when they *could* get it and generally unable to get it, were obliged to go into the country in search of food. To pay the reluctant peasants who produced it they took their jewels, their clothes, their household furnishings. The more they had the more food they could buy in this way. The supply was thereby reduced for the ordinary market. The poor suffered frightfully. The peasants preferred to sell in this fashion because the Government's fixed price for food was very considerably below the world market-price for their products. Some of these purchasers of their stocks were gamblers in food who sold to the big hotels for fabulous prices. The people's army determined to stop this. I learnt their method. It was certainly irregular. Was it effective? There were various opinions. It was frequently told me that the corruption had simply been transferred from one set of people to another, and that the wives and families of the soldiers of the people's army profited at the expense of the poor of every other class. Upon one thing those in authority were agreed, that to prohibit the Volkswehr from acting in this way would mean rioting and civil war, and possibly a Bolshevik revolution!

Crime, corruption, and dishonesty are the awful first-fruits of famine in all the countries of Central Europe. It is the calamity that the best people everywhere most lament. German students must fasten their caps and coats to their pegs with chains. Boots and shoes must not be left outside hotel doors in Poland. Sheets and blankets have been stolen off the hotel beds in Vienna. Railway trucks disappear regularly in Rumania and Russia. Bribery is the order of the day. Railway officials, hotel porters, policemen, soldiers, school teachers, University professors, legislators, generals, cabinet ministers, ambassadors—there is nobody in that part of the world who cannot be tempted, and very few, I am told, who do not fall. Complacent

English readers need not sniff superiorly. What would they do, if they saw their wives and children starving, and the wages for a month's hard work not enough to buy them shoes?

An Austrian friend of mine told me of his brother's experience on the frontiers of two Balkan states. This brother sent sixty truck-loads of goods from one country to the other. When he arrived in a passenger train at the frontier station he saw his sixty trucks, some of them broken open, standing in a siding. There were many trucks besides his own. As far as the eye could reach there was nothing but railway trucks, a wilderness of trucks, thousands upon thousands, halted for no reason that was apparent.

He made his way to the station official, and anxiously inquired about it. "When will my trucks be sent on?" he asked, with much concern. "It is most important that they should go without delay." The stationmaster grinned unsympathetically, and pointed to the forest of railway wagons stretching before them. "You want *your* trucks sent at once! Look you there. All those trucks came before yours. They must go before yours." And he prepared to walk away. "But I cannot stay here for months," replied the man in dismay. "I have very important work waiting for me. And the people in my city are badly in need of those things. If they stay here the peasants will steal everything. I beg you to send them out at once." But he argued in vain. The official was obdurate. Seeing that what he suspected was inevitable, the baffled trader drew out his pocket-book and asked the official to name his price. And he actually handed over to this corrupt servant of the public a sum which in the money of the country at pre-war values would work out at the rate of £100 for each of his sixty trucks! For this payment the goods were dispatched within a week.

Here is one little picture of Central and Eastern Europe which tells its story plainly. These bribes are not really paid by the trader. They are added to the price of the goods. The wretched consumers pay. The workless proletarian and poor peasant are the exploited; but the breaking point always comes. It will come in all the countries if international action to restore life to its normal basis be not taken in time. And that way revolution and Bolshevism lie.

At 6 o'clock on the fourth morning after leaving Berne I came to Vienna. The cabman who drove me to the Hotel Bristol, a mile away, charged 100 crowns. In pre-war values that would have been about £4. In present day values it is about 1s. 3d.! My room at the best hotel in Vienna cost 28 crowns a day. Before the war that was a guinea. To-day it is about 2d.! The meals at the Bristol were very ordinary, but the minimum decent meal cost about 150 crowns. Once that sum counted as £6. Now it is less than 2s.! The value of Austrian money has declined almost to vanishing point through the war and the peace.

I arrived at the Hotel Bristol before anybody except the night-porter was astir. He sleepily informed me that he could not give me a room until the secretary arrived. I had wired a week before and engaged the influence of President Seitz in addition; but the porter knew nothing about this. I sat in the hotel vestibule more than half asleep and feeling as though driven from home, when the secretary arrived, and from that moment all was well. The President had made secure for me a room in that crowded and popular guest-house, once the rendezvous of princes, now the abode of Entente Commissioners and the profiteers of all nations.

The traveller in the broken countries of Europe, enemy or allied, will see little of the real life and condition of the people if he live at the big hotels. This is true at any time, but more unfortunately true now; for the lazy and the prejudiced come home from their trips to write letters to the newspapers which give totally wrong impressions, and are meant to discourage every proposal to alleviate suffering. The same is true of every country in Europe which has been engaged in the war, the allied only less than the others. Perhaps Austria has suffered most; unless it be Russia. The country round is scoured to buy food for the big hotels. Even so the evidences of real poverty in the hotels were abundant in the patched and darned bed linen, the scanty blankets, the paper table-covers, and the entire absence of hot water, which was a luxury undreamt of at the time of my visit. Then, a cake of soap was a present of most conspicuous value to a friend in Vienna!

Fat cunning rogues ate (and still eat) plentifully of the food which in *their* real money they could buy more cheaply in Vienna than at home. No thought of the starving poor whose supplies they were lessening afflicted these gorging and guzzling adventurers, as busy with the pickings of profit as unclean birds tearing the last shreds of flesh off the bones of a corpse. Allied Commissioners by the hundred if not the thousand, with little or nothing to do, paid for by this starving little nation, were eating their heads off when I was in Vienna, whilst half-famished leaders of the proletariat struggled to keep down the spectre of revolution which the sight of so much abundance in the midst of starvation continuously tempted and provoked. I soon found it impossible to eat in the comparative luxury of the Bristol Hotel, and discovered a cheap quiet restaurant where well-conducted Austrians passed away the hours of their enforced idleness. Even there it was painful to eat. To be watched by dozens of pairs of envious eyes with every mouthful of the simple food one ate filled one with cold horror at the thought of what it implied, a slowly dying city of 2¼ millions of people. For the rest of my time in Vienna I contrived to share my meals with strangers whenever it was possible to do so without hurting their pride. And I found that pride is a plant which rarely survives where hunger and cold have starved the soil for several years.

What sad sights were there for the observant in the streets and cafés of the once gay city of Vienna! The postman who delivered the letters at the hotel was dressed in rags. The porters at the railway stations were in worn cotton uniforms, and were glad of tips in the form of hard-boiled eggs and cigarettes. Uniformed officers sold roses in the cafés. Delicate women in faded finery begged with their children at street corners. Grass was growing in the principal streets. The shops were empty of customers. There was no roar and rush of traffic. The one-time beautiful horses of the Ringstrasse looked thin and limp. Frequently they dropped dead in the streets, of hunger.

I climbed a hill outside the city, and from the many hundreds of chimneys of mill and factory no smoke was rising. At the Labour Exchanges many thousands of men and women stood in long lines to receive their out-of-work pay. I moved amongst them, speaking English, and heard no bitter word, saw no hard look from these gentle people who have been so grievously wronged by their own and other exploiters. In every one of the hundred one-roomed dwellings I visited were pitiful babes, small, misshapen or idiotic through the lack of proper food. Consumptive mothers dragged themselves about the rooms tearful about the lack of milk, which their plentiful paper money could not buy because there was none to sell. Gallant doctors struggled in clinic and hospital with puny children covered with running sores, with practically no medicines, no soap, no disinfectants. But for the magnificent help given by the American Relief Commission, the Society of Friends, and the Save the Children Fund, the coming generation would have dwindled out of existence and the problem of Vienna solved itself without the aid of the dilatory politicians of Paris by the simple process of the extermination of its population. As it is tens of thousands of child lives and old lives have been ended by famine and the diseases of famine; whilst over a long period the number of suicides from hunger and despair amounted to scores in every week.

The first call I made in Vienna was upon Lieutenant-Colonel Sir Thomas Cunninghame, at the headquarters of the British Military Mission in the Metternichstrasse. Sir Thomas is a tall Scotsman, buoyant, kindly and of progressive sympathies. He is slightly deaf, but spares no effort to try to understand his visitor's needs. He gave me generously of his time, to put me in the way of understanding Austria's problems. His sympathy for the unhappy people he had been appointed to watch over was very real, and the universal regard in which I discovered him to be held appeared to be thoroughly deserved.

I believe I have not erred in judgment in having formed the opinion that, so far as the higher officials are concerned, the British Missions in Europe, with one or two exceptions, have behaved with a consideration and a courtesy towards the people in whose territories they were planted which did them great personal credit and advanced the real interests of their country in a remarkable degree. Wherever I went, in Berlin, Vienna, Riga, Reval, I heard the men of our Missions spoken of in terms of the highest praise. Unlike the French and Italian officers of rank, the British officers frequently attended the opera and other public places in plain clothes, or at least without their orders. There was no swanking about the streets by the younger British officers. Rarely was there an ugly and tasteless demonstration of their position as the representatives of the conquering Powers, irritating and humiliating to the conquered, as in Wiesbaden, where, at a certain time, all business must cease and people stop and hats come off to pay tribute to the French flag, under pain of heavy penalties if it is not done. I have seen for myself the strutting about the streets and cafés of Allied officers, provocative of scenes like the one in the Hôtel Adlon where Prince Joachim got himself into trouble; but seldom did I hear of British officers of the higher grade behaving with the swagger and bluster of the man who tries to maintain his dignity by standing on it; and who never succeeds! The comparative liking for the English in spite of the Peace Treaties and the growing hatred of France all over Europe is due in no small measure to the better manners of British officials and the greater sense of responsibility of the men brought up in the British tradition for those placed in their care. *Noblesse oblige.*

The one criticism of Sir Thomas Cunninghame which I heard very mildly expressed by a man who had a genuine liking for him was, that he showed too great a fondness for the Hungarian aristocracy. This it was suggested weakened his usefulness to the new-born Austrian democracy.

The Hungarian aristocrats are charming people to meet in a drawing-room. They are handsome and clever and full of friendliness; but cruel as the grave when their passions are aroused and credulous as babies where their material interests are affected. The vilest murderer in the service of the Revolution, the pervert and madman Szamuely, was more than equalled in ferocity and blood-thirstiness by certain delicate Hungarian ladies I know with the best blood of Hungary in their veins. It needed a hard grip upon principle to turn from denouncing the Red Terror and hear the White Terrorists declare what they would do when they got back into power, and not determine to be silent in a contest where both sides justify the cruellest reprisals.

Looking on the poverty and misery of the masses of Austria and Hungary, a flood of deep anger came over me as I thought of the Hungarian in Berne who could think of nothing but the loss of her clothes and jewels and in particular of a pair of beautiful white boots.

"I would kill every Bolshevik if I could have my way; and they shouldn't die an easy death either. I would roast them in front of a slow fire. Think of what those dirty Jews have done to some of our best men. And all my clothes and jewels gone! I don't know what on earth we shall do. We have scarcely a penny in the world. Summer is coming and I haven't a decent thing to stand up in. My beautiful white boots are in Budapest. They are perfect dreams! And to think that those awful Bolsheviks have got them. Some horrid little Jewess is pulling them on to her ugly feet this very minute, I am positive. I could weep my eyes out. You have no idea how nice they are. The leather is perfect; and they come half-way to my knees. They are the smartest things ever seen. Oh, my poor boots!"

After the counter-revolution I saw her and asked if she had recovered her belongings. "Every stick, my dear. It is wonderful. See my boots?" And she stuck out two beautifully shod feet for me to see, her eyes sparkling with pleasure. "They hadn't touched a thing. I shall sell the jewels in America. They will bring in a handsome sum."

"Well, you at any rate will be able to speak well of the Hungarian Bolsheviks?" I asked.

"No, indeed. They are all filthy Jews, and they have behaved like savages. Do you know they hanged tiny little babies for the fun of the thing and old — —"

"Stop, for Heaven's sake," I cried. "Don't talk like that if you want to be taken seriously. It is too silly. You cannot prove what you say, and I, who am not a Bolshevik, know that what you say is not true. If you talk like that the only effect will be that you will make Bolsheviks by the dozen."

Concerning Entente officials and the counter-revolution, all I can say is this: That it is widely believed by responsible persons that there is some mysterious relationship which does not blend with the general tone of the Hungarian Peace Treaty. Hungary has all this time been permitted to keep troops far in excess of the numbers laid down in the Treaty. The anti-democratic policy of the present Hungarian White Government has received no rebuke from the Allied Governments. The guarantees made to the Social-Democratic Government which succeeded Bela Kun were openly flouted. Only the strong agitation by democrats in England saved the lives of Professor Agoston and his colleagues, guaranteed by the British representative in Vienna; and these men are still in shameful imprisonment. And whether it is the fear of France that the union of Austria with Germany has become menacing through the attempt to make it impossible by denying to Austria the right of self-determination in the Peace Treaty, and the hope that the restoration of a Magyar ruler under French protection would counterbalance such an evil, or whether personal matters and the obligations of friendship enter into the calculation at all, it is quite certain that the tendencies towards a restoration of the old order are receiving encouragement from some amazing quarters. In all this the public suspicion rests rather upon France than upon Great Britain. The utmost of which Great Britain is accused is weakness in following, and indecision in the failure to grapple with, the Imperialists of France.

The union of Austria with Germany was the declared policy of the Social Democratic Party which took the reins of government after the abdication of the Emperor Charles. Dr. Otto Bauer, the Socialist Foreign Minister, proclaimed this policy from the housetops, thereby alienating the Allies, who demanded and secured his resignation in favour of the more tactful and diplomatic Renner. When I questioned Frau Freundlich, one of the women members of the Austrian Parliament, on the unwisdom of so outspoken a declaration of policy at such a time, with the nerves of France still atwitter with fright, she replied that open diplomacy was more honest and straightforward than secret diplomacy, and that the Socialists meant to carry out this principle of theirs regardless of consequences. I could only agree with the first part of her remark, adding to my words of approval that, even so, there was a time to speak and a time to be silent, and that this noble recklessness of consequences might be justified in a Party or a person but was doubtful wisdom on the part of a Government whose people needed food from the foe to keep them alive! Like Kurt Eisner and his passion for free speech, the Social Democrats of Austria would permit of no compromise in the matter of the Party programme.

I met Dr. Otto Bauer at the house of my friend Madame Zuckerkandl. We were quaintly assorted guests. There was the grave and dignified City Councillor Dr. Schwartz-Hiller, whose care of little Jewish refugees from Galicia deserves the highest praise. There was the wife of an impoverished ex-diplomat, who had spent many years in China and who was starving on a pension of almost nothing a month; there was Baron Hennet, the charming and able young diplomat whom I had met in Berne, known in England for his informed interest in agricultural matters and his advocacy of Free Trade; and finally there was Dr. Bauer.

He is a man of medium height, with a handsome young face, inclined to roundness, and the dark hair and brilliant eyes of the Jewish race. He is justly reputed one of the ablest men in the European Socialist Movement. Common report had it at one time that he is a Bolshevik; but his enemies did that for him! I inquired about him at the British Mission and they denied this story. I asked Dr. Bauer directly if he believed in Bolshevism and received a smiling but unequivocal reply in the negative. At the time of our talk he was helping to edit the great Socialist newspaper, the *Arbeiter Zeitung*, in the absence of the regular editor, Dr. Austerlitz, who was lying ill. His influence was much feared by the French. And his policy appears to-day to be likely to succeed in spite of the prohibition of the Peace Treaty, which forbids for all time the union with Germany unless with the unanimous approval of the League of Nations. If the Allies had determined on an act which would help the Austrians to achieve their desires they could not have done better than make it a point in the Treaty. The manifest injustice of refusing to Austria what is granted in theory to every other country in the world, the right to determine its own form of government, has united with the Social Democrats thousands of Austrians who had previously opposed this political proposal. Now it is clear from the Tyrol plebiscite of 97 per cent. in favour of the union that the policy has become national and must sooner or later be successful. The language of the Austrians is German. There appears to be little hope of substantial co-operation with the succession states for a very long time to come. The Austrians are ill-disposed to the eternal spoon-feeding of the Allies, which must mean expensive and irregular meals, with a constant threat of the withdrawal of supplies if something does not please the nurses. To the overwhelming majority of the six millions of Austria's population the only means of living appears to be union with Germany, with a people speaking the same language and a country lying on their border.

But at the time of my visit to Austria there was a considerable difference of opinion in Vienna on the subject of the best future political arrangement for Austria. A number of people formerly of power and influence expressed hostility to the idea of union with Germany. They dreaded the merging of Austrian individuality in that of the stronger partner. They contemplated with real distress the future of their beautiful Vienna as a second-class city on the frontier of civilization instead of the sun and centre of culture which it had been. Some positively disliked the Prussian association because of its disciplined militarism. A few with the spirit of the flunkey desired to please the Allies. Others recognized the danger of flouting the Allies.

Of the various alternatives to the proposed union there were two which received noteworthy support, that which suggested union with the mild regime of a Bavaria independent of Prussia, and that which advocated what was called a Danubian Federation which should comprise the old states, and possibly Bavaria. The economic dependence of the states comprising the former Austro-Hungarian Empire was becoming clearer with every day that passed. The natural advantages as a clearing-house for trade and commerce of Vienna, in the centre of the system, as well as its amazing cultural facilities, provided every reason in common sense for a proposal of this sort. But hostile to the idea were those in Austria who would have welcomed an economic union apart from a political union, but who were unable to see how the one could be achieved without the other eventually following. The new states, particularly Czecho-Slovakia, jealous of any proposal which might restore to Vienna the importance they were determined to attach to Prague, pursued a policy of self-interest which menaced the very existence of Austria as an independent state, and looked askance at any idea of economic union between themselves and their ancient enemy. Anti-German feeling there was too pronounced for any other than the most individualistic action. Pro-German feeling in German-Austria favoured the union with Germany. The propaganda for the federation was conducted chiefly by agents abroad, and as I have already shown, a succession of events has made the proposal for union with Germany, originally the proposal of a party, a matter of united national policy.

Apart from its foreign policy the political problem of Austria appeared to be presenting itself along the line of peasant versus town worker. This is more or less true of every country in Europe. The peasants hated the city of Vienna. They had to maintain the two and a quarter millions of its population and got no adequate return for this in manufactured goods. The city could not manufacture for lack of raw materials and coal. The peasants disliked the "Red" Government because it fixed the price of foodstuffs in the interests of the poor of the towns careless of the reduced profits of the peasants. They disliked the towns because they were irreligious and full of the hated Jews. All these causes worked (and are working all over Central Europe and in Russia) at the time I was in Vienna.

"I very much fear," said Otto Bauer to me, "that the social problem of Europe for a generation or more will be the town against the country. And which will win?" The victory of the country seems imminent. It has conquered in Bavaria and, in a measure, in Austria. It will conquer in Russia. And the victory of the country in European politics does not mean maypoles and flowers and flowing beer and fat living for everybody. It means, at present, the reign of ignorance and bigotry and superstition and individualism, and the decline of all the things which make for a cultivated civilization.

The second party in the state then, the first at the present moment, was the Christian Socialist. How they got the name I have not yet learnt. There is no means of proving that they are not Christian; but they are certainly not Socialists! I imagine they came by the name for a certain historic interest in schemes of municipalization, but their chief leaders are big capitalists, and their chief supporters the small shopkeepers of the cities and the peasant farmers of the country. They approximate to the old Liberals of the Manchester school in England. Free trade is an important plank in their programme. Their efforts in 1919 were being directed against the decontrol of food, and Mr. Julius Meinl's theses on the subject have appeared in English in certain journals devoted to a similar policy. Dr. Redlich, the eminent writer, whose book on the British Constitution is regarded as the authoritative work upon the subject in much the same way as Lord Bryce's volume on the American Constitution is said to be the last word on that subject, is another gifted leader of this now dominant party. So far the moderation of its course has saved the country from the reaction that a too-swift swing of the pendulum almost invariably produces.

Amongst the women friends I made in Vienna one stands out with peculiar interest. She is the lady to whom I have already referred, Frau Zuckerkandl, the widow of a very eminent Austrian physician, and one of the most delightful women it is possible to meet anywhere. I saw her first in her dainty flat, dressed in a fluttering loose robe of diaphanous silky material, a fairy figure with heaped-up masses of bright hair and rather tired blue eyes. Less than fifteen minutes sufficed to teach each of us that there were intellectual and spiritual bonds between us that made friendship ripe at the first contact. Both of us are devotees of good music. Both passionately admire the drama. Both recognize in art the living spirit of a true and lasting internationalism. Both feel the service of the oppressed to be a glorious privilege. Only twice or thrice in one's life comes a friendship so rare and precious as I felt and feel this to be.

Frau Zuckerkandl's father was the editor and proprietor of a great newspaper. She is a writer of merit, and was the musical critic for a Viennese journal. We visited the Opera together several times. This marvellous people, half-famished and almost wholly despairing, crowded the Opera House night by night, to revel at the feast of song which was the only rich banquet left them, and the last table they would willingly leave. "We can live without bread, but not without roses."

My friend is related by marriage to the great Clemenceau. Her sister is the wife of "The Tiger's" brother. I think it was she who told me the story that was afloat in Europe at that time of how, when Clemenceau was charged by some of his insatiable fellow-countrymen with having made a peace bad for France, he replied: "But how could I do better, with a fool on one side who thought he was Napoleon, and a damned fool on the other who thought he was Jesus Christ?"

Another good story which was going the round of the Vienna cafés deserves to be repeated. In one of the cafés, years before the war, a young Jew sat sipping his coffee day by day. Nobody was in the least interested in him, and he was distinguished for nothing except a shabby dress and a wild mop of tangled hair. His name was Trotsky.

In those days everybody was talking about the Russian Revolution. Many were fearful of it. The Vienna Foreign Office was constantly being warned about its coming, and worried to death about the consequences upon Vienna of its coming.

Exasperated beyond endurance by the endless fears of his colleagues, and full of contempt for them, one of the higher officials exclaimed: "But what nonsense is this talk of a Russian Revolution; who is to make the revolution? There is nobody. Perhaps"—and here came a gesture of superb contempt—"Mr. Trotsky of the Café Centrale!"

A trip to Semmering was one of the excursions which consoled one a little for the desolate spectacle of empty markets and idle factories, of a disintegrating civic life. Semmering is a four hours' motor drive from Vienna, beautifully placed near the Styrian frontier. It is a health resort full at that time of rich refugees. At a simple guest-house on the slope of one of the hills President Seitz and his wife, with a few members of his Cabinet, recuperated during the week-ends for the arduous duties of the week. His secretary took me out there for the day. We were again a curiously mixed group. The overworked and courteous secretary was a baron of the old regime. Professor Leon Kellner, hearty in manner and ruddy of complexion, the famous Shakespearean scholar, was there; Otto Grockney, Minister for Education, gravely peering through spectacles at the new-comer; and Dr. Seitz.

Of this first President of the Socialist Republic of Austria, Karl Seitz, I have written before. He is a kind, amiable, benevolent, distinguished-looking man with a keen sense of humour. Someone hearing him thus praised exclaimed: "But what else do you expect from a President of Austria?" Looking at this polite and suave man of the world, every inch a president, it is with difficulty that one realizes that he was once on a time the fiercest leader of the Socialist Opposition in the turbulent Austrian Parliament. He started his career as an elementary school-teacher, became the fire-brand of the Lower Austrian Diet and ended as the President! He is a speaker of very great eloquence and power. He was always well liked, even by his opponents, and is extremely popular. Very few of the new type of potentate have the heart, the mind, the manners so ready to fit the new position.

Dr. Max Winter, the kind-hearted Vice-Burgermeister of Vienna, is the man to whom I owe most of my acquaintance with the civic life of the city. Day after day he or his secretary or his son, who had been a prisoner of war in England, took me out to see in particular what was being done for the children. Dr. Winter is always spoken of as "the children's Mayor," for the children are his very serious concern. In his company I saw the public feeding centres of the Americans, the clinics supervised by the Friends, the children's hospitals so sadly lacking funds, the open-air play-centres in the public parks, and the country schools. The houses of rich nobles who have fled and the palaces of the ex-Kaiser were used for this purpose. There was a particularly attractive little hospital and feeding centre in a corner of the Schönbrunn Palace for those children whose parents could afford to contribute a little towards their keep, I think two crowns a day, worth at that time about one penny. At the holiday camps in the parks the children ran about all day in bathing suits, and very brown and jolly they looked with the exposure to the sun and the regular, if scarcely sufficient, food. "Freundschaft! Freundschaft!" they cried, running to kiss my hand after the custom of the country. Sometimes they sang their little songs and danced their pretty dances. Beautiful brown-eyed Viennese children dancing in paper dresses, and crowned with wood flowers in the Wiener Wald! I see them now in the mind's eye, waving their thin arms and smiling sweetly, with not a thought of the bitter, cruel thing which is robbing them of health and life in their innocent young hearts.

After a sad excursion one day to the market, where little girls of twelve lay all night with their baskets waiting for the opening of the butcher's shop, and the scramble for the ration of meat for the family dinner, I found waiting for me in the hotel about twenty women and one child all robed in deep black. They had come with a petition. It was to ask me to help them to get their husbands out of Russia, prisoners of war there. Some had not been heard of for four years. Terrible stories of their sufferings had come through. The women were frantic with grief. They had been to the Mayor; he could do nothing. They had been to the Government; the Government had made promises but done nothing. They had been to the Allied Missions and had been sent away empty. They were beginning to believe that the Government and the Allies were in concert to keep the men in Russia because of their fear of Bolshevist infection—afraid that the men had become converts. Someone had suggested that perhaps I could help. They begged with quivering lips that I would do something. Suddenly the child, a little fair-haired thing, sprang from her mother's side, and falling on her knees at my feet, clasped her tiny hands and said in lisped English: "Dear kind English lady, do bring my daddy back to me." The women burst into tears, such a sobbing and a wailing as would have melted a stone. It was deeply painful. What could I do? I promised to interest the women's organizations of England and the Labour Party, and immediately wrote to both. Alas! when the relief came, thousands, tens of thousands, had died in exile, destroyed by hunger and disease.

The journey back to Berne was much quicker and more comfortable. By special permission I returned by the children's train. Six hundred small victims of the famine came every six or seven weeks to hospitable Switzerland; I travelled with one train load. I can add nothing to the description of the sufferers I have already given; but I can add a word of praise of the Swiss. They have raised for themselves a lasting monument in the affections of the Austrian people, and have set an example of practical internationalism which should shame all those whose faith in blockades and tariffs and embargoes and prohibitions is not yet dead. But for the Swiss and the Americans Austria's plight would have been beyond hope, and the world would be the poorer by the loss of one of the most cultivated, artistic and lovable races which have contributed to the happiness and elevation of mankind. Very late in the day the men of Paris have moved towards the relief of Vienna. Perhaps it is not quite too late to save the remnant. But the martyrs have been many, and the agony long.

CHAPTER VIII
AFTER ONE YEAR

At the first meeting of the International in Berne in 1919 I was very much interested in a lively little man from Alsace-Lorraine. His name was Grumbach, and he had a house in Berne, and a handsome wife with bright hair and a plump figure. In appearance he reminded me a little of an English coachman. He was smooth-shaven, with a bit of hair left on either cheek in the old-fashioned way. His face was round, and he had a sweet and rather childlike mouth. His eyes were very merry, and his manner kind. But the roar of him when he spoke was like that of a mad bull. He was very angry with the Germans, and could not contain himself on the platform, foaming at the mouth almost, as he lashed out at those unfortunate men on the front row. He made an excellent double bass to Renaudel's tenor and Thomas's baritone, whenever the wild music got going. And just as suddenly he melted into the utmost amiability. He disliked their past, and suspected the future policy of the Germans in relation to his own country. I have not seen him since the early days in Berne; but I have heard that his present discontent is with French administration and French behaviour in the restored provinces and that he favours an independent Alsace-Lorraine within the French orbit. I wonder what is true?

Another Alsatian of a different type was René Schickele, one of the leaders of the younger German poets. I met him also in Berne, but not at the Conference. This young and distinguished dramatist was introduced to me by Annette Kolb. He impressed me as shy and diffident; but that may have been the embarrassment of not knowing English. There is no barrier like that of not knowing the language of an acquaintance. He promised to learn English for our next meeting, and I promised myself to learn enough German to be intelligible. But how can one learn foreign languages when everybody abroad wants to practise his English?

During the war Schickele placed himself in opposition to the German Government. He was a German citizen then. Now he is in opposition to France. He is a French citizen now. The cynic would smile and talk of the passion for self-advertising; but I think there is a reasonable case for this position in a pacifist, who is out to smite the ugly spirit of militarism whenever and wherever it raises its offending head.

His play *Hans in Schnakenloch* was an attempt to give a just exposition of the psychology of French and Germans in Alsace-Lorraine. The Germans called it Francophile, the French considered it pro-German. It had an immense success in Germany in 1917, until it was suppressed by the military censor. Schickele belongs to the Clarté group. Fried, who died a short time ago, the kindly sentimentalist, but courageous Austrian pacifist, so long exiled in Switzerland, who won the Nobel prize, was another member of the band. René Claparéde of Geneva, Barbusse and Anatole France belong to the same group. Their policy is very much the same as that of the Union of Democratic Control in England. The poet's ultimate aim in politics is the friendship and conciliation of Germany and France.

When I was invited to attend the French Socialist Congress in Strasburg in January of 1920, exactly one year after the first meeting of the Second International, I thought of these two personalities, the only human connexion I had with Alsace, and hoped to meet again in their capital city of ancient fame and modern interest these two able men. Neither, however, was present.

But Renaudel was there, and Longuet and Marquet, and all the hosts of fighting French Socialism.

The battle of the two Internationals was by this time waxing fast and furious. The Italians had split in two, the French were about to follow, the British were threatened. My commission to the French congress was to convey greetings from the British Labour Party to the delegates; but also to make it clear that the Labour Party intended to cleave to the Second International in spite of the efforts of a few voluble *intransigéants* to draw it into the Third.

These various Internationals must be confusing to the average reader. The First was founded by Karl Marx and Professor Beesly in 1866, and dissolved in the wars of 1871. The Second was re-established in 1889, and discontinued its activities during the world-war. Its meeting in Berne I have already fully described. The success of the Revolution in Russia filled with arrogance the souls of the dominant Bolsheviks who determined to unite the entire world-Socialist Movement under their flag. They would dominate, command, discipline from Moscow every country in the world. They drew up twenty-one theses which they insisted should be accepted by all who would join them—the Third International. These included dictatorship instead of democracy, revolution by violence, and the abolition by force of the whole institution of private property, as against other methods of securing a just social and industrial order.

Round these two sets of proposals and methods the conflict has raged. Every Socialist Movement in Europe was split from top to bottom. America copied. New and ever new Internationals threatened to be born of the dissident sections. Capitalist Europe rocked with laughter. To keep the working-classes divided amongst themselves has always been the wisdom and the joy of the intelligent in the possessing classes. The Socialist Movement began to look ridiculous. It has not yet got back to common sense and sweet reasonableness. In the various national movements, arrogant and conceited young men are continually making fresh "caves." Offshoots of bumptious young people and venerable idiots, who think that wisdom will die with them, keep the general movement in a turmoil of quarrelsomeness whilst the enemy consolidates his ranks. The pity and the folly of it!

So far as I could discover there were at least five sections in the French Conference apparently hating one another far more keenly than the outsider. There was the Extreme Right, which had supported the war without question. There was the Extreme Left which had opposed it without tact. There was the following of Renaudel who opposed the Moscow International. There were the adherents of Vaillant-Couturier who supported it. There were the friends of Longuet, who did both. I do not mean that these last belonged to the cult of the jumping cat! They were not mean and "discreet." They simply wanted to leave the door open for a future reunion of the two bodies of disputants.

I spent the first day listening to the eloquent wranglings of the sections, and then went to view the city of Strasburg. The old parts are French, but the solid new parts of the city are German. It is a quiet old city of cafés and quaint streets and houses. It is dominated by its wonderful cathedral with the historic clock. The small hotel where I stayed, with its German proprietor, was a model of cleanliness. In front ran the canalized river. Bands of troops, black and white, marched through the streets, but the citizens paid little attention to them. Only once did I see a touching thing. A few bold boys marched singing a tune with a familiar sound about it. I stopped to look and listen. Near me was a student, a boy of twenty-three or four, with a broad round face and rather long fair hair. He had tears in his eyes, and held his cap in his hand. What had moved him? Not that simple, boyish singing? Was it the song? I caught the word "Heimland" as the lads marched past, and—yes—there was just one phrase in the song which brought to mind the English melody, "Home, sweet home!"

On the second day I made my speech. The gallant Frenchmen received it well, and I left the platform in a storm of cheers. But that was for the woman and not the speech; for they did not understand a word, and they voted heavily for the Third International at a subsequent meeting! The split was inevitable.

The next day I left for Berne *en route* for Geneva and the conference of the Save the Children Fund. I had to spend several hours at Basle and arrived in Berne at six in the evening. But what was the matter with the place? The station was as quiet as a church on weekdays. And the Hôtel Belle Vue was like a huge crypt, cold and clammy and empty. In that great lounge and immense drawing-room capable of holding comfortably a thousand persons, there were not three people! The drawing-room was dark; and the lounge lit by only a few dim lights. Were all the people in their rooms, or what was wrong?

"You are very quiet, aren't you?" I asked the hotel clerk as I signed the register.

"Yes, madam," he replied. "Most people are leaving Berne. Here are several letters for you which are probably from some of your friends."

I tore open the letters one after the other. Mr. Rudolf Kommer had gone to Berlin. Mrs. Lord was in Lugano. Prince Windischgraetz was in Paris. His wife had left for Prague. The group of German pacifists had returned to Berlin. Dr. de Jong was in Basle. M. Zalewski, the Polish Minister in Berne, whom I had met in England, and with whom I had renewed my acquaintance in Switzerland, was rumoured to have gone as Minister to Athens. Madame de Rusiecka, another Polish friend, was living in Geneva. Baron Szilassy and his sister were in Bex. Mr. de Kay was in Lucerne. Mr. Savery had been sent to the Legation in Warsaw—all, all had gone, the old familiar faces! And what a desolation they had left!

I gathered up my letters and prepared to take a walk to discover if there were anybody left. Was the Assyrian giant with the Gargantuan appetite still sitting in the Wiener Café? I have referred before to Dr. Ludwig Bauer, but he deserves another word. For he was a truly remarkable journalist. From the early days of the war he wrote every day, without exception, the leading article on politics for the Basle *National Zeitung*. His articles were always marked #—so he became known as the "Kreuzlbauer." They were read all over the country, a thing which happened for the first time in the journalistic history of Switzerland, it was said. The little Basle paper became suddenly an organ of national importance. The international representatives, diplomats, foreign correspondents, propagandists read the articles with great care. It is a curious fact that this Austrian was spoken of as "the only neutral in Switzerland." The French Swiss were more French than the French. The German Swiss were more German than the Germans. The Swiss Government tried to steer an equal course between the two sets of belligerents. There the Austrian journalist was useful. He expressed neutrality day by day. His articles were quoted in Paris and in Berlin. Occasionally his paper was excluded from one or the other, he himself being bitterly attacked by both sides. Most of all was he attacked by his Swiss colleagues who resented the great success of the foreign intruder, with a mentality more Swiss than their own. Another and a greater alien, Friedrich Schiller, whose "Wilhelm Tell" is the classic reading of Swiss youth, never saw Switzerland, but had caught the Swiss spirit better than some of the sons of the soil!

Dr. Bauer was not at the café. Neither were the jewelled and fragrant women who used to sip its sparkling wines, whilst they waited in the ante-chamber to Paris for their visa for the Heaven of their dreams. The war produced large numbers of this feminine type. I knew several of them. Sometimes beautiful, often wealthy, in spite of fallen money values, they played their game of coquetry in Berne to while away the time till better things came in sight. The ghastly tragedy of famine passed them by. The sufferings of the war left them cold. The colossal spectacle of Europe's downfall was nothing to them. Clothes, jewels, fine furniture, a good social position were the only things which counted with them. Their lovers from the broken countries they flouted. They had just enough practical sense to see that the things they wanted were not to be found in the land of their birth. Their men had become ineligible. They would take husbands from the lands of the conquerors. The "Entente husband" became an institution and the fair husband-hunters a joke. Beauty, wealth maintained by gambling in exchanges, in return for an "Entente husband" and a visum for Paris and the glory of silks and scents and a place with the conquerors! I know one such woman, a beautiful Pole—but let me be merciful!

On my return to the hotel I found a note from an American friend asking me to dine and saying she would call for me at eight. This was cheering. How it is known so quickly that one is in a place passes my comprehension! Punctually at eight she burst into my room, looking as radiant as the May, although she is nearly forty.

"Tell me," I asked. "How do you keep yourself so young, you amazing woman?"

"Simple enough," she retorted. "Massage and a blameless life, my dear."

We dined with several members of the Hungarian Red Cross, gone crazy with hate of Bolshevism, who talked themselves hoarse about the iniquities of the Jews and ate so many oysters that I began to be nervous for their constitutions. And so ended the last of my days in Berne.

I was too late for the Geneva Conference. The delegates had had their last sitting, and only a social function to say farewell remained. There I met a number of dear friends full of good works. I have written of Mrs. Buxton and her sister. These and their like compensate the world for the idle and mischievous butterflies waiting for their Paris visa and frocks and jewels.

At the theatre that evening a curious little international group talked of their many adventures of travel, with the difficulties of getting passports as a conspicuous item of conversation. One spoke of the amount he had had to pay in bribes in Rumania, another of having lost his passport. "But I had a receipted tailor's bill in my pocket. The Austrian Royal Arms were at the head. It was an old bill. And they accepted it as my passport without a question. It looked important and the fellow who looked at it couldn't read a word, so there was no trouble!" A little picture of Balkan Europe which tells a story one can read only too well.

Baron Ofenheim is reputed to be one of the wealthiest men in Austria. I only know him as the kindest of friends and the most tender-hearted of men. He has a connexion of many years' standing with England and is a man of great business capacity, which he has devoted to helping his unfortunate country out of her terribly trying situation. He was one of the most helpful delegates to the Fight the Famine Conference in London. He attended the Geneva Conference urging a better organization than he believed the Save the Children Fund had then achieved. He favoured activity on a larger scale by a more representative body of people than he considered the organizers of the Fund to be at that time. Doubtless the much superior organization that the Fund has achieved under the able secretaryship of Mr. Golden would satisfy the most severe critic, including the Herr Baron. With him was Sir Cyril Butler, at one time a British official in Vienna. With the opinion of these two distinguished men that Vienna would be a far more useful centre for the League of Nations than Geneva, I heartily agree.

Seven months later, in July, 1920, was held in this same city of conferences the second full gathering of the Second International. A further description of its proceedings is not necessary. Controversy followed the same lines as before. But there was a new tone, a better spirit. Germans, French and Belgians grew amicable once more, friendly without being effusive. The British Delegation numbered this time a few delegates of the "extreme left." They were attending an international conference for the first time. They found the quiet unity too tame. They spoke of the Conference, in private, as dead if not damned. They turned their eyes, if not towards

Moscow, away from the work in hand. With the mistaken judgment of the new-comer they made fiery propaganda speeches, forgetting that they were not talking at the street corners, but to a body of Socialists, many of whom were of the best and most intelligent minds in Europe, some of whom had suffered long years of imprisonment and exile for their political faith. They wanted a demonstration and welcomed the interruptions from the gallery which made Huysmans threaten to close it. The interrupters were a band of very young men with wild hair and red ties. A foolish business....

I had a call one day from Baron Bornemiza, the able Hungarian Minister to Berne, whose practical common sense is a great asset to his country, falling from a frenzy of Red fever into a fury of White. He speaks wonderful English and is not un-English in appearance, tall and straight and broad-shouldered. He was concerned about the cartoons of Admiral Horthy which the International was said to be exhibiting on its stall at the Conference. I imagine the local Socialists would be responsible for the literature stall. I never saw the alleged cartoons. They were probably as tasteless and vulgar as most such things. But it is a pity to pay any attention to them. In England one laughs when one is the subject of these exaggerated and generally offensive pictures. I told His Excellency so. Admiral Horthy must be like the King of England. The King is above the law of libel. Or at least he must not condescend to notice his traducers. To do that is to give them an importance they would not otherwise possess. The atrocities of the Hungarian White Terror, for which Horthy was believed to be responsible, would be the cartoonist's justification of his pictures.

One other person must be mentioned here and then this narrative closes. Dr. Marie de Rusiecka is a Polish lady doctor who served during the Serbian retreat. The stories she is able to tell of that appalling disaster to the Serbian Army make one sick with a shuddering horror. She became an enthusiastic propagandist for peace and all the things which make for peace. She exiled herself from her native land and took up her abode in Geneva. Like all holding her views she was persecuted and slandered. The terribly pro-French Genevese declared her to be pro-German and made life in Geneva impossible for her. She went to Berne. She did more than any other woman, and probably as much, or more, than any one person, to organize the League of Nations Conference. I met her there. Afterwards she took part in the women's conference at Zurich, and organized for Mrs. Despard and myself a highly successful meeting in Berne on the subject of the Treaty of Versailles.

She is a slight little woman, of fair complexion and energetic manner. She has a soft voice, but is quietly convinced and determined. No effort is too much which will advance the cause of peace. She is almost too grateful for any assistance. She is, I believe, deeply religious. She took rooms at the Hôtel de France, a small and humble hotel in Berne, and there she worked like a Trojan. I do not think she is a rich woman, but she must be spending the whole of her means on this work for peace.

Dr. Rusiecka has produced a French edition of *Foreign Affairs*. She is helping to edit a newspaper in Geneva along with the distinguished pacifist M. René Claparéde.

Nothing can discourage this gallant little woman. I have known things happen to her which would have driven most women into the haven of private life. But she goes on—brave, strong, defiant of wrong, and defendant of right. Wherever in Europe the word peace is spoken and meant the name of Dr. Rusiecka will be found to be associated with it.

CHAPTER IX
MORE ABOUT RUSSIA

I have told the story of my visit to Russia in a separate volume. A reference to the last chapter of "Through Bolshevik Russia" would help towards a clearer understanding of the few additional pages upon Russia which are all that can be spared to it in this book. That chapter speculates upon the future of Soviet Russia.

I have seen no reason since writing that book to revise in the slightest degree the judgment of Bolshevism there expressed. One of the points of criticism levelled against it by those who questioned the wisdom of its publication, but not the sincerity of its writer, was that I had not been sufficiently careful to distinguish between Bolshevism for the Russians and Bolshevism for this country. The one, it was argued, was necessary for the break-up of capitalism in Russia. It is unnecessary for the break-up of capitalism in a country where every adult person is equipped either with the vote or with the right of industrial organization.

With the argument I am not for the moment concerned; but I have indeed written foggily if it is not clear from my writing that *I am hostile to Bolshevism as a political creed and system,* and to its application to Russia only less than to its imposition upon England. The attempt to destroy an idea with guns is stupid at any time. To try to destroy it by force of arms in Russia was an unwarrantable cruelty on the part of the Allies, an impertinent interference in another country's internal affairs, and the crowning act of folly of an Entente which has distinguished itself for acts of madness since the days of the Armistice.

Perhaps it would be as well to state once again some of the reasons which moved me to criticism of the Bolshevik leaders, their programme and their policy.

First, let it be admitted once more, and emphasized in a manner which can leave no doubt in the reader's mind, that for the nameless sufferings of the Russian people from hunger, cold and disease, and for the state of war which has kept Europe restless, unsettled and distressed for the two and a half years since the Armistice, the Allied Governments must bear the chief burden of responsibility. During the whole of that time Russia was engaged gallantly beating off one military adventurer after another, equipped by the Allies with arms and stores. She did not want war. She desired above all things peace. With her wireless she filled the air with cries for peace even whilst she dealt triumphant blows to the right and left of her, as one foe succeeded another. These wireless waves struck upon the ears of the whole world and turned pitying hearts towards Russia who had no love for Russia's Bolshevism. Still peace was denied. France, crazy with fear of a possible Russo-German alliance, supplied one adventurer after another with the necessary equipment, in pursuit of a policy which made for the very thing she dreaded. England with her ships blockaded Russia's ports, sowing a deadly hatred for this country in the hearts of mothers and fathers of little children dead of hunger, and making inevitable a Russian policy in the East unfavourable to British interests.

But this fully granted, the Russian Bolsheviks must accept a very considerable part of the blame. These men and women are not fools. The chiefs are highly educated and widely read. They have an incomparable knowledge of world affairs. I very much doubt if there is a man living with a larger acquaintance with the foreign politics of the world than the brilliant Radek, or a woman who knows more of Socialist history and organization than Madame Balabanova. What outsider can judge with perfect fairness the act of a great man in the critical epochs of his country's history? It may have seemed to the Bolshevik leaders, in order to stop the fatal disintegration of Russia's economic life which was the first fruit of peace and the Revolution, of the first necessity to seize power and destroy the beginnings of democratic growth exemplified in the Zemstvo and the National Assembly. Their contempt for any democracy other than a Communist democracy may have sincerely justified itself in their eyes in the miserable circumstances of the time of the Second Revolution. I indict them much less for their swift deeds in the early days of the Revolution than for their settled policy after the Revolution was accomplished, although they must have known that both the one and the other would give the enemies of Russia in Western Europe the excuse for invading her for which they were looking.

No consideration was shown of the effect upon the Russian town populations of the attempt to carry out their complete party programme, with its consequent provocation of blockades, embargoes and wars, at a time when three years of war with Germany had used up even the vast Russian resources and worn her weary soldiers to the very bone and marrow of them. One noted Bolshevik met my remonstrances against the policy, which meant the wilful sacrifice of the entire population of Petrograd, with the words: "But the population of one city, what is that? Three-quarters of a million? Well, but there are plenty of millions left in Russia."

This is the true militarist psychology. I almost imagined I heard Mr. Winston Churchill speak; or General Ludendorff; or Marshal Foch.

The inevitable consequence of forcing a programme upon a people unripe for it, or unwilling, is tyranny and terror. In Ireland it is the tyranny of the minority. In Russia it is the tyranny of the minority. In Russia it is called the "dictatorship of the proletariat," a mere phrase, apt as most clever phrases to enslave and corrupt. The dictatorship of the proletariat means, in Russia, the dictatorship of a handful of clever political economists, very few of whom are proletarians, over an immense mass of peasants and workmen. Their intelligent support they drew from the workmen of the towns, their tacit support from the peasants, whom they bribed with the promise of land. Indeed, they established a system of virtual peasant proprietorship, creating a thousand vested interests where one had existed before, and yielding up the first plank in their programme in the very first hour of their power!

I do not charge the Bolshevik leaders with wilfully contriving terror and torture. I do not suggest they wallowed delightedly in the blood of fellow creatures. Ignorant and lustful brutes, self-elevated to power in remote towns and villages, did deeds in the name of the Soviet which make distressing reading. The official Terror of the Government was aimed at their own firm establishment and not carried on for the mere pleasure of killing. But the Communist philosophy predicates terror, and advocates its ruthless use against the adversary in the supposed interests of a glorious eventuality. To such lengths does the policy that the end justifies the means bring men and women otherwise humane! To such dangers is a population brought which permits its minority to ride rough-shod over the majority as in Russia!

That Lenin and the others sincerely desired peace in the beginning I am convinced. At Brest-Litovsk they issued a manifesto to the world which, for the idealism of its language and the beauty of its appeal, has not been surpassed in the political and diplomatic history of mankind. It was a plea to all the nations and their governments to stop fighting and to make peace upon the basis of self-determination for the nations and without penal indemnities for the conquered, the programme afterwards professed by Allied statesmen in order to undermine the resistance of the German people. The crime of rejecting this proposal rests with Germans and Allies alike. Mutual fears, hates, mistrusts were too strong, too deeply ingrained, and the Russian idealists were despised and rejected of men!

The Trotsky who raised the banner of universal peace at Brest-Litovsk, the prince of pacifists, became the prince of militarists, the great war lord of a hundred and fifty millions of people stung to arms again. The marvellously revived and sternly disciplined armies of Trotsky have performed miracles of soldier-craft which have filled an astonished world with reluctant admiration, tossing aside their enemies, Judenitch, Petlura, Koltchak, Denikin, and Wrangel, like terriers in a barn full of rats. Such exploits and the sympathetic agitation they aroused in the Allied countries compelled the Allies to face facts, always a difficult thing for them to do; and the outstanding fact of the situation is that, whether Bolshevism be approved or not, Soviet Russia must be taken into account in the shaping of the foreign policies of the Western Powers by a statesman who does not wish to go down to posterity as the worst kind of detrimental.

I am not a Communist in the Russian sense of the term. And the Communism of primitive Christianity, voluntary and unselfish, appears not to be practical politics at the moment. I believe that the system called Capitalism will have to give place some day to a collectivist internationalism which shall secure life and the fruits of the earth to its populations in proportion to their needs. I believe this change will come about slowly as the intelligence of the peoples develops, as they become acquainted with facts and see demonstrated before their eyes the insufficiency, insecurity and injustice of a system based upon production for profit rather than for use. Such things as are fundamental to life itself—land, minerals and means of communication—should not be at the disposal and under the control of a small number of private persons any more than the army, the navy and the arsenals. It is too unsafe. For the rest: Those things of which there is an abundant supply might not unreasonably be held privately; provided that nobody who desires them goes without, and nobody's private ownership inflicts injury on the community at large.

But the Russian Communists favour the complete abolition of private property down to the books one reads and the clothes one wears. This programme they have carried out by methods of wholesale and swift confiscation without the slightest consideration for the unfortunate owners, creating new injustices in order to remove the old, and provoking thereby the inevitable reaction. This is of the essence of the revolutionary method. It is not happy for Russia. It would be just as unhappy for England or America.

The Bolshevik Government is now in the fourth year of its existence. This fact is adduced by its admirers in this country as a mark of super-excellence. Truly at a time when European Governments are changed with the regularity and rapidity of moving pictures at a theatre some credit is due to a Government which can survive the shocks of war and revolution through nearly four years of Europe's stormiest history.

But the long life of the present Russian Government is due to three or four primary causes. It is due to Allied support of counter-revolutionary movements, which drew every section of the Russian population together for common defence against the foreign intruder. It is due to the fact that no alternative government has presented itself with a programme which would give more food and furniture, clothes and medicines to the people of Russia. It is due to the fear of the Extraordinary Commission with its agents and spies and prisons and executioners. But above all it is due — and particularly in these latter days since the fear of foreign invasion has departed — to the acceptance by Lenin and his friends of moderate counsels, and the gradually achieved ascendancy in the government of the nation of the more moderate men amongst the Bolsheviks.

It is, and always has been, a mistake to assume that all the Bolshevik leaders are equally extreme. It was not true when we visited Russia in May, 1920. It is much less true to-day. During the period of civil wars and Allied invasions the extreme element was dominant. Now the moderates rule. Lenin has never wavered from his fixed idea of world-communism and world-revolution; but he has proved his greatness to his friends and has confounded his enemies by yielding to the necessity for compromise, making deals with the alien capitalist governments and with the native individualist peasants alike.

Turning to my other pages on Russia for the estimate I there recorded of the keen-brained, merry-eyed fanatic of the Kremlin (for the wisdom and statesmanship of twelve months later have astonished me as much as they have surprised most people), I discovered the following sentences:

> "He (Lenin) impressed me with his fanaticism. This is surely the source of his driving power. And yet I am told that compared with the really fanatical Communist Lenin is mildness itself, and should be classed with the 'Right.' It was rumoured that he is engaged on a new book to be given the name 'The Infant Diseases of Communism,' or some such title, which suggests an honest confession of mistakes made in the early days of the commune. If this be true there is hope of happiness for Russia yet. But I must confess his firm belief in the necessity of violence for the establishment throughout the world of his ideals makes one doubt miserably."

I no longer doubt Lenin's capacity. More than that I am inclined to believe that history will accord to him one of her foremost places when the tale of these times comes to be told, in spite of the terrible blunders and awful crimes for which he will, in part, be held responsible. It takes either a true lover of his country or one who having tasted power knows how to keep it, to confess his mistakes in the ear of a listening world apt to say "I told you so." If Lenin loves power and means to keep it, I, who differ from him in aim and loathe with a deadly loathing his past methods, declare my conviction that it is for no selfish end that he seeks to preserve his hold upon the Russian nation, but for the good of his cause and for the ultimate realization of his dreams that he has risked unpopularity with his extreme supporters, and has met half-way the capitalists at home and abroad. The following sentences extracted from his speech to the Annual Congress of the Russian Communist Party held on March 7, 1921, promise a bright era for Russia yet:

> "As far back as April, 1918, it was thought that the civil war was concluded. In March, 1920, the Soviet Government supposed that a period of peace was beginning, but already in the following month the Polish attack was launched. This experience teaches us that we should not cherish undue optimism, although at the present time there is not a single enemy soldier on Russian territory. Our internal affairs are concerned mainly with problems of demobilization, food supplies and fuel. We have made mistakes in the distribution of the food supplies, although these supplies were much greater than in previous years. Difficulties with fuel were due to the fact that we began to renew our industries at too rapid a rate. We over-estimated our powers in the transition from war-time to peace-time management. Agriculture is passing through a period of crisis, not only in consequence of the imperial and civil war, but also because the new State mechanism is building up its methods of work only by a gradual process, and for that reason it still makes mistakes from time to time. The most important political problem of the present period is the relation between the peasants and the industrial population which in Russia preponderates to a considerable degree. The international situation is marked by an unusually slow development of the revolutionary movement throughout the world, and in no case do we look for its speedy victory. The Soviet Government is therefore

considering the question of the necessity for an agreement with the bourgeois Governments, which would result in the granting of concessions to foreign capitalists in Russia. The agricultural population, which supposes that the Czarist generals are no longer a menace to it and that it is receiving too small a share of industrial products, considers that the sacrifices demanded of it are too great. We must show consideration for the efforts of the agricultural workers. We are introducing a natural food tax which will be distributed in proportion to the resources of the peasantry, and will give a free scope of activity to their material interests. This tax will absorb only a portion of the agricultural worker's produce. What he has left he will be able to sell by means of local markets and trade. And just as the concessions are to provide us with the means of production for our industries, so, too, by showing consideration for the wishes of the agricultural worker, we are at the same time mitigating the agricultural crisis and improving at the same time the relationship between the working classes in the cities and the peasantry. The question of the natural food tax is the most important problem of the Soviet policy. The accomplishment of this task is beset with serious obstacles, and demands the closest concentration of the Party, as well as a clear understanding of the difficulties delaying the dictatorship of the proletarist in a petty bourgeois state."

Thus passes at a stroke the communal ownership of the fruits of the land as well as of the land itself! Thus return the bourgeois institution of private trading and the ancient exploitation of the concessionaire! It was inevitable, and the wise man bowed to the necessity. Lenin's line is the one upon which I hoped and believed that Russia's future *might* develop, the line which, but for the fanaticism of a comparative few, once including Lenin, might have been taken very much earlier with advantage to Russia and the rest of Europe.

But whether this line of slower and more peaceful development will be permitted to Russia remains to be seen. I sincerely hope it may. There are discontented democrats, however, rightly insisting on the speedy restoration of democratic political methods. They want the Zemstvo restored and the National Constituent Assembly. They want simple and equal adult suffrage, as much for the peasants as for the townsfolk. They want vote by ballot. They want freedom of thought, of speech and of the press. They want restrictions on labour removed and freedom of contract restored. They want free trade. Will these good things be given back to the Russians at an early date? I am very hopeful. A good beginning has just been made.

If Lenin has restored to himself and his Government by his drastic reform of the levy on the peasants, those vast millions of Russian folk, he can, if he chooses, continue his regime for an indefinite time. With such modifications in the system as I have just named this would be the best way out of Russia's present distressing state, for, should counter-revolution arise and spread, a new chaos would almost certainly follow, opening up dreadful possibilities for the population; and for the watchful and greedy adventurers, out to carve a kingdom for themselves from Russia's enormous territories, or thirsty to exploit her unimaginable resources of precious metals and rich forests in their own selfish interests, would present the opportunities they are palpitating to use.

But there is yet another element threatening the future happiness of Russia—her own Napoleons, and the flushed and triumphant militarism which supports them. Trotsky has the reputation of an extremist. There is said to be a coldness between Lenin and himself. It is commonly believed that he will not readily disband the army that he has created and employed with such signal success. Not only that, but he believes with many others that Bolshevism can only survive if a strong, active and triumphant army supports it. He believes that the conquest of the East for Bolshevism will not only keep the soldiers busy and add to the glory of Russian arms, but will menace the proud empires which have caused so much unnecessary suffering to his people, and which are still opposing the interests of Russia, though in less apparent fashion. It is openly said in Moscow that Trotsky himself is the coming Napoleon.

The Russo-Polish peace signed at Riga on March 18, 1921, and ratified by Poland on April 16 points rather in the other direction; unless, as is suggested, it was signed through fear of defeat or in order to clear the way for a concentration of warlike operations in the Caucasus and the Near East. The fear of defeat it is impossible to believe in. Russia is too big to be defeated.

The recent news from the Caucasus, however, supplies conclusive evidence, as far as it goes, of a distinctively imperialist policy, which recks as little of the right of self-determination as the policies of capitalist governments. A treaty with Kemal Pasha and joint action between the

Turkish Nationalists and the Bolsheviks against Armenia (that pitiful victim of Allied policy), and Georgia, promised self-government and independence by Moscow only a few months previously; the domination of Azerbaijan from Moscow for the security to Russia of the oil supplies of Baku; the intrusion of Soviet politics into Persia with its intended threat to British interests in India; Bolshevik propaganda marching with the armies or bulging from the portfolios of the political and diplomatic agents of Russia—these things and others, have an alarming appearance of old-fashioned militarist Imperialism very disturbing to those who wish well to Russia, and who long desperately that she shall not copy too closely the aims and methods of the discredited diplomacy of the Western Powers, even though it be on behalf of the whole nation and not of a single class that the methods of conquest and spoliation be employed.

The alliance between Kemal Pasha and the Bolsheviks can have no other meaning than a common design to embarrass the Entente's plans in the Near East, and to menace British and French capitalist interests in India, Mesopotamia and Angora. Kemal Pasha is no more a Bolshevik than the man in the moon. The cynical Radek is clearly aware of all this. He wrote in the Moscow *Pravda* of January 26, 1921, examining the possibility of the revision of the Treaty of Sèvres and the consequent desertion of themselves by Kemal and his army:

> "Which way Kemal Pasha will choose we certainly cannot say; but we have never been so simple as to throw ourselves unreservedly in the embraces of the Nationalists of the East. It is an absolute necessity for us to be on guard, and not only to be awake but to act also. The stronger we are on the Caucasus the more solid our position in Turkestan, the more real our assistance, the more certain shall we be to hasten the development of the East in the direction and in the interests of world revolution."

He rejoices in the same article on the complete Bolshevization of Georgia, the recalcitrant, whilst his colleague, Steklov, in *Isvestia* of January 30, 1921, wrote with equal cynicism of removing "the black point" (Georgia) from the Caucasus, and so making easy joint action between the Kemalists and themselves against the armies serving the interests of the Entente. Thus, in spite of solemn pledges, promises of protection, League of Nations covenants and the rest, the wretched Armenians are tossed into the laps of new tyrants, the close associates of the old, whose unspeakable cruelties towards their hapless dependents have scandalized mankind for generations; whilst the unhappy Georgians have had to stop their constructive work for social democracy to defend themselves almost with bare fists against the faithless Russian hordes whose leaders had guaranteed their independence. Of this I shall write elsewhere.

Writing these words in the warmth of a bright April sun, within sight of trees weighed down with vast masses of snowy blossom, the pink and white of the cherry and the apple, a soft wind from the valley blowing gently in at the tiny casement window, the mind turns to the quite other scenes of exactly a year ago. In the imagination are pictured the endless plains of Russia with the patient peasant walking at midnight behind his span of oxen and his wooden plough; the brown, muddy waters of the rolling Volga with its picturesque rafts carrying whole villages; the red-robed Kalmuk priest in the cold moonlight; the glittering domes of Moscow's thousand churches; the dull, pale-faced hungry crowds of Petrograd; the happy children, utterly fearless, on the great estates of vanished proprietors; the lazy routine of numberless offices; the careworn and incompetent high officials, with their indolent staffs and littered desks and stuffy buildings; the talkative Commissars; the strife, the passion, the idealism of it all.

In Moscow sits Tchicherine, master of the foreign policy of a country the size of Europe. Who would have expected Tchicherine to achieve such an exalted position in so short a time who had seen this delicate man fidgeting on the edge of his chair in the office of the National Council for Civil Liberties, seeking the help for Russian prisoners in England of the Council's Executive Committee? His thin, artistic fingers tapped the table nervously as he spoke in a high-pitched rather strained voice. His manner was shrinking. He lacked the usual voluble earnestness of the Socialist exile. He suggested the gentle and refined artist, the man of taste and leisure. He was full of a timid courtesy. His diffidence was a temptation to the coarse and undiscerning to be rough and contemptuous of the suppliant.

When we saw him in Moscow he looked as though all the woes of the world had been laid by force upon his frail and inadequate shoulders. His clothes appeared to be many sizes too big for him. He looked over his collar like a frightened owl over a hedge fence. Soft and slow of speech, but of quick intelligence and with the clearest outlook, his true friend would none the less wish him a happier fate than to be Minister of State in a country so full of tangled problems as Russia in these dreadful days. Making beautiful music to a company of congenial souls, the samovar steaming merrily and the song going gaily behind warm, close curtains, in the light of a bright fire, till the dawn on the horizon told of the coming day, is the proper life for this gentle Minister, whom to know is to like. Perhaps such a dream-picture comes to him in the small hours of many a weary morning to cheer him to renewed efforts in the cause which alone, he believes, can make his dreams come true.

"You will never go to Russia again, of course," said a friend. "They would never let you come out alive." But I shall go to Russia again some day. I shall go because Russia is the kind of country which, having once won you, claims your interest and affection for all time. You cannot escape the love of her. She draws in a fatal way all who have come under her magic spell.

Russia is crammed full of mystery. Nobody can define her. Her people are lovable, beautiful, idealistic, spiritual; but coarse and cruel too. They are a race of artists with gifts of this sort for mankind that have not yet been dreamt of. Russia is not Bolshevism. This hard, cruel phase will pass, is already passing. What the next chapter in Russian history will be who can tell? What Russia's contribution will be to the world's political problems who will dare to prophesy?

A generation is growing up in Russia which has seen fearful things and done dreadful deeds. Its children have grown weary, toying with corpses. But in spite of that I am sure that Russia will justify the brightest hopes of her. That her gift to mankind will be a great contribution both materially and spiritually I am convinced. At present the land of mystery calls for our aid and co-operation. She will give to us more than we can give to her. But for many years to come she will be clothed in mystery for most, until the material blends with the spiritual and the oneness of life becomes known to all the nations of the earth.

I must tell a true story of Moscow. Hauntingly, like a strange, sad dream, comes the remembrance of that nightly experience in the big city. Every morn, at the same hour, the hour when the last rays of twilight give instant place to the first beams of morning light, the hour of two, a woman's clear voice rang out in a mournful strain, sometimes piercingly shrill, sometimes pathetic; sometimes a tender moan, sometimes a scream of agony; never joyous, ever tormented. The singing seemed to come from the building opposite the hotel where we were lodged, a building which looked like a factory. The song was always the same.

Larghissimo e con angore.

The key was changed for every repetition of the wailing song. Sometimes a line was omitted. Sometimes only three or four notes of a line were sung. A pause of the proper length was made whenever notes were left out of a line, or for the whole line when this was not sung, and the tune resumed at the end of the pause, thus:

Larghissimo e con angore.

The effect was weird and torturing. Whom could it be? What could it mean? Was some sick creature housed opposite? Was some poor woman kept a prisoner by force? Was it a piece of religious ritual? Was somebody mad?

I spoke to one or two of my colleagues about it. They slept soundly and heard nothing. I inquired of the Bolshevik servants. They knew nothing about it. A Bolshevik secretary had the room next to mine. Often he typed all night. Sometimes he paced the room till the day dawned. He could scarcely fail to hear the voice. But he could not help me.

Perhaps some Russian reading this book will write and tell me the meaning of that torturing cry, of that singing ghost which is one of my liveliest memories. She shall be, till then, the symbol of all Russia, tragic, seductive, mysterious; the bride of the East calling to the bridegroom of the West to come and set her free for the marriage which is to be fruitful for the happiness of mankind.

CHAPTER X
FROM RUSSIA BY SWEDEN AND GERMANY

On our way from Saratov on the Volga, to Reval, the interesting old capital of Esthonia, my colleagues and I discussed the possibility of returning to London via Berlin. Dr. Haden Guest and I were especially interested in the condition of child-life in the German cities, he from the point of view of a humane medical man, I as a member of the Executive Committee of the Save the Children Fund, charged with the administration of large sums of money for the relief of the suffering children of Europe. A view of the problem at close quarters would be valuable to our various committees, and useful to ourselves as propagandists.

Reval is a quaint old city, with odd winding streets and cobbled roads. Its harbour is very fine; but at the time of our visit in June, 1920, it showed very few signs of an awakening commerce. The position of the Border Republics was very uncertain, both politically and militarily, and the social condition of the people was lamentable. The fear and hatred of Bolshevism was upon them. The minefields of the Baltic had not been cleared up, which added difficulties to the trade with Sweden, prolonging the voyages and reducing the number of sailings owing to the necessity of careful and roundabout navigation. Finland was too poor to attempt to sweep them; and perhaps a little reluctant through fear of Russia, her powerful neighbour. The Allies were indifferent, and still giving aid and comfort to counter-revolutionaries of all sorts. Anything which added to the miseries of Russia they were slow to destroy; but Russia's near neighbours suffered also.

Poverty and hunger abounded in Esthonia. The shops were almost empty of goods. The value of money was incredibly low. Enough roubles to paper a room could be bought for an English pound. The British Military Mission was obliged to have a large part of its necessary stores sent from home or from Denmark on account of the scarcity; which added to the cost of the mess and made the hospitality so freely and graciously offered a gift of more than ordinary value.

What extraordinarily good fellows were those British officers in Reval! It would be invidious to mention names; but it was perfectly clear why they were so universally popular. A well known and genuine interest in the people they had come to help was the foundation of it.

Mr. Leslie, the able and courteous young British Consul, facilitated our departure from Reval to the best of his ability, and we cast off from all Russian or related contacts on the third day after our arrival in the city. Our destination was Stockholm, where we hoped to get the necessary visa for Germany.

No words can adequately describe the voyage through those lovely Finnish islands. The nearest approach to it is the trip through the Canadian Lake of the Woods or the Greek Archipelago. The little islands stood out like emeralds against the clear horizon line of glowing pink, yellowing into the deep blue of the night sky, with its crescent moon and evening star. The ice-blue waters were as placid as a lake, and no sound but the swish of the ship's propeller disturbed the heavenly stillness that held us through the greater part of the night. Wealthy Americans who rush to Europe to see beauties which abound in their own country might do a service to mankind by popularizing this tour.

We were compelled to submit to medical examination both in Reval and Stockholm, but this being satisfactory, we proceeded to our hotel. The trip to Russia obliged us to spend two weeks in Stockholm, one week each way, because of the infrequency of boats to Russia; which gave us the opportunity of making some interesting acquaintances, and seeing with some degree of thoroughness the most beautiful city of Northern Europe, well wooded and spotlessly clean, and threaded through and through with canals and waterways—a veritable "Venice of the North."

Amongst these new acquaintances was a lady I first met in Geneva at the conference of the Save the Children Fund. The Countess Wilamowitz-Moellendorf is a lovely woman of about thirty-two years of age, tall and graceful as a lily, with a lily's whiteness in her skin, and a lily's pale gold in her hair. She has a soft voice and a gentle blue eye, which occasionally sparkles with pure mischief. She possesses the elegance and simplicity of manner of the *ancien régime*, to which she belongs, and has the gift of humour, suggestive of the Irish strain that is actually hers. Her distinguished husband died during the war at Bagdad and lies buried there. She has an only child, a graceful girl of sixteen growing up into the likeness of her beautiful mother.

This charming woman and devoted mother, Swede by birth and German by marriage, is giving herself without stint to the work of saving the starving babies of Europe. She also has ideas on Labour and International questions which would raise the ghosts of many of her departed friends did they but know these. She attended with me a meeting at the Volkshaus in Stockholm to hear an address by a Labour speaker, and I saw with what regard she is held by the Radical forces of the city.

One day she came to the British Labour delegation to ask their interest in a matter of relief. The Swedish Red Cross, hearing of the epidemics in Russia, and particularly in Petrograd, organized a relief expedition comprising sanitary engineers, plumbers, doctors and nurses to the number of almost a hundred, with supplies of medicines, soaps, disinfectants, and all the equipment of a sanitary and medical expedition. Prince Charles, President of the Red Cross, was extremely anxious that the Mission should set out. He had written twice to the Russian Foreign Office offering his gift; but, although weeks had passed, there was no reply. Would it be possible for us to see Tchicherine and get something definite from him, either an acceptance or a rejection, so that in the event of the latter the Mission might proceed elsewhere?

Some of us saw Prince Charles and heard the story from his own lips. His sincerity was impressive. We promised to do what we could. This grave Swedish prince is a man of distinguished appearance, with a manner of great reserve. He is tall, grey haired and blue eyed, with strong, fine hands. His royal reserve melted for a moment and his blue eyes softened with appreciation when I ventured softly to commiserate him on the death of Sweden's popular Crown Princess, who had died the preceding day. We left his presence reinforced in the belief that humane feeling and practical social service are the disposition and occupation of no particular class. They are the characteristics of the generous and refined of all classes. We told the story to Tchicherine when we saw him; but I very much doubt if the royal gift were accepted. The Russians trust only the Society of Friends. All other relief organizations do propaganda against the Soviet Government, they allege.

One of the most interesting personalities I met in Stockholm was the great traveller and scientist, the friend of kings and kaisers, the distinguished supporter of Germany, Sven Hedin. I lunched at his house in company with some of my fellow delegates. It is a lovely home, especially his own room. This room is lined with exquisitely bound books and filled with curios of priceless value collected during many marvellous journeyings. Signed photographs of numerous monarchs stand in the recesses and on tables. Rich Oriental carpets cover the floor, and precious hangings of rarest quality add colour and character to the room.

He is a remarkably handsome man, with a mass of raven hair slightly tinged with grey, brushed but rebellious; and brilliant eyes, flashing thought. He has a happy manner, full of little gallantries. He possesses the great and saving gift of humour, can be gaily ironical and ironically severe. He is unmarried; but is tenderly devoted to his adoring family of aged mother and gifted sisters. He has an astounding capacity for work, sleeps a little in the afternoon and then works till 4 o'clock every morning. We had great argument with him, which changed neither his opinion nor our own. But there was no crudity of speech or manner on either side to spoil our reputation in a neutral city, or to lessen the quality of his generous hospitality.

The Countess succeeded in getting permission for us to go to Berlin. She introduced us to the German Minister to Sweden, and Prince Wied of the Legation, who were touched by our interest in the children of Berlin. The tax upon aliens entering Germany—at this time about 60 marks—was graciously remitted in our case as we were going on relief work, and we booked our places on train and steamer and began to pack our bags.

The last day in Stockholm was spent most happily with Mr. Branting and his gifted wife at their country house two hours' distance up the straits. Mr. Branting was at this time Prime Minister of Sweden, whose Government was preponderatingly Social Democratic. He and his colleagues in the Cabinet had richly entertained the British delegates to Russia on their way out. This meeting of the great man in his home was of a more precious and intimate character.

The good-natured statesman at home is all that his kindly personality promised it would be. Considerate of the guest who took no wine he had provided specially for her needs. We had lunch in the garden, our table shaded by trees from the hot sun and placed in view of the quiet waters of the channel. Neighbouring houses embedded in foliage peeped at us from leafy bowers. There was no trace of a wind. Bright sunshine filtering through the leaves made a pattern upon the short smooth grass. It was an ideal place for a tired politician seeking to escape for a while from the sordid squabbles and bitter feuds of his profession.

The first time I saw Mr. Branting was at an Allied Socialist Conference in London. His burly form and erect grey hair, standing squarely off a broad forehead, as if seeking to escape from the brush of a pair of fierce, shaggy eyebrows, his large powerful hands and the broad shoulders of a Viking gave him a command over the assembly which a rather weak voice and a slow and deliberate speech might otherwise have diminished. He speaks several languages well, although one who speaks these better, an impish member of the fraternity of the press, whispered to me in Berne that "Mr. Branting confuses the delegates admirably in seven languages!"

On this occasion his wife was dressed in forget-me-not blue, which matched her eyes and set off her fair skin to perfection. Her light, fluffy hair was softly tucked under a large garden hat designed for the sun. She has the strong prejudices mingled with the charm of the French-woman that I am told she is. Mr. Branting is her second husband, and her son has adopted the name of his step-father. She is a writer of books with some claim to serious attention, but I have the misfortune not to have read any of them. She is a delightful hostess, a devoted wife and a very charming woman.

Branting was at this time gravely concerned about the effects of the Peace of Versailles and the Allied policy towards Russia. His Allied predilections during the war entitled his opinions to the gravest consideration, and he expressed himself of the opinion that the conduct of both France and England towards Germany and Russia was conceived in a spirit hostile to true internationalism, and was calculated to produce new wars by reviving old hates. The claim was being made that Russia should pay for the damage due to her withdrawal from the war. Russia retorted by demanding payment for damage done in Russia by counter-revolutionaries paid by England and France. Branting agreed there was logic in the retort. Anti-Bolshevik to the last ounce of him, he none the less regretted a policy which he believed could only have the effect of strengthening the Bolshevik power.

We bade farewell to our good friends at the water's edge and boarded the steamer for Stockholm and the night journey towards Berlin. The Countess accompanied us, and she and I shared a compartment. The swift Swedish express brought us by morning to the Trellborg-Sassnitz steamer which conveyed us across waters as smooth as a lake to the German side.

We could only spend four days in Berlin. We had therefore carefully to map out a programme so as to accomplish as much as possible. There were the courtesy calls at the British Embassy and the British Military Mission to be made first. At both places the greatest interest was manifested in our trip to Russia. We told the story to Lord Kilmarnock over a pleasant cup of tea at the Embassy, and repeated it to General Malcolm and his staff at the Military Mission during lunch.

But I was extremely anxious, if it could be done in the time, to see representative men and women of every shade of German politics. The Countess was of the greatest possible help in bringing us into touch with one section. The German Foreign Office was equally obliging. British newspaper men gave a hand, with the result that we actually accomplished our desire in this respect, and left Berlin having seen the spokesmen of every party in the Reichstag. We found time to visit the Reichstag in session, and had the experience of hearing the speech of Herr Fehrenbach and seeing the dignified temper of the Assembly under circumstances of extreme trial and provocation.

The Allied representatives in Berlin were seriously concerned at the time with Germany's alleged defaulting in the matter of disarmament. Our generous Britons, with not an ounce of ignorant hate in them, were not quite sure that Germany was not playing a game of gigantic bluff. It was impossible for me to believe that, after talking with many cultivated and sincere Germans. Fear of Communists on the part of the middle classes as strong as the fear in France of Germany; fear of the Junkers and the middle classes on the part of the Communists (of whom it was alleged there are 500,000 in Germany), was responsible for the charges of concealed guns and hidden rifles freely made by both sides. The Communists had thousands of rifles hidden in the woods, it was wildly said. The Junkers had quantities of ammunition and machine-guns secretly stored for future use against the common people was the counter-charge. It was this fear that put the Englishman Phillips Price on the side of the Allies in their demand for Germany's complete disarmament. This interesting character has given up his wealth in England, embraced political Communism and married a German workgirl. When I saw him he looked very happy, rejoicing in the birth of a child to him. He, as guileless as many another, believed that France would disarm when the Germans were made helpless. With a truer estimate of the realities Germany refused to be convinced. Hence the passionate plea from her political leaders for more consideration of her difficulties, which had been interpreted by the Allies as a crafty attempt to evade the terms of the Treaty.

Amongst the politicians I saw in Berlin was a little group of German Nationalists. The most distinguished of them was the uncle of my gentle Swedish friend, a scholar of international reputation whom the great Universities of this country delighted to honour before the war, Professor Wilamowitz-Moellendorf. He is a proud and gentle old man, whose white hair only gives the impression of many years, with a grave scholarly manner, and an air of great distinction. His reasonable and proper regret was that scholarship and culture should have steeped itself in the vulgar passions of the slum and the gutter during the years of war, forgetting their dignity and worth in the disgusting welter of political hates. All the time his speech about England was courteous and kind, and though his Oxford friends had given him just cause for resentment, he kept his happier memories of her green. His was not the anger of that other scholar, Herr Edouard Meyer, half mad with the sense of injustice and wrong.

This little group of German Nationalists met me in the splendid lobby of one of the big Berlin hotels, and in a quiet corner we discussed the then political situation and the ominous signs of the times. There was the usual keen interest in the Russian adventure. Professor Wilamowitz-Moellendorf was not present on this occasion.

The most remarkable personality of the group was a tall soldierly man whose stern expression of face and grey hair were possible relics of bitter war experiences. After a few idle phrases in complimentary vein, he turned suddenly upon me and demanded fiercely: "Mrs. Snowden, why have you come to Germany?"

The sudden question startled me, but I concealed my surprise and replied: "Ever since the publication of the Peace Treaty I have been trying to come to Germany to tell the people here that there *are* men and women in England who do not break their pledged word and who want a square deal even for their foes. I want to shake hands with everybody here who is willing, along with us, to help to mend a broken world."

His reply was startling: "When I came into the room just now I shook hands with you and I am still suffering from the surprise of it. I had taken a vow that never again would I touch the hand of an English person, man or woman. I had believed in your nation. I had thought it would honour its pledged word. I was foolish enough to think that British statesmen meant what they said, and that Wilson's programme was seriously intended. I was wrong. I made that vow. And I took your hand just now. I was wrong again."

"I think I understand," I murmured. "In the same circumstances I should have felt as you feel."

"*Do* you understand, I wonder? Do you understand that for us Germans there is nothing left but black despair? Do you realize that our children are dying of hunger? Do you understand that our young men have no careers open to them? Do you understand the pain of being spat upon, the torment of being thrust down every time you attempt to rise? Do you know what it is to be robbed of your faith in idealism, your belief in goodness, your hope for mankind? I find it difficult to believe that you understand."

The pain in his voice, the look in his eyes hurt. He went on: "If there is any gleam of hope for Germany to be found anywhere it lies in religion. No, no," he said hastily, noting my glance of inquiry, "I do not mean the Churches, although there must be Churches to give form and substance to the thing. The Churches must remain, but they must be reformed and reformed from within. By religion I mean that looking and striving upwards for better things without which the world perishes. If my unhappy people can lay hold again of that and keep it, there may be a little hope for them. For myself there is no hope. Everything is gone. My country is utterly destroyed. There is nothing left to live for, unless" —and here a new and fiercer light came into his tired eyes— "unless after all the Communists are pointing the way. Russia's untold millions and our officers. It may be so."

He was quiet for a moment. "I do not like Communism. I do not want to see Communism in Germany But when our position is so bad that nothing we can do will make it worse and something we may do might make it better, what would you?"

Another and a longer pause, and then came his final word: "If our enemies refuse to give us a gleam of hope for the future, and if the Communists of Russia *have* shown us the only way to throw off the intolerable burden of insult and oppression, *I go with them*. And there are many like me in Germany."

And I learnt before leaving Berlin that of the many like him, General Ludendorff was one.

From this interesting gathering I betook me to the house of the Socialist President of the German Republic, President Ebert. I found him seated in a comfortable library chair, in a pleasant room overlooking a garden, a plain-spoken simple old man, of a natural and pleasing dignity. He could speak no English, but there was an interpreter present. Also, the Ex-Chancellor Müller, looking much better in health than when I saw him in Berne, stood behind the President's chair whilst we talked. Once more we related our adventures in Russia and drew from the President that the Communists of Germany were a troublesome and incalculable element, complicating the situation woefully for those desirous of keeping order till Germany was out of her difficult debate with the Allies.

I could not help comparing President Ebert with the two other Socialist Presidents of my acquaintance, Herr Seitz of Austria and Herr Eisner of Bavaria. Herr Seitz was professional in style, well dressed and bourgeois in appearance; Herr Eisner was Bohemian in appearance, not very clean in his dress and style. President Ebert was suggestive of the typical English Trade Union leader, good-tempered and comfortable looking, as good as most and not so clever as many, less liable to rouse antagonism than a more brilliant person; more apt to steer the ship of a troubled country across a stormy sea than a steersman given to taking risks with rocks and whirlpools in order to reach the haven a little sooner. I must say I liked the homely President of the new Germany.

That same evening we assembled in one of the private rooms of the Kaiserhof the leading lights of the Independent Socialists. To our regret Herr Kautsky was in Vienna, but there came to drink coffee with us the Herren Breitschied, Dittmann, Ochme, Kuenzer and Oscar Cohn, an amiable and interested group. We wanted them to talk about Germany, but they preferred to ask us questions about Russia. Most of them were about to leave for Russia on a similar expedition to our own. We answered their questions rather wearily, for the story had become very stale by this time. These men left us with two distinct impressions. The first was that the Socialists of Germany are for the most part disinterested in the Peace Treaty, and their minds are not engrossed to an appreciable extent with such questions as the distribution of coal, the assessment of reparations, the disarmament of Germany, or the mad designs of French Imperialists. They look upon all these things as so many inevitable steps in the dissolution of the old order. They see representatives and supporters of the old order, as if maddened with lust and revenge, doing their very best to make sure the passing of their authority, and they smile and pursue their various avocations, calm amid the storms that stir the breasts of the petty bourgeoisie and the impoverished aristocrats. Their only apparent political interest lies in the future and how that is to be shaped. Shall they follow the leadership of Russia? Or shall they make their own way in their own fashion out of the chaos which the world's capitalists and militarists have created? As a matter of fact, the same debate is exercising the Socialists of every country, and the Second International (Berne) and the Third International (Moscow) are the symbols of the conflict.

To my regret there were no Socialist women in this little party. The rush into Berlin without letting anybody know I was coming, and the rush out again at the end of a few days, made it difficult to see all those it would have been pleasant and useful to see. In the Reichstag building I had counted seven women members of Parliament seated at their desks, and thought of our hard-working and courageous Lady Astor still unsupported by a single woman colleague. I believe there are many more than seven women in the German Parliament, though exactly how many at the moment I cannot say. But they looked very normal and thoroughly competent, and mingled with their fellows in an accepted comradeship of political labour very pleasing to observe.

I met Herr Dernburg at the Club House of the Democratic Party. He assembled a few like-minded people to meet us. Most of them spoke excellent English, all appeared to understand it. I like Dernburg very much; but for some he has an unfortunate manner which makes enemies. His frankness is regarded as mere brutal bad manners. It is nothing of the sort, and I like it. It makes for clearer understanding than the polite pretences of the less courageous. I cannot reproduce in his exact words what Herr Dernburg said, but the substance of part of his long and able discourse was the cruelty of the starvation policy of the Allies and in particular in its effect upon the children. "Your people come to Germany and report that we are pretending to be poor. They see our good clothes, neatly brushed, and our generally tidy appearance and they say that Germany is better clothed than they are. They do not realize that we are reaping now the reward of our habits of thrift. The clothes that we are wearing are many years old, taken out of wardrobes and altered as best might be to suit the fashion of the hour. Women's dresses are frequently made out of the dyed linen, bed and table, which every German girl begins to accumulate for her marriage as soon as she leaves school or earlier. Many of our children wear paper clothes or garments woven of grasses. Always are our clothes kept well brushed and used with care. It is a feature of the German character, this neatness, cleanliness and industry. Look at Berlin. Would you think that a city so full of woes could find time and heart to be so clean and trim? And yet, compared with the Berlin of pre-war days, she is soiled and stained almost beyond knowledge to those who knew and loved her well. Our hotels are crowded with rich gourmands chiefly from foreign lands; but go into our little homes, the homes of the miners in the Ruhr, the homes of the workers in Leipzig, Frankfurt, Nuremberg, Hamburg, and see in the wan, pinched faces of the children and their mothers what the peace is doing to those whom the war did not kill."

There were those in Berlin who had carefully preserved the speeches of British statesmen during the war. One such drew out of his pocket a whole note-book full of phrases from the speeches of Mr. Lloyd George and Mr. Asquith. "Listen to me," he said, "and I will read you what your rulers said, and what the new-born Germany believed, to its present sorrow." He fingered the loose news-cuttings and selected one from the rest. Clearing his throat he began: "Mr. Lloyd George on January 5, 1918. 'The destruction or disruption of the German people has never been a war aim with us from the first day of this war to this day…. Our point of view is that the adoption of a really democratic Constitution by Germany would be the most convincing evidence that in her the old spirit of military domination had indeed died in this war and would make it much easier for us to conclude a broad democratic peace with her!' Mr. Lloyd George on November 12, 1918. 'No settlement which contravenes the spirit of justice will be a permanent one. We must not allow any sense of revenge, any spirit of greed, any grasping desire to override the fundamental principles of righteousness.' Mr. Lloyd George on the same date: 'We shall go to the Peace Conference to guarantee that the League of Nations is a reality!' Mr. Bonar Law, September 24, 1914: 'We have no desire to humiliate the German people.' Mr. Lloyd George, September, 12, 1918: 'We must not arm Germany with a real wrong. In other words, we shall neither accept nor impose on our foe a Brest-Litovsk treaty.'"

"Enough," I said, "I know all these speeches by heart. It has hurt me just as much as you that the Peacemakers have departed from their promises!"

"No, no," he said sharply, "not so much, not nearly so much. It has *hurt* your *pride*, but it is *killing* our *children*. Where is the comparison?" And he turned away in disgust.

The Hôtel Adlon is like the Hôtel Belle Vue in Berne and the Bristol in Vienna, full of the oddest assemblage of human curiosities that the storms of war have tossed together. The Countess and I dined there one evening after the opera to amuse ourselves with the spectacle. Every table was crowded. It was with the greatest difficulty that we secured places. Eventually, and with the aid of a little English silver, we were invited to take seats in the corridor leading to the main dining-room. Herr Stinnes, the great man of industrial Germany, the coal king, iron master, high financier, newspaper proprietor, political "boss," millionaire—large-eyed, impressive—the most powerful magnate in Central Europe at the present moment—sat at the next table to our own. In the corner was a famous dancer, impudent and vivacious, a dainty profligate. There were the German *nouveaux riches* in unaccustomed corsets and high-heeled shoes, hot and miserable under the brilliant lights. A group of fresh-looking British officers gave the wholesome touch to a hectic scene. Hysterical women, half-dressed, sang snatches of accompaniment to the waltz strains of the orchestra. A French officer made undisguised love to a fascinating brunette at a near table. Two out of three had the brilliant eyes and swarthy skin of the Jew. Every language under the sun could be heard. It was a veritable Tower of Babel. It suggested nothing so much as a company of condemned criminals spending a last riotous night before the hanging in the morning.

A pleasanter meal was eaten at the House of the American High Commissioner. America still being at war with Germany had no ambassador, but his equivalent, Mr. Drexel, was our courteous host on this occasion, and at the same table I met my old acquaintance of the American Legation in Berne, Mr. Hugh Wilson. Mr. Wilson is a delightful young American diplomat of wide sympathies and progressive views. I made his acquaintance through the kind offices of our friend in common, Mr. William Bullitt, the courageous young American who resigned his position as part of the American Delegation to Paris when he discovered that the Peace Treaty violated every one of President Wilson's Fourteen Points.

Mr. Wilson is small and slim, with a winning smile of extreme good nature; but he is very impatient, and properly so, with the selfish dogmatists who do not mind if the world be destroyed if only they may attempt to force everything and everybody within the four corners of their particular creed.

America's diplomacy is rich in talent if it possesses many young men as able as Mr. Hugh Wilson and his friend, Mr. Bullitt.

In one of the children's clinics in Charlottenburg I saw the saddest sight since my visit to Vienna, crowds of little girls and boys, stripped for the doctor one by one, pitiful pale faces, ribs sticking through their bodies, hollow chests, fleshless arms—doomed to die from pulmonary disease, the helpless innocent victims of the war and of the peace. The physician received us coldly, and we could see that he felt bitter; but his manner was correct, and he warmed a little as he gradually realized that no impertinent curiosity but a real desire to understand and help had brought us to his clinic. "The next generation of Germans will be three parts diseased," he said in a dead level voice more terrible than passion. "Is that what your people wish?" I assured him that our people did not know what was happening, but that it would be our business to tell them. Since that time the British miners alone have subscribed more than £12,000 to the fund for relief. And it may be the miners, whose standard of living is threatened at this time, who will be the first great body of workmen to learn, and the first to teach the connexion between foreign politics and the daily circumstances of their lives. The ruin of the English export trade in coal is the direct outcome of that part of the Treaty of Versailles which provides that Germany shall supply to France coal so much in excess of her needs that, not only need she not import coal from this country, but she can export it to other countries which were formerly our customers.

With the artistic life of Berlin I was not able in the short time I was there to get into close contact. Some day it will be my object to do so. The world of politics is not the only world, nor the best. The world that interprets the world, the world that takes you out of the world, the world of art is the best of all worlds. And when the passions of living men, tearing and wounding the innocent, sicken the soul, the exploits of the dead, read by the fireside, or rendered in song and dance and drama, offer a refuge for weary body and mind, tired with their fruitless protest against cruelty and wrong.

One interesting artist of Germany I may call my friend, Karl Vollmoeller, author of *The Miracle* produced in London at Olympia in 1911. He is sometimes spoken of as the "Voltaire of Würtemberg" because of his physical likeness to Voltaire. He is small and pale, with fair hair, and thin, rather pinched features. I imagine he is very delicate in constitution. He is a scholar, a poet, a man of the world, one of the leading German neo-romanticists. He spoke to me and another of the time when Lord Northcliffe, whom the flighty young Radical intellectuals of this country have dubbed, "Alfred and Omega," ironical of his pretended omniscience, boomed *The Miracle*, turning what threatened to be a failure into an overwhelming success. Whimsically he spoke also of Charles Cochran, who organized the Olympia "Miracle" season of Max Reinhardt, and who is now supposed to be the leader of the campaign against German plays.

Vollmoeller told many amusing stories of the rehearsals at Olympia, of Engelbert Humperdinck, the composer, Maria Carmi, the actress who played the Virgin, Max Pallenberg, the greatest comic actor of the German stage, Trouhanowa, the dancer, and so on.

Some time later Vollmoeller's *Turandot* was produced at the St. James's Theatre and *The Venetian Night* at the Palace. The latter caused considerable friction with the Lord Chamberlain. The performances were stopped for a day or two. Finally there was a compromise, and the performances were resumed. These reminiscences of the artist were full of a quaint interest. They revealed the utter folly of war and materialism in the light of the universality and beauty of art.

At the end of our four days we left Berlin, travelling *via* Cologne. There was a compulsory break of twelve hours there. It gave us an opportunity of seeing the city under Allied occupation, and of taking a trip up the Rhine. There were no outward and visible signs of unhappiness in the people; but I have long since learnt that the broad highway is not the place where respectable misery flaunts itself. That hides itself behind closed curtains and thrusts its children out of sight of the pitying eye of the foreigner. Still, the general appearance of the people was better here than in Berlin. They had more colour. They were not so thin. The middle-class crowds which came on to the steamer at Bonn and other towns as we sailed up the beautiful river to the cherry country of the Drachenfels were glowing with health by comparison with the anæmic Berliners, dragging tired feet along the hard and unsympathetic pavements. The Rhine is a glory. And the view from the top of the Drachenfels exhibited a panorama of soft wooded beauty which made the hot air of the city cafes a nightmare memory.

From Cologne to Antwerp, a ten hours' journey through land almost literally flowing with milk and honey! Belgium is the richest war country in Europe. Her fields were brown with waving corn. Her fruit trees were laden with fruit. The restaurant on the train was packed with food, ample supplies of rich butter and milk and cream; eggs in abundance. Coming straight from the starving cities of Germany and Russia, the abundance of Belgium was a relief to the mind. And there are generous hearts in Belgium (as in France) which some of her politicians belie.

There is nothing so disgusting about war psychology as the willingness with which decent men and women will listen to any story which discredits the enemy. Whether it be true or not is no concern of theirs. They believe it *could* be true. So it must be true!

A rumour was set afloat in the Allied countries that Germany was converting the money which was being raised in America for relief purposes to political uses through the German Embassy in the United States. What was the fact? It was simply that the money raised in America was used by the German staff for its own expenses, and an equal amount credited to relief accounts by the Government in Germany in order to avoid the risks from torpedo activity of sending the money by ship. The rumour was, of course, an attempt to prevent relief being sent to little German children. But it failed; as it deserved to fail.

Thank God, there is one thing which unites the great masses of men and women of all nations, whether in peace or in war; and that is a tender concern for children. When Nature fails there, and children are deliberately sacrificed to satisfy the ambitions of men, the end of the world will come, even though all the guns be cast into the midst of the sea, for the belief in immortality, which is implicit in the love of men and women for children, will have given place to a calculating materialism in which the be-all and end-all is self. And selfishness is of the very essence of corruption.

CHAPTER XI
CONCERNING THE JEWS

"I hear you are going to Georgia," said Mr. Macdonald to me as we sipped our coffee in the hotel breakfast room one morning in Geneva. I had heard nothing about an expedition to Georgia and expressed my surprise. "Well, I happen to know that arrangements are on foot for a delegation from the Second International to visit that country and that we shall be amongst those invited to go. Will you accept?" he continued, lighting his pipe and rising to go.

My first impulse was to say no. I had been home from Russia barely four months. Anything remotely connected with the Russia I had seen had not the faintest attraction for me, and the Caucasus was only recently a part of the great Russian Empire, and enjoyed an independence of doubtful quality and stability. Apart from all that, the journey was frightening, not because of its dangers, which were real but not known, but because of its fatigues, which were numerous and foreseen.

When Tseretelli, the handsome and distinguished Georgian who represents his country in Paris so ably, and whose revolutionary career during the old regime in Russia included several years of solitary confinement, approached me with a cordial invitation to visit his country, instead of refusing I took a day on the hills on the French side of Geneva to think about it and promised a definite answer on the following day.

A Polish fellow-delegate, K. Czapsritski, came with me, and I told him of the scheme. He neither spoke nor understood English, and my German was negligible; but we contrived to understand each other in a curious mixture of French and German. When I spoke of the Georgian enterprise he waxed suddenly warm and eloquent.

"Why don't you come to Poland, comrade? You go everywhere—to Petrograd, Moscow, Berlin, Vienna, Paris, Geneva, but never to Warsaw or Cracow. Why not? We need you in Poland more than they need you in Tiflis. Surely Poland has as good a claim as Georgia?" I had praised the hills by which we were surrounded. "We have beautiful mountains in Poland, far more beautiful than these," he said, waving his arm in the direction of the Alps, shimmering in the mists of a summer morning. "Our mountains are wild and solemn. And very, very beautiful"—his voice grew tender. "Come to Poland and read Heine in the Polish hills." I had brought a copy of Heine's shorter poems with me, and we had read them together at a wayside inn where we called for coffee. I shall remember that little inn for another reason, not so happy. The last time I saw my friend Mary MacArthur in the flesh was when she flashed past that tiny inn in her automobile, on her way to Italy in a restless search for health, never found.

"But the Labour Party has already sent a delegation to Poland along with other Socialist nationals, Mr. Tom Shaw, M.P.——"

"Yes, yes," he interrupted, "it is true. But we want more to come. We want a woman to come. We should like you to come. Our condition is very bad. We need help and we need understanding. We think the world does not like us very much."

"But why do you say that? Some of us are inclined to think that Poland is the spoilt darling of the Entente. Surely France, at least, likes you very much!" I said, with a quizzical look at his dark, rather heavy good-natured Jewish face. He appeared to be a well-educated specimen of his race with the broad forehead and developed cranium of so many intellectual Jews. He was certainly very widely read in Polish, French and German literature.

"But perhaps you fear the Bolsheviks?" I ventured, inquiringly. "I gather from the newspapers that Trotsky's generals are massing their troops for a triumphal entry into Warsaw."

"Trotsky will never enter Warsaw," said my colleague confidently. "I do not believe we have anything to fear from the Bolsheviks. There are very few of them in Poland, practically none amongst the peasants; and the Socialists of the towns are very largely Social Democrats."

"But your fellow-countrymen in this city, to whom I spoke last night, do not think with you on this matter"—and I mentioned the names of a group of Polish exiles in Geneva whose chief preoccupation of mind was the almost certainty that Poland was about to be overrun by the armies of Russia. "They are very nervous and anxious. They imagine that British Labour has more power than it really has, and are trying to get permission from the French Government to travel by Paris to London in order to interest the British working-class leaders in their side of the story. And they are quite right," I added, "for Labour will one day be all-powerful in England, and at the present moment the British Labour Movement is convinced, rightly or wrongly, that the heavier share of the blame for this fighting belongs to the Poles. They believe the Poles began it by attacking the Russians."

I made this statement to M. Gavronsky of the Polish Legation in Switzerland, and he promptly retorted that it was not true.

"But it is not enough that I go home and say to British Labour that it is not true the Poles began it. I must have positive proof of this if I am to do you any good."

"Well, I can give it to you," said M. Gavronsky. "But I should like to go to London myself and give it to the Labour leaders personally. It is, of course, very difficult to apportion the blame in any conflict, to say who began it and when it began. The raids upon the homes of the Polish peasants by the ravenous Russian troops, who stole all the food and clothing they could lay their hands on, burnt the farms where there was any show of resistance, and ill treated the women were the beginning of the trouble. Very properly the peasants hit back when they could. If your people call this resistance to Bolshevik violence beginning the war, there is nothing more to be said. But I don't. I admire them for it. What do you suppose Englishmen would have done in the same place? The same thing, of course. I have lived in England. I know them. But"—and here he sprang to his feet and began pacing up and down the room, his handsome face distorted with rage—"the most awful thing these damned Bolsheviks have done is the ill treatment of our prisoners. The brutes have sent Polish officers back to their camps mutilated in the most horrible fashion. That we shall never forget nor forgive."

To what extent these charges and counter-charges of horrible atrocities are true I am not able to say. They are made by every army in Europe against its enemies. I can speak with definiteness only of those things I have seen, and with confidence only of what I have heard from those witnesses whose calm and dispassionate judgment and power to sift and weigh evidence I know; whose cool blood gives their testimony a certain value. But there was no doubt whatever in the mind of this ardent young Polish patriot and supporter of Pilsudski that the most awful outrages had been perpetrated upon Polish soldiers helpless in the hands of their enemies.

M. Gavronsky is related to the great Polish family, the Radziwills. Despite his aristocratic birth and connexions he is, I am convinced, a man of genuinely democratic sympathies. He is very English in appearance, tall and fair and fresh-complexioned. He speaks English better than most Englishmen. He joins to a delightful boyishness and engaging frankness the elegant manners of a finished specimen of our race. At his request and that of his friends, I introduced him to Mr. Sidney Webb and Mr. J. R. Macdonald, and left him to make upon these two such impression as he could.

Soon after this the situation on the Russo-Polish front completely changed, to the astonishment of the whole world. Warsaw forgot its follies and rose like one man to resist the invaders. The failure of supplies and the breakdown of discipline caused the Russian armies to be driven back. Warsaw broke into a mad riot of joy. The restraining influence of the Allies, whose experience of Russia had developed a certain wisdom in them, saved the jubilant Poles from the stupid blunder of a vindictive pursuit. Some sort of a peace treaty has been patched up between them; but like every other peace treaty made during the last two and a half years it is scarcely likely to prove worth the paper it is written upon.

I asked my companion of the hills to tell me more about Poland. "The trouble with you Poles is that you will not stop fighting. You are everywhere looked upon as the *enfant terrible* of Europe. Your ridiculously disproportionate army of 600,000 men not only keeps your naturally rich country poor, but is a disturbing factor to the whole of Europe. Of course," I said hastily, not wishing to hurt, "I know quite well that, as a Social Democrat, you are personally hostile to all militarist enterprises. I say what I have said because I am really sorry for the unpopularity which Poland will bring upon herself when it is discovered whose restlessness it is which is preventing Europe from settling down. You are helping the opinion to grow that the small nation is a big nuisance whatever may be said of the theory of self-determination." He grinned understandingly, and continued his interesting talk.

Poland's lot during these years of war has been a particularly sad one. Her plight has at times been terrible. Her fields have been trampled by three armies: the Russian Imperial, the Russian Bolshevik and the German. Whole villages have been razed to the ground. People have died by the roadside in tens of thousands, of hunger, cold and fever. Flights of refugees and cruel evacuations have cost the country untold lives. I was told by a British General, concerned himself with the evacuation of one Polish city, a frightful story which he knew to be true, and one of many equally horrible and equally true.

The weather was intensely cold with the unimaginable cold of Poland in winter. Food was difficult to get and clothing almost impossible. The evacuation was conducted on foot, in open carts without springs or in slow railway trains without any heat. A young mother and father with three small children were amongst the travellers in one of these trains. The cold snow and bitter wind blew in through the broken windows. The children sobbed with cold and hunger. As the train crawled miserably on the sobs became pitiful moans for water. Soon the moans of two of them stopped altogether. They were frozen dead to the seats! The train stopped at a tiny station. To save the last child the frantic mother leapt out of the train for water and, returning, had the agony of seeing husband and child and corpses carried away from her by the rapidly vanishing train. She shrieked aloud. They arrested her for being without a passport. She was conveyed to the police station, raving. Some days later she died, quite mad.

The soil of Poland is very rich. If her armies could be disbanded and set to work upon the fields, Poland could very speedily feed not only her own starving children but millions of other children also. When one of the organizations for relief heard from the beautiful Princess Sapieha the story of the appalling suffering of Poland's children, the wholly sympathetic committee, whilst promising help, felt bound to point out that it was like pouring money into a sieve to send it to a country for ever challenging the fortunes of war. It is, alas! French policy which is responsible for the militarist spirit and the military adventures of Poland. French officers train the regiments. French soldiers fill the cafés and theatres. French promises keep the people happy. It is the fashion now in Poland to worship the French and to imitate them. But the day will come when Poland, along with the rest of Europe, will discover to its infinite cost that the evil of militarism is just as menacing and corroding to civilization when dressed in the uniform of a French General as in that of a Prussian Guard.

Russia and Poland are popularly conceived to be the pivot and centre of what is called the Jewish problem in Europe. The outrageous anti-Jewish propaganda which is being conducted all over the world is a disgrace to our modern civilization. There is a certain reasonable explanation of it, so far as the people of Central Europe are concerned, in the paralysing fear of Bolshevism which possesses them, invariably associated with the Jews. It is astounding how many otherwise perfectly intelligent human beings believe Bolshevism to be an emanation from the Jewish brain. Trotsky is a Jew, Radek is a Jew, Zinoviev is a Jew, Balabanova is a Jew, Bela Kun is a Jew, therefore all Jews are Bolshevik and all Bolsheviks are Jews; which is absurd! As a matter of fact, only two out of the seventeen or eighteen members of the Bolshevik Cabinet at the time of the British Labour delegation's visit to Russia were Jews. The most commanding personality in Russia at this hour is not a Jew. He is, if anything distinctive, a Tartar.

"I like your book 'Through Bolshevik Russia' very much indeed," has been said to me over and over again, "but you are too kind to the Bolsheviks. Surely you are aware that the whole Russian business is part of a Jewish conspiracy hatched in New York with the idea of getting possession of the whole world, in order that the Jews may be revenged upon mankind for the things they have suffered in every country since the beginning of the Christian era?"

"Rubbish," I have said with more force than politeness. "Surely you know that nursery-maids since the beginning of time have frightened little children with bogey stories of just this sort. Don't be a child"; this to a pale and agitated young man who accompanied me home from one of my meetings, and scarcely knew how to contain himself for horror of the thing he believed.

"But," he continued excitedly, "there's Trotsky in Russia, Bela Kun in Hungary, Adler in Austria, Shinwell on the Clyde; there was Liebknecht in Germany, Holst— —"

"Stop, for Heaven's sake!" I interrupted. "Before you go any farther I want to tell you that I know personally both Shinwell and Adler. Shinwell is no more a Bolshevik than you are. The biggest Bolshevik in this country comes from South Wales, and he is made of lath and plaster. A lion on the platform, he roars as gently as a sucking dove when negotiating with the employers. You need have no fear of him. I hear he has been found wanting by his fellow-Bolsheviks and his resignation has been called for. As for Adler, he is one of the most courageous of living men, and has saved Austria from the Bolshevism that for a time captured Hungary. Liebknecht is not a Jew."

"Well, you can't deny that there are a million and a quarter Jews in New York and that the East End of London is full of them."

"But they are not necessarily Bolshevik," I replied. "The rich Jew is rarely, if ever, a Bolshevik. He is like the rich Gentile, he has too much to lose. The rich Jew is not only an anti-Bolshevik; he is sometimes anti-Jew! That is, he loses his sense of Jewish nationality in his citizen's pride in his adopted country."

"Henry Ford doesn't take so easy a view of it as you do. He is putting up a great fight against the Jews in Detroit. What about Italy? What about Ireland?"—here his voice fell to a fearful whisper—"Sinn Fein, you understand? De Valera is a Portuguese Jew."

"How do you know that?" I had heard this wild story before and had made careful inquiries in Ireland. It was denied amidst shrieks of hilarity. But if it were true it would have had no terrors for me.

"Lord Alfred Douglas— —" he began; but I stopped him, tired of it all at last.

"Then that is all?" I queried. "*Plain English* and, it may be, the *Morning Post* is your authority for all this nonsense? Here is where you forge your mighty weapons?" He nodded. "Well, I happen to like the *Morning Post*. I like its brutalities. I admire its consistency. It delivers frontal attacks upon its enemies. It makes no pretence of friendship it does not feel. It is as full of vices as most newspapers, but you know where you have it. There is no flirting with the thing it hates. It is against every political principle I stand for; abuses like a fishwife everything I cherish. It fills me with blind fury on occasion. But it does not cook its news and — well, I like it. But beware of its prejudices in estimating any cause it attacks."

I paused to ponder whether the *Morning Post* would welcome an unsolicited testimonial of this particular sort, and then continued.

"Some newspapers and many men and women have certainly allowed their judgment to be clouded by their prejudice over this question of Bolshevism. To associate Communism with the Jews is also as serviceable to their commercial jealousies as it is to their racial antagonisms. And Bolshevism is only the inevitable throw-up of four years of the most terrible war that ever was waged. I know people in Europe, men of wide culture and of high social standing, who actually profess to believe that it was not the German Kaiser, nor the Austrian Emperor, nor the Junkers, nor the militarists, nor the capitalists, nor the stupid, ignorant millions of deceived and tormented people who caused the war. It was the Jews! The whole wicked business was conceived in the Ghetto! Can raving anti-Semitism go farther?"

"But surely there must be something in it when such people as you describe, men of good brain and fine character, hate the Jews? Why, the whole world is beginning to be up in arms against them. The whole world cannot be wrong. There is something in it."

"There is exactly this much in it and no more," I said, picking up a notorious anti-Semitic journal and reading slowly, "'De Valera's mother was an Irishwoman, and, *judging from the wonderful organizing ability he possesses, his father must have been a Jew!'* What do you think of that for evidence? Judging from the wonderful organizing ability he possesses Mr. Lloyd George's father must have been a Jew; yet I am sure he was a very much respected Welsh Nonconformist. Judging from the wonderful organizing ability she possesses Miss Pankhurst's father must have been a Jew; yet I know he was a much esteemed Gentile lawyer of Manchester. The thing is absurd."

Prejudice was too strong. He left me, unconvinced. But it is simply incredible how many sane people build up a case against a person or a race on evidence as worthless as that which I have just quoted.

The Hungarian Communist Jew, Szamuely, has been proved to have been guilty of frightful atrocities. It is alleged he killed for the joy of killing. He hanged people with his own hand for the pleasure of witnessing the better their dying agonies. He was a madman and a pervert. He finally shot himself; but the Hungarian White Terror has paid this pervert the compliment of imitating him. It has visited upon thousands of miserable Jews of the poorer sort, innocent of crime, the most hideous punishment for this madman's deeds, and a campaign against the whole Jewish race is employing certain Hungarians of my acquaintance abroad in a manner highly destructive of their reputation for sanity.

The popular argument against the Jew is one of crafty exploitation. It runs something like this. The Jew shopkeeper charges extortionate prices for his goods. He cruelly sweats his workpeople. He watches and waits for the misfortunes of his neighbours to trap them into his power by the offer of loans at extortionate rates of interest. They toil and slave to be rid of their debt. They cannot shake it off. He exploits them for life. He robs the heir of his patrimony and the children of their bread. And all because he hates the Christian. He has even been known to steal Christian children and sacrifice them at the Feast of the Passover. The story is good enough to excite a pogrom anyhow!

I know of no more striking case than that of the Jews, and the things which are said against them, illustrative of the fact that two and two do not always make four. In other words, the fact is not always the truth. It takes more than a statement of fact to make a statement of truth. An unsympathetic statement of the strictest accuracy as to fact may leave the same impression as the most calculated lie.

The fundamental facts of the controversy about the Jew are at least two: Firstly, the success of the Jew is due to good habits and an inherited gift of intellect. Secondly, the objectionable characteristics of the Jew are the direct consequence of persecution.

Consider the circumstances of his life in those Central European countries where Jews abound. The land system of Poland, for example, is the fundamental cause of the misery, not only of the Jews, but of the entire peasant population. A Galician village is ofttimes a very nightmare of filth and poverty. The peasants have not the heart to improve their lot. Improvements on their farms are not paid for. There is no fixity of tenure. Rents are high, and are exacted with great severity to supply the needs of gay landlords dancing in Paris or Rome.

Alcohol is a State monopoly in Poland. It used to be in Russia. It is a valued source of revenue to many European Governments. Who is to manage this highly important Government industry? The peasants are slow, ignorant and unreliable. They drink heavily. The Jews do not drink. A drunken Jew is a thing unknown. The very words are a contradiction in terms. It is a temperate and sober race. The Jews must manage the liquor shops. To the Jews are given a very large proportion of these positions in the interests of the State, and not because of any partiality to the Jew. The drink-shop in a village very naturally becomes the village store. The Jew is the storekeeper.

"We had to cease giving soap to the peasants in Czecho-Slovakia, although they needed it so badly, because they would sell it to the Jew for vodka," said the lovely Countess Döbrenszky.

"Why not prohibit the sale of vodka?" I suggested. She smiled and shook her head. "It could never be done."

As the servant of the State the Jew is expected to encourage the sale of drink in those countries where it is a State monopoly, and it is easy to see how everything else follows.

The second of the two bottom facts of the Jewish side of the controversy is the undoubted hatred and envy by the Gentile of the superior Jewish intelligence, particularly in commerce, but as certainly in everything else. Nothing can keep the Jewish race from excelling. Ages of ancient wrong could not do it. Present-day oppression cannot do it. In some countries still the Jew is not allowed to own land. In others, Rumania for example, he is not permitted to enter the profession of lawyer, doctor, or teacher. In the old Russia he might not go to the Universities. In Poland he can exempt himself from army service and consequently is denied citizenship. Cruel as it all seems, and is, there is an underlying instinct of self-preservation at the foundation of it, for, given equal chances in the race of life, the Jew will ofttimes leave the Gentile laggard far behind.

In the early 'forties an enterprising statesman of Vienna began to train young Jews in journalism, and now all the important papers of Vienna are run by Jews. Since the opening of new doors to them in Germany they have dominated the artistic professions in Berlin, and have contributed overwhelmingly to the intellectual life of Germany. The greatest continental authority on Shakespeare, Professor Leon Kellner, is a Jew. Professor Einstein is a Jew, Professor Ehrlich is a Jew. These two great scientists are distinguished in a host of learned Jewish men of science. Maximilian Harden, eminent journalist, is a Jew. Max Reinhardt, composer, is a Jew. The list of famous living Jews is too long to be given in full. In England they distinguish themselves chiefly in politics—Lord Reading, Viceroy of India, Sir Herbert Samuel, High Commissioner in Palestine. And the Jews are dominant in the Socialist politics of Europe, not because of any deep and treacherous design against humanity they possess, but for precisely the reason they are dominant in other spheres, because of their good brains, logical minds, keen perceptions and rare artistic abilities.

If the economic domination of the world by the Jews should come to pass it will be in no small measure due to the historic fact of the persecution and exclusion which have necessitated to a great extent the expression of the rich mental life of the race along one narrow channel for two thousand years; and it will be due in some degree to the comparative self-indulgence and contempt for hard intellectual labour of the Gentile section of the world community.

This excursion into Poland, and the question of the Jews which the discussion of Poland always invites, has postponed for several pages the trip to Georgia. I had the intention to go to Warsaw this month, but a charming young Pole, a lovely girl of twenty, has come to stay with me for some months. Her cousin tells me she is Poland in epitome and advises me to stay at home! Wanda is still too young to be other than a fervid nationalist and patriot. She is full of the poetry and romance of things, and the love of dainty dresses. She is filled with the vague longings and sadness of youth, and likes the autumn better than the spring, which is exactly as it should be in sentimental twenty. My only trouble with my guest is one of race and upbringing. I have an unconquerable and brutal British habit of saying "yes" when I mean "yes." She says "yes" when she means "no," because to her it is polite and proper to say the thing you imagine you are wanted to say. The consequence is that I am in danger of killing her by dragging her from her books over the hills and dales of an English countryside, to put roses into the pale cheeks, and a bright light into the grey eyes which have seen too much of sorrow and suffering for one so young and fair.

CHAPTER XII
GEORGIA OF THE CAUCASUS

M. Camille Huysmans persuaded me to accept the Georgian invitation. "The Georgians want you to come very particularly because you were in Russia recently. They want someone who can make comparisons between the Bolshevik Government of Russia and the Social Democratic Government of their own country. It would be helpful to them, and would be interesting and useful to you."

The delegation was selected from the Second International. Besides myself, Mr. J. R. Macdonald and Mr. Tom Shaw were invited from Great Britain; Messieurs Vandervelde, de Brouckere and Huysmans from Belgium; Messieurs Renaudel, Marquet and Inghels from France; and Herr Kautsky and his wife from Germany. Several Georgians and Russians with their wives were also of the party, and we were joined in Paris by Madame Vandervelde and Madame Huysmans and her daughter. The Kautskys joined us in Rome, travelling thither from Vienna.

Camille Huysmans would have to occupy a central position in any picture of the personalities of the present-day European Socialist Movement. His is a figure of more than ordinary interest. He is tall and slender, with an attractive mop of fair, curly hair. He possesses a keenly intellectual face, like that of Lasalle, delicate featured, but with a slightly cruel mouth. His eyes are restless and his general movements, except in speaking in public, are nervous. He has an extraordinary capacity for organization, and speaks four or five languages with equal fluency. His knowledge of the history and the present position of the world movement for Socialism is unrivalled.

His knowledge of the private histories as well as the public records of his Socialist colleagues in all lands is also very complete; which makes him a terror to evildoers. I have heard attributed to this knowledge the fact that the Russian Bolsheviks have left him severely alone. It certainly cannot be because he has spared them, for his hatred of their undemocratic form of government he has cried from the housetops.

His is the artistic temperament, and he is passionately fond of music and the drama. He loathes all the naked ugliness and stupid self-repression that passes for Puritanism in the minds of the soured and disappointed. He professes no personal religion, but temperamental leanings towards the forms of Roman Catholic worship are discernible in the expression of his general views of life. The pictures, the colour, the incense, the music of the æsthetic temples of every great Faith would probably be implicit in his scheme of things, for the sheer beauty of them.

I have a great liking and admiration for the secretary of the Second International; but it requires a sense of humour and a certain gift of scepticism to make him understood of the great mass of his more sober Saxon comrades. "You can as easily make an Englishman musical as a Belgian moral," he said gaily into the shocked ears of at least two English persons present, delighted to be taken seriously when he only wanted to draw us into a debate. His eyes twinkled mischievously as he spoke. He is the Puck of the International, the tormenting imp who likes nothing better than to stab with little darts of irony the self-important people who take life too seriously.

On public occasions he appears the most self-possessed of men; but he told me once that he suffers an agony of nervousness when called upon to meet strangers. His public speech sparkles with wit. He can laugh, sing, dance and shout with the abandon of a schoolboy; but when some piece of stiff business arises and he has to calm a raging storm of passion between two sets of nationals in a conference his peculiar genius shows itself, and he restores order and amity with the hand and voice of a master. Without Camille Huysmans the ship of the International would sail very unsteadily upon the turbulent waters of present-day politics. Huysmans is a member of the Belgian Parliament, and if there be anything in present signs and portents he is marked out by circumstance and his own commanding abilities to play a prominent part in shaping the future fortunes of his gallant little country.

"La petite Sara," as his gifted young daughter was called by the Georgians, helps her father, whom she adores. She has his charming personality and marvellous facility for languages, with an added seriousness and self-sufficiency, if not a slight stubbornness of character, which will not detract but rather add to the quality of her international work. She is a very pretty girl, with large, serious grey eyes, dark fringed, and a complexion of cream and roses. All the young men of the party fell in love with her and lived in hourly, jealous fear lest some dancing Georgian rival should persuade her to marry him and carry her off to his mountain home.

M. Louis de Brouckère, tall, handsome and dignified, another of our Belgian companions, is the perfect scholar and gentleman. Could more and better be added to that?

M. Emile Vandervelde, the Belgian Minister for Justice, is a portly figure with a ruddy complexion and wonderful blue eyes, clear and limpid as a child's. He is slightly deaf, which obliges him to lean and strain to catch the words of a speaker. He professes not to speak English, but that is all nonsense. He both speaks and understands it very well. His wife is an Englishwoman.

Of French he is a master. He is one of the greatest of living orators. As chairman of the Delegation he spoke on almost every occasion. So perfect is his art, so entirely matchless is his choice and use of word and phrase, so magnificent the roll and crescendo of his argument that his listeners stood fascinated as he spoke, or leaned forward in their chairs, their faces aglow with enjoyment of gesture and speech, even when they did not understand a word. To the understanding the speech was ever a marvel of beauty and delight, holding them spellbound to the last triumphant word and overpowering gesture. The theme in Georgia was the same for us all, and for all occasions: sympathy for the Georgians in their effort to build up peacefully and on Social-Democratic lines the Socialist Republic; offers of help in our various home countries; condemnation of Bolshevism; praise of Internationalism.

M. Vandervelde is one of the most brilliant supporters of the Temperance Movement. He is by preference a total abstainer, although he is often placed by his public life and on foreign travel in circumstances where it is very difficult to indulge his taste. In some of those Eastern lands the water is tainted with germs and poisonous to the last degree. When it comes to a choice between typhoid and alcohol, the choice usually falls upon alcohol! Sometimes bitter offence is given where it is highly important good feeling should be maintained if a guest declines to drink wine with a host; incredible in these days, but true; impossible in this country now, but in Eastern Europe of the greatest frequency.

It was in the company of this distinguished statesman that I visited the wine-cellars on the estate in central Georgia of an exiled Russian Grand Duke. We entered the vast chambers led by smocked peasants carrying torches. They bowed till their beards almost swept the ground as we thanked them for their pains. Vast, gloomy, mysterious in the light of the flaming torches, the cellars were not so attractive, we thought, as the enchanting garden under the moon, and the voices of the villagers singing their folk songs on the lawn; so we left the rest of the company and sought the road back to the palace ourselves.

"What do you think will happen at the next election in Belgium?" I asked my companion.

He shrugged his shoulders and spread his small, white hands with an expressive gesture. "I cannot tell. There will probably be little change. I shall have to be home by then."

The sound of the music came through the trees, guiding our steps. "I should like to understand Belgian politics better," was more than a polite observation on my part. It represented a genuine regret that I was so ignorant.

"The Belgian Socialist point of view was not understood during the war by the English comrades," said the Minister. "And even now we are roundly abused for joining the Government, even by a section in Belgium. It is always the dividing line. Shall we stand outside and be simply a propaganda body? Or, having secured a certain position and membership, shall we take the responsibility for carrying out as far as we can our political doctrines, recognizing that in a composite Government we can go neither so fast nor so far as we might wish? The workers' party in Belgium is now the largest party in the State. Can the largest party in the State refuse to share the responsibility of helping in the country's government? Camille thinks not. I have thought not. Now I sometimes doubt the line we should take. We shall see how things develop; what the result of the election is. But you must come to Belgium and tell us about Russia, and we will show you anything and tell you anything you wish to know."

At this point we emerged from the thick wood into full view of the palace. Servants were lighting paper lanterns. The clatter of plates and cutlery spoke of the coming revel. The choristers burst into a new song as we approached. The bright moon lit up the magnificent range of mountains in the distance. It was fairyland come true, making the things of this world, its dirty politics and mean diplomacy, look small and poor.

A tall English blonde of very great charm of manner when she chooses is Madame Vandervelde. When she does not so choose she can be ruder in three languages than any woman of my acquaintance knows how to be in one! I do not in the least complain of her conduct to me. We got on extremely well. We were sufficiently candid with each other to be able to maintain to the end a good comradeship in spite of the very trying circumstance of joint sleeping quarters. My one quarrel with my fellow-countrywoman was on account of the number of trunks she carried. It was almost impossible to turn round in that small state room because of the array of bags, boxes, suit-cases, hat-trunks piled into the room and occupying every available inch of space. One member of our party, the little French bride of a Georgian physician, who was carrying her trousseau to her new home in Tiflis, lost on the Italian railway a trunk containing two thousand pounds' worth of valuable hand-made clothes, laces and household goods which she never recovered. An old empty trunk with her original label attached was found in its place. It may be the effect of the war. If four Prime Ministers in Paris can steal several colonies in Africa, if fat profiteers can rob the dying Austrian children in their thousands of their food, surely one little Italian railway porter can annex one trunk without blame? Whatever the reason, it is certainly true that, on more than one continental railway at the present time, the only way you can assure the arrival of your trunk at its destination is by sitting on it.

Madame Vandervelde contrived to bring all her goods safe into port without sitting on them. She pressed into her service the gallant men of the party. There are some women — and my friend is one of them — who by reason of their presence of mind and absence of conscience can command the services at all times and in all circumstances of even the men who dislike them. And apparently there are men who like being kicked!

But I do not want to imply that any man on this trip found his service a trial. I am sure the beautiful Lalla commanded the whole-hearted service of her numerous cavaliers. They liked her free manners and fascinating personality. They delighted in her racy talk, daring jests and semi-Bohemian tastes. The least that ought to be said about her is that her impish delight in shocking people and in saying teasing things kept the whole company titillating with expectant amusement or nervous fear. Nobody could be dull in her society; and, after all, dullness, which is always a nuisance, becomes a positive crime on an excursion of this sort, which compels twenty persons to live very closely together in ship or train for fifty days and nights.

Of the remaining women of the party, Madame Huysmans is a pretty dark woman, full of gentle kindnesses and not without the gift of humour. Madame Dvarzaladze is a magnificent beauty of the gipsy type. Madame Skobeloff, one time a prima donna at the Petrograd Opera House, was the very incarnation of her favourite heroine — Carmen — and by the skilful glances of her glorious black eyes and her coquettish manner brought the passionate lady off the stage to live amongst us for several days.

M. Dvarzaladze conducted the expedition on behalf of his Government, and was the kindest of hosts. M. Skobeloff assisted him. The latter is as fair as his wife is dark, with the Russian breadth both of figure and of face, and a mass of light silky hair brushed back from a square forehead. He was Minister of Commerce in the Kerensky Government. Something in his speech and manner gave the impression that he regretted a little the Bolshevik Government, and would have liked to participate in it; but I was confidently assured that I was mistaken.

M. Nazarov, as a student in Petrograd, embraced Bolshevism with great enthusiasm. When student days ended he came back to his original faith of Social Democracy. He acted as secretary to the expedition and was, without a single exception, the most consistently courteous and considerate person I have known who has ever occupied so difficult and thankless a position. Early and late he was engaged in looking after the comfort of everybody. Pestered to the verge of insanity, as he must have been with the requests of various members of the delegation, his manners never for an instant forsook him, and the remembrance of him alone would make the visit to Georgia unforgettable.

Of the three delegates from France, M. Inghels is the typical bluff and substantial Trade Union leader, a representative of the textile workers; M. Marquet is tall and slim and elegant, faultless in dress, of impeccable manners, leaving on the mind the impression of easy victories with women; M. Renaudel has already appeared in these pages, the man of robust proportions and prodigious appetite, of matchless eloquence in speaking, with a voice of great beauty.

There remain only the English delegates to describe, and one of these was a Scotsman, Mr. J. R. Macdonald, of the dark eyes and wavy hair of silvery grey, of the calm judgment and austere outlook upon life so valuable to the leader of men, and so necessary for the safeguarding of inexperienced Labour representatives in England come new and defenceless against the seductions of wily enemies in the House of Commons; and Mr. Tom Shaw of the Lancashire Textile Unions, stout and ruddy complexioned, full of fun and good-natured banter, the best of travelling companions and the kindest of men.

The delegates met in Paris at a dinner given to them by M. Tseretelli, the Georgian Minister. Preliminary to this was the tiresome and disgusting business of inoculation. The wily Georgians had said nothing about this in Geneva. Had we known then of the ravages of the pest, and had we been told we must be inoculated against bubonic plague, it might have affected our decision about going. For some time we resisted; but on the very earnest solicitations of our friends, and because it was suggested that by not being vaccinated we might endanger the lives of other people, we weakly yielded and consented to allow ourselves to be ill-treated in this peculiarly objectionable manner! I have never been able to reconcile myself to the deliberate poisoning of my blood at intervals during my life, and have always felt triumphant when the healthy blood I inherited from plain-living and high-thinking ancestors refused to be poisoned by the filthy injections.

The journey from Paris to Rome occupied two days, with a change of train at Turin. The one memorable thing about this journey was the descent through the Mont Cenis Tunnel into the Italian valley, with its villas and vineyards and sun-steeped fields.

We stayed a couple of days in Rome awaiting the date for sailing and to complete the passport business. Into those two swift days we crowded as much sight-seeing as possible—the Forum, the Coliseum, St. Peter's Church and the Appian Way. There are some travellers whose sole happiness lies in being able to boast of having seen something which nobody else has seen, or to have got ahead of the party by doing something it never occurred to the others to do. You praise the sunset. "Ah, but you should have seen it an hour ago," is the remark which cools your enthusiasm. You are pleased with the dinner. "But it is nothing like so good as yesterday's," is the observation which robs you of half your pleasure. You are enraptured with the song. "Oh, he's gone off lately. You should have heard him a year ago," is the comment that leaves you flat and disappointed.

"How wonderful is the Coliseum!" exclaimed one of the delegates to the rest of us.

"But did you see it by moonlight? No? Then you have not seen it. You must see it by moonlight if you really want to see the Coliseum." And we left Rome with the feeling that there was nothing to be done but to return to Rome to see the Coliseum by moonlight, or our visit to the city would be mere fruitless folly.

I discovered the Corso to be no place for a woman walking alone. As a matter of fact, reputable Italian women do not walk in the streets of Rome unattended, particularly at night. I was ignorant of this, or had forgotten it, and did as I am accustomed to do in my own country, when I speedily discovered one difference between an English and an Italian city which pleasantly distinguishes the former; for there are very few places in England where a modest woman going about her legitimate business unattended would be stopped and spoken to in a familiar way in a public thoroughfare. In the streets of Rome the sun at midday is, apparently, no guarantee of impunity for women from the annoying familiarities of unknown and undesirable men.

Taranto, the port of sailing, is a quaint old city of antiquarian interest situated on a beautiful bay. The museum is filled with ancient statuary and pottery excavated from the ruins of a still older city, dating back to the days of the ancients. We spent some hours in the building, examining the tessellated tiles and old Greek vases under the guidance of the elderly curator, who, as he said good-bye to us, broke two delicious pink roses off the rose tree in the courtyard, and, with a graceful old-world bow, his hand upon his heart, gave one each to Miss Huysmans and myself.

Taranto comprises two towns, the old and the new. The new is set upon a hill, the old lies about the port. The new has an American look about its new white stone-fronted buildings, the old has the stamp of the Middle Ages upon it. The streets of the old are winding and so narrow that the people on opposite sides of the streets can in some cases shake hands from their bedroom windows. They are paved with cobblestones, and there are no sidewalks. The houses have tiny windows and the top storeys project. The shops, as a rule, have no windows at all, but are open to the street along the whole of their front. Some of the cafés are underground cellars. Men and women meet in the shops for gossip, and in the cafés for scandal and politics. Work is leisurely. The men are mostly engaged in fishing, net-making and basket-weaving. The women wear native peasant dress, bright coloured, and attend to their houses or help the men with the nets. Donkeys are numberless. Huge masses of fruit, notably grapes and water melons, are piled up on the stalls and barrows that line the street fronting the sea. It is a city of amazing picturesqueness, astounding squalor and incredible smells.

Our ship was an Austrian vessel, part of the Italian share in the spoils of war. Her commander was an easy-going Italian with a tremendous admiration for Lord Fisher. He refused to promise us fine weather, and, even as we entreated, the sun entered a cloud which, before evening, had spread gloomily over the whole sky!

We sailed pleasantly amongst the Greek Islands, sighting Corinth and Athens and the Hill of Mars. We steamed slowly through the canal cut through the Isthmus of Corinth, a marvellous feat of engineering. We crept gently past Gallipoli and gazed with dim eyes on the graves of the gallant dead. The sea near the shore was full of ships, sunk by the fire from the Turkish forts, and the captain told us that here careful navigation was very necessary and we might not go nearer the land; but with the aid of field-glasses we marked the blasted hillsides and battered fortifications of the Turk. Here and there a broken gun rusted on its side in the scorched and trampled grass. Hearts felt sick for the sacrifice that the politicians were threatening to make vain, and we silently renewed our vows to devote our lives to the building up of such international organization as should make such sacrifices unnecessary in the future.

On the fourth day after leaving Taranto we sighted Constantinople. This city was the most completely satisfying of all my childhood's dreams come true. I recollect how disappointing to me was my first glimpse of the Niagara Falls. So it has been with many of my friends. Such beauty as that grows upon one, but at the first visit one expects too much. One expects something more and bigger than can be taken in with a single glance of the eye, a wilderness of waters, something stupendous, to send one reeling! One sees a vast and steady tumbling, a roar like a Tube train entering a tunnel, and feels the lack of mystery. I am inclined to think the injury is done by the aggressive and vulgar civilization all round: the tawdry town, the eating-houses, the electric-power stations, the street cars, the vendors of toys and ice-cream and picture post cards and penny buns. Seen and heard in the vast spaces and awful silence of a desert it would be altogether different.

Constantinople fulfilled every wish, satisfied every expectation. Magnificently set upon its several hills it appeared the queen of cities enthroned above the worshipping waters, crowned by the moon, and glittering with ten thousand jewels of ten thousand shimmering lights. By day her beauty changed. Unlike Moscow, whose domes and minarets gleam golden in the sun, those of Constantinople have lost their radiance, but they stand out nobly against the clearest of blue skies, the mosques on the hills of Stamboul competing for praise with the vast modern palaces at the water's edge. The Golden Horn, classic symbol of plenty, was crowded with shipping, a pleasing contrast to the stagnation of Astrakhan.

The streets of Constantinople are a kaleidoscope, a mass of jostling humanity, white and black and brown. The Turkish fez predominates. The dark-skinned Jew and the cunning Greek vie with the crafty Armenian in the business of stripping the guileless stranger of his money. Thick-lipped Nubians are as common as flies. Black-veiled Turkish women add a distinctive note to the scene. Water-carriers sell their water to thirsty traders in carpets and embroideries. Anatolian peasants bring their fruits to sell. Turkish princes flash past in shabby automobiles. Gay French officers on horseback menace the careless foot-traveller. Young British officers on polo ponies rush laughingly by. The big hotels are filled with the usual crowd of foreign Military Mission folk, big business men, pseudo-politicians; youthful, *very youthful* diplomats and soldiers, profiteers, adventurers, wives of officers and women of the underworld—gay, charming, lovely and dangerous. No sign there of the bitter hate that sits on the brow of the Turkish café habitué, who deems the least tolerable part of his burden the position of dominance over him given to his ancient insolent enemy, the corrupt and perfidious Greek.

I shall write more about our doings in Constantinople later. We sailed through the Bosphorus in a calm sea and into the dreaded Black Sea after the third day. The beauty of the Bosphorus suggests the exquisite reaches of the Rhine with its ancient castles and woody crags, but with a gentle softness for the Rhine's proud strength. The Black Sea belied its name, and our passage was without a break in its comfort and content.

We rested for a day outside the port of Trebizond. There, to our amazement, was flying the red flag of the Bolsheviks, whose co-operation with Kemal Pasha had evidently not been misreported by the Press. Kemal's headquarters were in Trebizond. Several boat-loads of Bolsheviks in khaki uniforms and peaked caps came to inspect the ship. Some came on board. They were perfectly civil. No attempt was made to interfere with the passengers, who were strongly urged by the chief officer on board not to risk a landing. We took on board many new passengers here and at a previous stopping-place, the name of which escapes me. These were of various nationalities, chiefly Turks, with their carefully segregated and veiled womankind carrying large quantities of fruit, and themselves hauling on board loads of wonderful Turkey carpets. A few long-bearded Greeks and swarthy Jews were amongst the new-comers, and several fascinating black-eyed children. These people shared the lower deck with the sheep and goats. The sheep were penned, but the goats escaped, leaping all over the deck and chewing to tatters the sailcloth and the ropes, to the anger of the sailors, who, with all their nimbleness, were no match for the goats.

Below in the hold were the horned cattle, bellowing their protest at two days and nights of painful thirst in their hot and crowded quarters. The way in which these poor beasts were treated made us sick. They were hauled from the small boats on to the ship and into the hold suspended by the horns from the ship's crane. Their eyes bulged out of their heads, their legs beat the air as they swung up and then down, their heavy bodies pulling at their horns. A young Englishwoman expressed her detestation of the performance in a full company, when, with a grin, a facetious foreign gentleman exclaimed with his hand upon his heart: "Ah, mademoiselle, you English, you have pity for ze poor animals but none for ze poor men. We break our hearts for ze mademoiselle and she care not. But ze horses, ze cats and ze dogs, she adores zem. It is desolating." And he made a frantic gesture of despair.

"What do you say to the idiots who talk like that?" I inquired, sorry for the cause of that angry flush on her pretty face.

"I say nothing," she replied; "but I begin to feel thankful that our quarrel with the German people is only skin deep."

One night more and we were in Batoum, beautifully situated on the slopes and at the foot of great, wooded hills which make a sombre background to the white houses. As the noise of the ship's engines ceased, distant strains of music crept into our ears. It came from the shore, which was black with people. I grew nervous and apprehensive. I opened the cabin door. I strained forward anxiously to hear. I was not mistaken. My first fear was realized. It was the "International," the song which brought Russia back to mind, the jingling melody that I had heard, at a modest computation, a thousand times in Russia alone!

I rushed to the ship's side and, borrowing a field-glass, stared out to shore. Yes, yes, it was all there, the familiar circus; the bands, the crowds, the carriages, the flowers, the red flags and bunting, the photographer and cinema operator—all so kind and well-intentioned. I looked at Tom Shaw; he grinned back at me. There was nothing to be done but resign ourselves to the inevitable and look as pleased as we could.

We clambered down the ship's side on a shaky, swinging ladder to the waiting tender and steamed away to shore. The kindest of welcomes awaited us. Our arms were filled with flowers, and after the usual courteous preliminaries we were led off amidst deafening cheers to receive the official welcome at the City Hall.

The City Fathers gave us greeting in a few short and well-chosen phrases to which Mr. J. R. Macdonald suitably responded. We then proceeded for a similar function to the headquarters of the Social Democratic Party. Five thousand people assembled in the street to be introduced to us. The introductions were made from a balcony. Each delegate was brought forward separately and named, with certain of his gifts and exploits. Then the crowd yelled with delight. M. Vandervelde on our behalf acknowledged the courtesy and struck the international note, and we were released for lunch and a subsequent tour of the city's chief points of interest.

The tightness about my heart left me after the first hour amongst these happy people. What, I asked myself, had I really been afraid of? I had feared to see a starving company drawn up in stiff lines giving us welcome by compulsion. I remembered how, in Petrograd, loss of work or of ration was the punishment for non-attendance at these formal ceremonies. The cruel fatigue of many hours of waiting in biting wind or blistering sun was the price paid there by thousands of underfed and underclad workmen and women for a sight of the foreign delegates. I felt it quite impossible to endure this sort of thing again.

But in Georgia it was different. The experience in Batoum was the same everywhere. There was no compulsion to meet us. The people came because they wanted to come. They moved freely amongst us, without restraint of speech or manner, laughing, shouting, singing. The brown-eyed children climbed into our laps. They shyly played with our watches or examined our clothes. In all those merry faces turned up at us on the balcony I saw not one look of bitterness, no tightening of thin lips, no burning hate in the eyes. One jolly giant, whose curly grey-black hair waved a head's breadth above the crowd, led the cheering, which was caught up by the crowd in unmistakable sincerity. They ran by the side of our carriages, flinging red roses into them and blowing kisses to us as we gathered up the roses and pinned them to our coats as the red emblem of international solidarity.

We spent a pleasant afternoon in the Botanical Gardens, rich with every kind of tropical and semi-tropical fruit. The head gardener boasted with joyous pride the possession of sixty different varieties of orange. There they hung, yellow and tempting. Visions of Southern California surged up, the blue Pacific at San Diego, and the big glowing orange broken off the tree, ripe and delicious, for the daily breakfast. From the figs and grapes, the lemons and bananas of these gardens, we proceeded to the tea plantations and the bamboo woods, and saw two infant industries developing themselves, the one under the care of a skilled Japanese. Georgia's industry needs development on modern lines, with modern machinery and by modern methods. At present production is slow and old fashioned. A common sight on a Georgian landscape is a wooden plough, hand guided, drawn by eight pair of stout oxen. This is mediæval.

In the evening we were entertained by the Batoum Municipality to a dinner on the enclosed veranda of a large public ballroom. A Georgian dinner is a thing to be remembered, and this, the first of many, lingers pleasantly in the mind. Flowers and climbing plants adorned the glass-covered veranda on the outside, palms and flowering trees decorated and scented it within. The long table accommodated two hundred guests. At one end of the room a choir sang songs, and an orchestra made merry music whilst we ate. Course followed course of the most deliciously cooked food. Enormous epergnes, filled with glowing peaches of incredible size and huge black grapes, adorned the table at frequent intervals of space. There were sparkling wines of rich vintage and various colours, exquisite in the soft light from the shaded lamps. This dinner could not have been surpassed for the completeness of its appointments by the most expensive mountain hotel in America. Torrents of summer rain and vivid flashes of lightning added to the sense of comfort and jollity within.

The speeches at a Georgian banquet are delivered between the courses. After the speeches, before the speeches, furtively during the speeches, the toasts are called. Never in the world was there anything like this mad passion for toasting one another. Every guest is toasted at least once. The health of every lady is drunk at least ten times! If the wine does not give out, absent friends and popular causes, the cook in the kitchen and the butler in the pantry supply excellent excuses for a further riot of toasting.

Conversation waxes louder and more excited with every glass. Eyes begin to shine with the moving spirit of alcohol. Strange stories of gallant adventure are told aloud. Wild gestures are flung about. Out of the storm of confused tongues and frantic gesticulations, from the far end of the table comes a faint voice softly singing a slow song. Others take up the strain. In less than two minutes the entire table is singing, each person roaring his accompaniment at the very pitch of his voice. This song sounds like a Scottish psalm tune, but it is the Georgian equivalent to "He's a jolly good fellow." It is very impressive and runs something like this; I give it from ear:

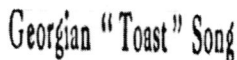

Georgian "Toast" Song
Very slowly.

Perhaps twenty times in one evening this song is started and taken up by the company. Each time it is a compliment directed at some special guest, and concludes with the clinking of glasses and a roar of cheers for the honoured one, who bows his appreciation of the kindly courtesy.

A distinguished general of the *ancien régime* was my *vis-à-vis*. He delicately complimented me upon the few words those gallant Georgians would have me say, and afterwards sent to Tiflis a large basket of delicious red roses for the ladies of our party. On my right sat several young nobles in the handsome native costume. They wore long grey coats, full skirted and with belts at the waist. Underneath was a high-necked blouse, buttoned at the front. Each side of the coat was ornamented at the breast with a row of pockets for single cartridges. Ornamental cartridge-cases were fitted into these pockets. The round hats were of white astrakhan, and they wore soft leather Russian boots which came high in the leg and were seamless and unlaced. Each carried a dagger at his side, with richly chased silver handle. When the spirits of the company had risen sufficiently high, two of these young princes rose and danced a graceful Georgian dance down the whole length of the corridor and back on the other side. The guests accompanied with a monotonous clap, humming softly a suitable melody. One arm held gracefully above the head, the left hand on the hip, the feet moving intricately and delicately, the body swaying ever so slightly from the hips and seeming to float upon the polished surface of the floor, there is nothing that dance resembled so much as a sailing ship on a placid lake gently moved by a soft wind.

The absence of rancour, the atmosphere of friendliness, the fellowship and intimacy of it all, charmed us, and we left for the night train and Tiflis with regret at having to part so soon with these new friends.

The special train had been a royal train. It was replete with every comfort. There were bathrooms even, and an excellent kitchen. The food department was in the hands of a Russian family, a widowed mother and three children. They were a family of good birth whose fallen fortunes had been relieved in this way by the Social Democrats as a reward for saving the life of the President, always in danger from the violent extremists of both sorts. The mother was a stout, comfortable body, and the girls beautiful creatures of the Slavonic type.

We were received in the waiting room at Tiflis by the President, M. Jordania, and his suite. The floor was carpeted with rich and costly rugs. On the walls hung portraits of Karl Marx and the principal Georgian Socialists. An orderly crowd waited outside and cheered us as we left for our quarters in the residence of the departed American Commissioner.

Our first business in Tiflis was to attend the special session of Parliament called in our honour, to hear a speech of welcome from each of the eight political parties represented in that Parliament. The Georgian Parliament is elected on a franchise which gives every man and woman of twenty the vote. At the last election, which was conducted on a basis of strictest proportional representation, 102 Social Democrats were elected out of a total of 130. The nationalities represented by this 130 are six, and there are five women in the House. The secretary to the Speaker is also a woman, and a very able one. Distinctions of sex do not exist in Georgian politics or in Georgian industry. Equal pay for equal work is the ruling economic dictum.

For the purposes of an election the whole country, with a population of about 4,000,000, is one constituency. As a natural corollary of this the districts have almost unlimited powers of self-government. The model is a combination of Swiss and British. There is no second Chamber. The President of the Republic is also the Prime Minister. He is elected annually, and cannot hold office for more than two consecutive years. Elections are organized and carried through by national and local Election Commissions. The twenty-one members of the national Election Commission are elected by the Members of Parliament. The insane, the criminal, deserters from the army and insolvents may not vote.

The domestic policy of the Socialist Government of Georgia is the gradual socialization of land and industry. Having guaranteed themselves as far as possible from enemies within the State by establishing themselves upon a thoroughly democratic basis, they have sought to accomplish what was expected of them by disturbing as little as might be the private interests and ordinary pursuits of the citizens.

They have established a system of peasant proprietorship. This it was less difficult to do than might have been expected on account of the fact that 90 per cent. of the land had already been mortgaged by spendthrift proprietors. The law establishing the land in the hands of the peasants was finally promulgated on January 25, 1919. The amount of land allowed to each peasant is strictly limited to seven acres, or thirty-five acres for a family of five. The old landlord may have his seven acres if he will cultivate it himself, or within his own family. I met landlords who submitted cheerfully to the new system and noble ladies who rejoiced in their new-found economic liberties.

But again I say, a knowledge of newer methods of production is necessary to make the rich soil yield all that it is capable of yielding, and quantities of machinery must be imported if the area of soil under cultivation is to be increased. Only 24 per cent. of the land in Georgia was cultivated as against 31.5 per cent. in Russia, 55 per cent. in France and 57.4 per cent. in Italy in pre-war days.

There is an excellent Co-operative Movement in Georgia which is working up a national co-operative scheme of production and distribution for the peasants. By this means it is hoped to guard the interests of the consumer, so apt to be at the mercy of the cultivators of the soil in a country of fallen exchanges, and at the same time leave the peasants free in the possession and cultivation of their land.

No attempt, so far as I could discover, has been made to destroy private industry and individual enterprise, nor even to interfere with either beyond the need for protecting the vital interests of the workers and the necessity for safeguarding the interests and liberties of the country. The shops and bazaars of Tiflis were open, not closed and their windows boarded up as in Moscow and Petrograd. The principal streets of Tiflis and Batoum were a pleasant contrast to the Nevski Prospect.

The Ministry of Labour consists of two Commissars. For its purposes Georgia is divided into four districts: Tiflis, Koutais, Sokhum and Batoum. The officials of the Ministry are chosen from candidates elected by the Trade Unions. This important department has five sections: (1) the Chamber of Tariffs, which fixes wages and salaries; this is controlled by a committee comprising ten employers, ten workpeople and one representative of the Ministry of Labour; (2) the Chamber of Reconciliation; it is not obligatory that an employer or union should appeal to this body for help in the settlement of a dispute, but once having appealed its decision is binding upon both; (3) The Commission of Insurance, which insures workpeople against accidents of all kinds; (4) The Committee of Relief, which insures against sickness and old age, and (5) The Labour Exchange, for the supply and regulation of labour. There is a universal eight hours' day in Georgia. Overtime is permitted in certain circumstances, but must be paid for at the rate of a time and a half. Holidays are fixed by law, and those who are obliged to work in holiday time must be remunerated with a double wage. Employers who dismiss workpeople must provide compensation, a law which does not invariably work out happily for workpeople or for masters.

The price of bread in the open market at the time of our visit was 30 roubles a pound. For the workers the same bread was 5 roubles. It was possible for us to buy 3,800 roubles with an English pound.

All this interesting information was given to us during numerous and protracted interviews with members of Government departments and Trade Union officials. The most distinguished of this number was M. Jordania, the President Prime Minister. He is a man of tall and stately and even aristocratic bearing. But there is not the slightest shadow of doubt of his democratic sympathies and real belief in Socialism. He wears a well-trimmed beard, has fine dark eyes and sensitive, shapely hands. He speaks well and clearly, has a rich fund of humour and is adored by his people.

We had the pleasure of meeting the President's aged mother in her simple home at Goria. She was dressed in the native woman's dress, a stiff, black silk skirt, very full and touching the ground all round. A long-sleeved jacket covered the embroidered blouse. Over her head she wore a white veil which was attached to a black velvet circlet fixed squarely on the head. The veil fell down the back almost to the edge of the skirt. On either side of the sweet old face were old-fashioned ringlets, a part of the general costume and style of the women. This tiny old lady of lovely and hospitable spirit could not understand or appreciate a subdivision of land which robbed her loved son of a large part of his patrimony; but with gentle firmness he pointed out that the new law was for all alike, the rich as well as the poor, and that those who had more must give to those who had none.

In a quiet part of the garden is a sacred spot where a loved child lies buried. It is beautifully kept, and a garden seat facing the west is placed near the grave. We bent our heads at this sacred family shrine in a common feeling of sympathy and understanding.

The foreign policy of this Socialist Republic is better understood when a little of its history is known. The Georgians are a race of enormous antiquity. Their exact origin is still a matter of dispute amongst the savants. It is now generally believed they are descended from the ancient Babylonians. They are certainly not Slavs. Nor is their language a Slavonic language. They are usually a dark-skinned race, tall and graceful, with aquiline features and flashing black or dark brown eyes. The typical Georgian man is superbly handsome, passionate in love and brave in war. The typical Georgian woman has a world reputation for beauty, too often blighted, as in most countries of fighting men, by the hard tasks which ought to be done by men.

A treaty with Catherine the Great guaranteeing their independence to the Georgians did not save them from definite annexation to the Russian Empire in 1801. Since then it has been a hundred years of struggle for freedom for a gallant people whose unfortunate land lay in the route of march towards the realization of Russia's age-long ambition, the possession of Constantinople and the command of the Straits.

In the hope of achieving their freedom through the overthrow of the Czars the Georgian Socialists took part in the abortive Revolution of 1905. As a result their leaders were either thrown into prison or exiled to Siberia. Then followed a period of terrible repression and reaction. When the Revolution of 1917 came the Georgians helped it, and some of them took office in the Kerensky Ministry.

Kerensky's magnetic personality and very real gifts of eloquence and idealism could not hold a position difficult enough by reason of the war, but made immeasurably more difficult, in fact impossible, by the disastrous policy of the Allies towards Russia and the unscrupulous machinations of the Bolshevik Party within the country. The mild policy of the Kerensky regime left Lenin and Trotsky, with other leaders of the Bolsheviks, free to subvert the loyalty of the soldiers in burning speeches in the streets of Petrograd. Kerensky fell and fled, and Lenin assumed his position. But not until May of 1918 was the independence of Georgia duly recognized by Russia.

This recognition was always half-hearted and unreal. It was looked upon as a temporary necessity meant to relieve the Bolshevik Government of one complication in their very dangerous international situation. With a cynicism unsurpassed by any Foreign Office of a capitalist country a Bolshevik dignitary in Moscow informed me that neither Azerbaijan nor Georgia must expect to continue independent of the Moscow Government. Russia must have the oil of Baku. It was a necessity of her very existence; and Georgia was too important for Bolshevik policy in the East for them to allow either of these countries permanently to be independent. So long as Georgia remained non-Bolshevik, she was a stumbling-block in the path of that policy. If she became Bolshevik absolute independence became a matter of no importance. She then entered directly into the Workers' Confederation for the world-wide destruction of the capitalist system, and national boundaries lost their significance in such an enterprise.

The Georgians desire, for economic reasons and for mutual defence, the establishment of a Federation of Caucasian Republics. With the idea of creating this they called three conferences in 1918, 1919 and 1920 respectively, with the sister republics of Azerbaijan and Armenia. The breakdown of the conference in 1918 was due to the Armenians, whose timidity or reluctance to take any definite and independent action could not be overborne. They declined during the second conference to make a definite alliance to prevent the return of the Czars. In 1920 Azerbaijan was *intransigeant* under the pressure of the Bolsheviks. These conferences were abortive as to their purpose, but useful for preparing the ground for future action. A Treaty of Transit with Armenia was actually signed.

Tchicherine in Moscow, as Minister for Foreign Affairs, invited the Georgians to join in the attack against Denikin. This their policy of strict neutrality forbade. On the same ground they had refused help from both the English and the Germans, the one eager to employ anybody against the Bolsheviks, the other ready to engage anybody against the Allies. The Bolsheviks, angry at this refusal to help them, invaded Georgia from Vladicaucasia on May 17, 1920, but were successfully repulsed. So far so good. But we saw clearly when we were in Georgia, and at every point, that the situation there was anything but stable. From the Kemalists on the one hand and the Bolsheviks on the other, the population was in constant danger. The young general who accompanied our expeditions travelled almost literally with his hand upon his sword, and the statesmen were full of care and anxiety.

The main points in the foreign policy of this young Socialist Government besides that of strict neutrality, which has already been mentioned, and the establishment of normal relations with the Western world, are the recognition of Georgia's independence by the Allies and the inclusion of Georgia in the League of Nations. They strongly desire federation with the other Caucasian republics. Some of them anticipate with clear intelligence the time when they will be compelled by economic necessities and the development of internationalism in politics to enter one of the large political systems, possibly Russia; but before that happens—and when it happens it must come peacefully—they want to see Russia quit of all her tyrants, Czarist and Bolshevik alike, and established upon a genuine, democratic basis with a representative National Assembly.

CHAPTER XIII
MORE ABOUT GEORGIA

After three interesting and informing days spent in Tiflis, a city beautifully situated upon many hills, we left for a ten days' excursion into various parts of the country. The first trip was to Kasbec in the Caucasus Mountains.

Eight automobiles, with a complete camera and moving-picture equipment and a couple of newspaper men, drew up in front of our door at 7 o'clock one morning. The rain poured in torrents. The air was hot and sultry. We were advised, none the less, to take with us the warmest wraps we possessed, as we were to climb several thousand feet before the end of the day and sleep in the mountains. I made an *entente cordiale* with two of the Frenchmen in order to exercise my French, and we three packed ourselves into one of the roomy cars very comfortably; and off we went.

Despite the weather, it was a gay cavalcade which dashed along the great military highway, one of the finest engineering feats in the world. The rain became steadily less persistent after the first half-hour. The clouds began to disperse and the sun to peep out at us. About two hours' distance from the city we were hailed by a brown shaggy figure standing in the middle of the road. On either side of the road was a group of picturesque peasant folk in their rough, homely garb. The men were on one side, the women on the other. An ancient priest was amongst them. The chief peasant advanced to the first car bareheaded, carrying bread and salt. His companion held a large horn of sour, strong wine. We were invited to break bread, to eat salt and to taste the wine, all of which we did punctiliously. Their faces broadened with happy smiles as they passed from car to car. Huge bunches of grapes followed. The women threw flowers to us. The lips of the bearded priest moved as if in prayer, and his hands were raised to bless. The little children broke from the side of their mothers and clapped their tiny hands. At last the horn sounded, the signal for departure was given, and to the roar of cheers, the waving of hands, the curtsying and the smiling, we left this patriarchal scene full of thoughts of early Bible lessons and the pictures of the shepherds of the East. Some of the young men wore curious yellow wigs of unsewn sheepskin, which looked like a mass of tangled blond curls, contrasting sharply with their laughing black eyes. One young giant, wearing a sheepskin wig and carrying a heavy stick, suggested the traditional Esau tending his herds and flocks.

On we flew, through richest scenery hourly becoming more mountainous. The road continued admirable. The sun broke dazzlingly through the mists. The aspect of the country was that of a soft, delicate patchwork in shades of green and gold. There were no hedgerows. There were no glittering scintillations of light and atmosphere, no hardness of outline as in Switzerland. All was soft, suggestive, seductive. Little wooden houses perched upon the rocks and ledges. Large patriarchal farm-houses lay in the valleys. Bright rivulets flashed in and out of the sedge. Occasionally we passed a broad stream or a lake, or paused to drink from a sparkling waterfall. Higher and higher we climbed, the sweet air growing rarer, the habitations less numerous. Eagles screamed aloft. An ancient castle or faded monastery, incredibly old, stood out here and there upon the landscape. Everything spoke of a peaceful, happy, peasant life, of rich flocks and autumn plenty.

At intervals the cars were stopped for some radiant welcome of us by happy villagers. Sometimes we made little speeches to them, which were translated by a young Georgian officer. Bread and salt, wine and fruit, song and dance, merry words and gentle prayers and fierce patriotic vows—it was all very wonderful and very moving to the men and women from the West. A tiny peasant boy danced for us shyly at the little town where we lunched, and imagination removed that boy to the Opera House in Petrograd or to the Alhambra in London, there to delight the sophisticated city folk with his mountain-born grace and incomparable agility. The Georgians are a race of dancers. Their feet and hands move instinctively to a gay tune. The lilt of the song is in my ears as I write:

Georgian Dance Song (to be sung to the clapping of hands)

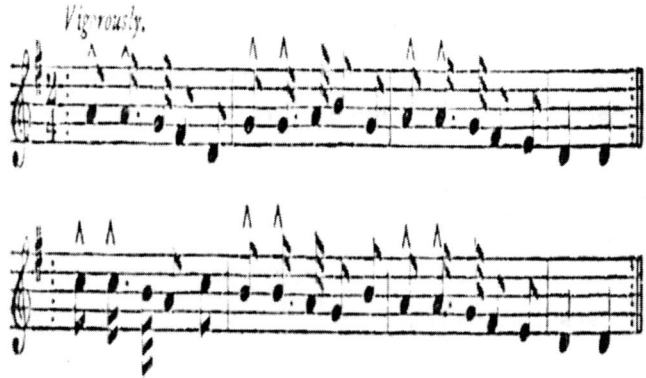

Georgian Dance Song (to be sung to the clapping of hands)
Vigorously.

On and on we went, higher and yet higher. The sun was beginning to go down. Should we reach Kasbec before it quite set? Should we see the great peaks before darkness came down upon us? We wished that we might. We wrapped our furs more closely around us. It was really cold now. Our faces were sore with alternate cold wind and hot sun. We chaffed one another on our personal appearance, our red noses, suggestive of a certain want of sobriety! The peaks grew higher. Round first one and then another, we dashed at the maddest pace on those narrow roads. Up and up we went. Now the road narrowed dangerously, the valleys darkened, the gloom gathered on the hills. The solitary peasant at the head of the pass stood gazing after us with astonished eyes, leaning upon his staff. Round the last corner we panted, our machines steaming their protest, when suddenly there burst upon our awestruck gaze Kasbec, the prince of mountains, its immense snow-covered peak glowing rose-pink in the last rays of the setting sun. One glorious instant, and it was gone, shrouded in shadow and mysterious gloom. Up one more slight incline, and then began our descent. It was quite dark by this time. We settled down to quiet reverie upon the majesty of the mountains and the beauty of the starry night.

With startling suddenness wild shrieks tore the air, and the mad clattering of innumerable horses' feet coming towards us along the pass. We sat up startled. What on earth could it be in that solitary place? It was not the screaming of eagles, nor the roar of wild animals in pain. That steady patter of feet growing ever louder was of horses ridden by human beings. We were within a few miles of the Russian frontier. Perhaps this was a raid of hungry Bolsheviks. If so, what were we to do? Unfortunately for our safety, the Georgians carried arms. At one of our pleasant stopping-places they had practised their arms on improvised targets. The picturesque Mayor of Tiflis, for a wager, had hit the bull's-eye at thirty paces, the target being a piece of white handkerchief on the branch of a tree. There would certainly be fighting in the event of a collision with the Bolsheviks. And then—what?

The foremost emotion was curiosity, not fear. Renaudel stood up and peered into the blackness. Marquet mounted the seat. I hung out of the car at the side. We could discover nothing. The sounds were coming nearer. They came from either side as well as in front. Shots rang out. Wild whoops added to the mystery and the clamour. Suddenly from out of the mountains on both sides, almost into the cars where we sat, leapt ferocious horsemen, black and bearded, by the score. They were dressed in native peasant warrior style, with swords and pistols, curved scimitars and studded shields. Their head-dress was of various kinds, round astrakhan caps or the captured peaked caps of the enemy across the border. The heads of most were uncovered. Broad, spreading square-shaped astrakhan capes, a family inheritance perchance, covered the more sober riders.

They rode hardy mountain horses or shaggy ponies, and rode them with amazing skill, picking up their dropped swords as they galloped and performing other feats of astounding dexterity. They were of several tribes, these peasant soldiers of Georgia, of terrifying aspect, wild and untamed, but withal the merriest, most engaging lot of black-eyed brigands that ever stepped outside a cinema show. We were out of the modern world and had moved back through a thousand years of history.

This gallant company had assembled to conduct us into Kasbec, the most original guard of honour that ever took charge of the guests of a Government. At their head galloped a particularly attractive ruffian carrying a red flag on a long wand. How he contrived to carry this heavy pole in one hand, holding it perfectly erect, and to control his spirited horse with the other, was one of the wonders at which we marvelled greatly. It seemed as easy as falling off a log to him. He led the procession in the three-mile gallop to Kasbec. On either side of the cars ran torch-bearers on horseback. The fifty attendants grew to a hundred as we neared the city, the hundred to two hundred, the two hundred to three, four, five hundred. In addition were women and children in the town, waiting to help with the songs and the dances.

The old church in which the address of welcome was to be delivered was too small for the company assembled. We held the meeting in the churchyard and spoke to the people from the top of a broad wall. I never heard Mr. Macdonald speak better than he did to those grim but simple mountain warriors, reminiscent as they were of the shaggy Highlanders of his native Scotland three centuries or more ago.

I cannot write about the hotel in Kasbec. It was unbelievably awful in its primitive arrangements and its dirt. The food was abundant and of good quality, and the host was more than kind. To make us feel more at home and more secure, exuberant young warriors during the whole night at intervals flashed past the hotel on horseback, firing shots as they galloped! And towering high and white in the risen moon, like a stern but indulgent father, was Kasbec of the everlasting snows.

On the morrow morning we took a trip to the Russian frontier to pay our respects to the Bolshevik guards and to give some of our friends the satisfaction of saying they had set foot in Russia in defiance of Lenin and Trotsky. There the poor fellows stood, in frayed uniforms with the red star in front of their peaked caps, looking dull and lonely and tired. They were very pleased to see us, and our cigarettes and chocolates gave them great satisfaction. "Poor devils!" said a sympathetic delegate. "They must have an awful time in this lonely, God-forsaken spot." No attempt was made to engage them in argument nor to weaken in any way their adherence to their Government, but one young fellow volunteered to us in excellent French as we parted: "Nous ne sommes pas communistes; mobilisées!"

Perhaps in some respects the most amazing reception we received was at Koutäis, the ancient capital of Georgia. Literally the whole city turned out to receive us. Masses of people assembled outside the station. Beautiful white-frocked children, with wreaths in their hair, lined the road from the railway cars to the carriages, throwing flowers in our paths. The streets were lined half a dozen deep for the mile and a half to the public park where the great demonstration was held. Here there was an enormous concourse, and we had a great time with these happy folk.

Börjom is perhaps the most beautiful of all the cities of Georgia. It is in the very heart of the mountains and is famous for its mineral springs. The surrounding country suggests Switzerland, with this difference, that for nine months of the year there is a warm and sunny climate and a profusion of sub-tropical fruits of the greatest variety. As we wound through the woods and climbed the great hills on the mountain railway we felt a regret that Georgia and its beauties are not better known and more accessible to European and American travellers after health and pleasure. Otherwise it could not fail to attract thousands of people content with lesser beauties at a greater cost.

At a place called Ikan, about three versts from Börjom, is the palace of the Grand Duke Michael Nicolaivich, whose ancient and impeccable servitors, long-bearded and profound, ministered to our needs during the whole of a long summer's night. Of this I have already written.

The port of Poti we saw through a flood of rain which filled the streets with miniature lakes and roused to malignancy a veritable plague of mosquitoes. These vile insects made the hours in Poti a time of intolerable torture; but the ladies of Poti were most kind in their ministrations, and made matters as easy as they could. In an immense church which had not then been consecrated, reminiscent in size and austerity of St. Paul's Cathedral, we held a meeting, beginning in the early afternoon and continuing until the light had faded and the fitful gleam of torches lit up the faces of the speakers to ten thousand eager, patient, curious spectators of a dozen nationalities—Turks, Armenians, Jews, Tartars, Russians and native Georgians; Christians and Mussulmans; soldiers and peasants; princes and workmen; women with and without veils, little children on their mothers' laps, all congregated to see and hear the strangers from the unknown lands of the West.

Our practice was to travel all night and speak and visit during the day. Sometimes we did not leave the train but spoke to the people from the steps of the railway carriage. Sometimes the platform was placed in a field adjoining the railway station, to save the time of the delegation. Often carriages were in waiting to take us into the larger towns, where we were shown the more important of the civic institutions. Frequently we spoke four, five, six, or seven times in one day. I think the minimum number of speeches was four. And always there were bouquets of flowers and baskets of fruit as a reward. The Georgians are indeed "given to hospitality" of the most generous sort.

Amongst the interesting experiences they gave us was a visit to the manganese mines. Georgia has some of the richest deposits of manganese in the world. There are already mined vast quantities of this mineral waiting the restoration in Europe of the amenities of trade and travel for shipment abroad. In the case of this important industry the principle of nationalization has not been adopted. A heavy percentage on profits is paid by the companies to the Government. The managers of the mines are of several nationalities—Belgian, German and English. The Englishman we met appears to be a favourite with the men. The Belgians were less popular.

The German overseer of coal mines with whom we spoke gave the usual impression of very great efficiency, and obviously commanded respect. The rich coal deposits need capital for their adequate working. The two thousand miners to whom I spoke appeared to enjoy the novelty of a woman speaker.

But to say everything that might be said about this gallant little Socialist Republic, or even one-half of what we ourselves saw during our two weeks' visit, is out of the question. The impressions formed need time for their ripening, but on certain matters we formed very clear and definite judgments.

The Republic of Georgia, about the same size as Switzerland and with the same population, is equally beautiful if it is not even more lovely. It has a good soil, very fertile, with useful deposits of valuable minerals and a rich supply of oil. Its industries might be made very productive if modernized and supplied with the necessary capital. Foreign capital is shy, however, since the Russian Revolution. It fears confiscation by even the moderate Socialist Government of Georgia, and is certain of it if Georgia comes to be Bolshevized either by Lenin from the outside or revolutionaries from within.

Georgia needs peace and security for her happiness. There is no immediate prospect of either. From the Turks on one side and the Bolsheviks all round she is in constant danger.

I had the very strongest impression when in Georgia that the population was overwhelmingly against Bolshevism, and that their support of the Social Democrats was founded on the love of the peasants for the land and the fear of the bourgeoisie and aristocracy that a worse fate might befall them. I believe it to be true of Georgia, as of other countries whose ancient orders have been overthrown, that the vicious terms of the various Peace Treaties have united all classes in support of a party which has not failed in government because it has never been tried, and which stands for the national existence against a world of foes combined. In other words, there is a thick streak of nationalism running through every Socialist Movement of Europe, not excepting the Russian, whose chief leaders only, and not the rank and file to any extent, are believers in that anti-nationalism they falsely parade before the world as internationalism. Surely there can be no internationalism unless there are nations out of which to make it.

Since the writing of the above I have received this letter from Paris. President Jordania is there, in exile. He writes in French, but I have translated the letter:

Paris,
April 9th, 1921.

Dear Madam:

I enclose the manifesto signed by my comrades and myself and addressed to all the Socialist parties and workers' organizations. You will find in it in detail the latest events in Georgia. This exact document gives in brief amongst other things, the purpose of our action in Europe: it is to expedite the evacuation of Georgia by the Bolshevik troops.

The war is not yet finished in Georgia, but it has taken a new form: it is no longer the Republican army which desperately resists the invaders, it is the whole country which fights against the armies of occupation as it has formerly fought against the power of the Czar.

The issue of this conflict depends very largely upon the attitude of the workers of the world. Each voice of protest raised against the invaders of Georgia strengthens the power of resistance of the Georgian democracy and quickens the day of its deliverance.

In thanking you warmly for all you have done for the cause of Georgia I count upon your support, dear madam, in this new campaign.

Socialist greetings,
N. Jordania.

Madame Snowden,
London.

It is a thousand pities that the enclosed manifesto, signed by the Minister for Foreign Affairs, M. Gueguetchkori, the President of the Constituent Assembly, M. Tcheidze, and the Minister of the Interior, M.

Ramichvili, in addition to President Jordania, cannot be reproduced in full, for it is interesting and valuable history; but in the fears for Georgia already expressed I had foreshadowed only what has unhappily come to pass.

The substance of the document can be given in a few words. It begins by pointing out the importance of Georgia in Bolshevik policy in the Orient and of the desire in Moscow to accomplish its conversion to Bolshevism. For a long time it was hoped to do this by subsidized propaganda from the inside. In spite of a wealth of money poured into the country, this plan failed. Then came an attempt to do so by force. This also failed. A Russo-Georgian Treaty secured the recognition of Georgian independence by Russia on May 7, 1920. In November of the same year Trotsky, speaking to the assembled secretaries of the Communist Party, declared: "The establishment of the Soviet in Armenia is the end of Georgia." The Russian General Hocker was asked to present a report on the number of soldiers and equipment required for the conquering of Georgia. This was in December. The general pointed out that it could be done only with the co-operation of Angora; but from this moment began the massing of Bolshevik troops on the Georgian frontier, notwithstanding the vigorous protests of the Georgian Foreign Minister. Although it had been clear for long that the Russians meant to attack Georgia, they sought to find some excuse that would satisfy exterior public opinion by discovering a quarrel between Georgia and Armenia over some disputed territory. Part of the Bolshevik army attacked from the Armenian side, Armenia having been compulsorily Sovietized also in the interests of Bolshevik policy in the East. This enterprise was undertaken at the very time when M. Chavordoff, the Armenian Bolshevik, declared his willingness to negotiate with Georgia the disputed districts. Another section of the Russian army began to close in from the side of Azerbaijan. Instructions were sent to the Bolshevik representative in Tiflis to join his agitation to the efforts of the army in the hope of counter-revolution within. Tiflis was occupied after valiant resistance. The Turkish Kemalists, assisted by Bolsheviks, attacked and captured Batoum. The whole country was given over to its enemies, who cared nothing for treaties when something crossed their path.

Since all this, a treaty between the Turks and the Russians has been signed at Moscow, in which the Bolsheviks are recognized as the masters of Georgia. The Kemalists renounce their aspirations after Batoum, receiving for themselves the two disputed districts of Middle Georgia, Artvin, and Ardahan, and a part of the province of Batoum.

Georgian National Anthem

Georgian National Anthem

Lenin is making a great effort to reconcile the people of Georgia. He has urged his representatives in Georgia to find a way of reconciliation and a common platform with President Jordania and his friends. But so far the Georgian people have shown no sign of going over to the enemy and forsaking their old leaders and elected representatives. And Jordania, an exile, writes from Paris.

As I write my mind travels first to Russia and the dying population of Petrograd, then to the merry Georgian peasants with their cakes and honey in the fields on the way from Kasbec, and finally to the unforgettable national song which poured from a thousand throats when patriot-soldiers swore to defend their country's liberties with their blood, like the loving sons of every land.

CHAPTER XIV
HOME THROUGH THE BALKANS

After a very happy two weeks in Georgia, we left for the homeward trip. The special train brought us to Batoum overnight. The day we spent in wandering about the city's bazaars. Everything was ridiculously cheap for those possessed of English money, though for some curious reason which I never explored the Turks and Armenians whose shops we visited were forbidden to accept English pounds. Some did accept them on the guarantee of our guide, an English-speaking Georgian, that no evil would come to them as a consequence. We bought astrakhan caps, Russian boots, silver-mounted daggers, drinking-cups, silver chains, furs, and jewelled belts for a mere trifle. In one shop there was a magnificent set of ermine skins for £70 which would have sold for ten times the money in England or America had any one of us had enough business instinct to buy. Persian and Turkish carpets were selling for a mere song!

The British Delegation of three kept together during this promenade. There is no reason for making a special note of this fact except this—that each of us can testify to the falsity of a Reuter's report circulated throughout England at a later date that Mr. Ramsay Macdonald was mobbed in the streets of Batoum by a number of Bolsheviks! Mr. Macdonald was one of our party. We saw no Bolsheviks in Batoum. And the only semblance of a crowd was when, in a Turkish quarter, the unveiled Englishwoman showed herself in the shortest dress that had been seen in that quarter since the last batch of American women passed that way! The Turkish women go black veiled still, generally by their own choice, and their dresses almost touch the ground.

Before the steamer sailed M. Marquet and I drove along the sea-front to inspect the tents we imagined we saw from a distance, bordering the coast. They were not tents in the regular sense, but rude shelters improvised with poles and tattered garments, which sheltered the most miserable and squalid mass of wild-eyed human beings it has been my lot to see. It was said they were Greek refugees who had fled the approach of the Nationalist Turks. A pro-Bolshevik critic of the Georgians censured them severely for not having provided for these unfortunates; but when huge masses of people suddenly hurl themselves upon a community out of nowhere, organization is not simple, especially when means are limited. The condition of some of the German prisoners' camps in England in the early days of the war was very far from perfect; but the suddenness of the contingency, no less then the proportions of the problem, offered a reasonable explanation of the unsatisfactoriness of things.

The steamer which took us back to Constantinople brought Herr Kautsky and his wife to Georgia. Kautsky had been detained in Rome with fever for two weeks.

We had a perfect voyage to Constantinople. The sea was as smooth as a mill-pond, and a heavenly moon lighted our path across the waves at night. At Trebizond several of the party went on shore and braved the questionings of the Turko-Bolshevik Governor; but they saw nothing for their pains but a bazaar which was very much inferior to those of Constantinople.

We spent two days in Constantinople waiting for the transcontinental express. During those days I talked with several people who claim to speak authoritatively about affairs in Turkey, and checked my impressions of the earlier visit. Lunch at the British Military Mission and an interview with a Turkish prince of the blood rounded off an experience of the city and its problems, too brief to justify the record of anything more serious than general impressions, liable to be modified upon closer acquaintance.

And perhaps the clearest impression of all that I received was that of the disinterestedness of the British Government in Turkish affairs. France and Italy were clearly up to the eyes in intrigue for positions of commercial and industrial advantage in Turkey. With this in view they were manifestly encouraging in his defiance Mustapha Kemal Pasha, even whilst they were conspiring to perpetrate the Treaty of Sevres. Greece likewise was adopting the insolent attitude of the conqueror, more galling to the Turks than the domination of any other foe. Upon the Commission instituted to govern the affairs of Turkey in general and Constantinople in particular, England glanced with wary eye at the deeds of her colleagues, France, Italy, and Greece. It might be urged that England has quite enough to do with her own vast territories and enormous responsibilities without adding to the burden by taking more than a nominal interest in the development of Turkey. Against such a view the men on the spot protest with indignation. There is a land of inestimable fruitfulness. It lies on the route of valuable British possessions. It is possessed by a race holding high repute amongst the peoples of that part of the world which is not averse to England. Widely advertised Armenian massacres ought not to be permitted to blind the untravelled to the fact that the Turk is regarded very highly by most people who know him well.

His faults of cruelty and corruption he shares with all Eastern peoples. His virtues of cleanliness, sobriety, and (in the country) honesty and industry mark him out for peculiar admiration. I have to confess that I met nobody who expressed dislike of the Turk. I met everywhere people who spoke with contempt of the Greek and the Armenian.

"Tell me," I said to a British officer in Constantinople, "why does everybody hate the Armenians? I do not myself know any of these people; but I can find nobody with a good word to say for them. I have just heard one educated man declare that the only thing to do with the Armenians is to massacre them."

"It is certainly true," he replied. "There is a saying in this part of the world that it takes two Jews to make a Greek, two Greeks to make a Levantine, and two Levantines to make an Armenian. Perhaps that explains it."

"You mean that they are notorious beyond all words for commercial dishonesty and extortionate dealing? But is that all? That is very bad, of course; but does it explain all the bitter hate?"

"I don't know; but I don't believe for a moment that it is purely a hatred of Christianity. The Turks are a warlike race. They hate the pacifism of races like the Jews and the Armenians. To them it is effeminate weakness. They despise the drunkenness of Christian tribes. They are abstainers by religion. And the plundering of the peasants by Christian extortioners has done more to set the Crescent against the Cross than any preaching of Christian doctrine could have done by itself."

"I am proposing to return to this part of the world to visit Armenia in the spring, unless the Bolsheviks from Angora capture it between now and then."

"Well, good luck to you!" said the young Englishman. "Nothing would tempt me to go. Please remember that if half the Armenians reported to have been massacred had really died, there would not have been any Armenians left to visit!"

The Bolsheviks have captured Armenia, and the Allies do nothing to help. Therein the Armenians have a real grievance. Their really marvellous propaganda had secured them the sympathy of the whole Western world. They had received distinct or tacit promises from the Allies and the League of Nations. But neither the one nor the other has done anything to save them from their frightful fate at the hands of Russian Bolsheviks and Kemalist Turks.

Prince S——, the nephew of Abdul Hamid, is a cultured Turkish gentleman of the very first order. His beautiful little daughter was educated in England. She speaks perfect English, her father admirable French. Over the Turkish coffee, thickly sweet and delicious, we discussed the future of Turkey. I had met the prince and his daughter first in Switzerland, at Caux, overlooking the Montreux end of the Lake of Geneva. The Castle of Chillon, and mountains of Savoy on the French side make a picture of extraordinary beauty. Then, as in Constantinople, he spoke warmly of England. I have seldom met a foreigner who had a higher opinion of England and English institutions. In Turkish matters the prince appears to stand half-way between the Turkish Nationalists and the representatives of the old order. He looks for the day of an independent Turkey, self-governing and governing with intelligence; but he appears to think that day has not yet arrived. Before that, there should be universal education for Turkey, free and progressive. The rich, natural soil of agricultural Turkey should be subject to intensive cultivation on modern scientific lines. Land should be made available for all would-be cultivators; estates limited in size, but not alienated from the owners by the State.

Till the day of its emancipation arrives this patriot prince would have for Turkey the assistance of England. It was obvious to the least interested amongst us that Constantinople suffered atrociously from the divided authority of the Allies. Who were their masters—French, Italian, British, or Greek—the wretched Turks really did not know. Each set of nationals in authority got into the others' way. There were general suspicions and dislikes. Could the prince have had his way, Turkey would have been ruled jointly by Turks and British until education in responsibility had gradually but surely fitted the Turks to be absolute masters in their own house.

This amiable cultured Turkish gentleman admitted the awful atrocities committed by the Turkish Government in the past against the Armenians, and regretted them. His secretary and not himself spoke of equally fearful cruelties practised upon the Turks by Armenians—the same dreadful game of reprisals with which a mad world appears to be anxious to destroy itself.

A marked feature of the British personnel in Turkey is the extreme youth of most of its members. Those who do not take themselves and their work very seriously do not suffer. Those who are conscientious and have their country's interests really at heart suffer acutely, not only through the physical strain of getting things done against indifferent officialism in a country of unequalled opportunities and matchless interest, but from the mental pain which is born of seeing great opportunities passed by, or seized by wiser people in the interests of nations other than England.

There is a new-born Socialist Movement in Constantinople—at least, it calls itself Socialist. It came into being as the result of a successful tram strike. As a matter of fact it is really a Trade Union Movement. It has little knowledge of the economics of Marx. Its leader would be described as a Radical in England. I have the same view about the Socialist Movement that Prince S—— has about the Nationalist Movement—that a period of education would be a valuable and is, indeed, a necessary precedent to the agitation for Socialist government, even municipal government.

When we boarded the train in Constantinople it was intensely hot. Within an hour of leaving it blew so cold that the women of our party were constrained to put on their furs. For two days the intense cold lasted. Not until we had passed over the bleak moor and forest lands of Bulgaria, reminiscent of certain parts of Scotland, did we begin to feel anew the warmth of autumn days. Milder Serbia warmed our blood, and we ventured to make an excursion into Belgrade, where the express rested for four hours. Tired of train food, we betook ourselves in a party to the Hôtel Moscou and enjoyed a first-rate supper amongst the joyous Serbs.

I hope to see Belgrade by day in order to revise my opinion of the city. As it is, I have the poorest opinion of it. Its streets are paved with cobble-stones and are full of shell-holes which would hold the proverbial horse and cart! In the pitch black of the night—for the streets were either badly lighted or not lit at all—we were constantly tumbling into the smaller of these unspeakable holes or twisting our ankles on the round cobble-stones. One required the feet of a mountain goat to maintain oneself erect in such abominable thoroughfares.

But a pleasing experience superseded the unpleasant memory of Belgrade streets. I had been given a letter to post to Budapest by a lady in Constantinople, who feared it might be opened if posted in that city. I had given a solemn promise that this should be done. To venture into those Belgrade streets alone was impossible. I had to wait until my fellow-delegates had done feasting. Time passed, and still they ate and ate. Soon it would be impossible. The train was due to leave in a little while. I waited. The eating went on. I rose to go alone. M. Marquet's kind French heart was touched. He went with me. We wandered over half Belgrade before we found the post office, and when we found it it was closed! We walked to the back of the premises, and there were two young men packing letters into bags. In a mixture of French, English, and German we contrived to make them understand we wanted a stamp. One of them, smiling broadly, took out his pocket-book and produced the necessary article, sticking it on to the letter himself, which he then pushed into his bag. We laid down a substantial coin. But with a graceful bow and a fine smile he declined payment. We shook hands cordially and parted, the travellers with a happier estimate of Belgrade than its stones had supplied!

If one can in any real measure judge a country's state from the railway train, Serbia and the highlands of Jugo-Slavia are enjoying considerable prosperity. At the time we passed through the country the same abundance of produce was everywhere visible as in Belgium. In addition, the little pigs for which Serbia is renowned were numberless. They ran all over the lines at the railway stations and clustered in herds round every cottage door. The neat, bright comfort of the mountain farms of the Tyrol made a very profound impression, and were a real joy to those of us who were on the look out for as much happiness and prosperity as we could discover in a world torn with sorrow.

A rush round the city of Trieste, a long wait in the railway station in Venice on account of a serious railway accident just ahead, a peep at Milan, a glimpse at Lausanne, and we were on the last stage of our long journey to Paris. The journey had been fairly comfortable with the exception of the last day. There was no water for washing in our carriage. I mean by "our carriage" the one in which the English delegates were. We gave mighty tips, but the attendant would not be comforted and refused to get us more water! He protested savagely at the amount of water the English people used. He complained of the number of times we thought it necessary to wash ourselves. We were thoroughly in disfavour. We bore the discomfort and the feeling of not looking our best till we got to Paris. There came relief, cleanliness and good coffee. Twelve more hours and we should see the home faces once more and recount our adventures to interested friends.

Every one of us vowed we would not go abroad again for a very long while. Every one of us has broken that pledge. It must be so. The human spirit, once having escaped from the circumscribing atmosphere of native city or even country, will never more be content to be environed perpetually by so much less than it has known. It must go out again and again to the scenes and the people it has known in other lands, or break its wings against the bars of its cage, imprisoned in the infinitely small and narrow. Let all who can travel, for the broadening of their minds, the widening of their outlook, the strengthening of their sympathies. And let those who cannot travel read, so that they may know what the men and women of other lands are thinking and feeling, and may co-operate with them in the shaping of brighter and better things for mankind.

CHAPTER XV
THE DISTRESSFUL COUNTRY

Late one evening I was returning home from a Fabian lecture when a tall, middle-aged man, with slightly wavy hair and a pair of merry blue eyes, accosted me. He carried under his arm a large and rather untidy brown-paper parcel, which looked as though it might contain groceries and gave him the appearance of the middle-class father of a family. His voice was soft and pleasant, his accent unmistakably Irish.

"Pardon me, madam, but are you an Irishwoman?" he asked interestedly.

"No," I replied. "I was born in Yorkshire. But why do you ask?"

"Forgive me, but your voice carries a long way, and I could not help hearing a part of your conversation with the lady who left you at Hampstead. You were talking about Ireland. Your voice and the kind things you said about Ireland made me think you might be an Irishwoman."

"No," I said again; "I am not Irish, but I am going to Ireland to-morrow."

"Ah!" he said, drawing a deep breath. "And why are you going to Ireland at a time like this? Surely not for pleasure?"

"No, indeed; there can be no pleasure in Ireland for anybody with a spark of human feeling. I am going to Ireland to try to discover the truth, if that is possible."

"You are a newspaper woman, then?" was the next query. I made no further answer, feeling that the conversation with a perfect stranger, albeit a courteous and sympathetic one, had gone on long enough, when he began to speak with added warmth both of speech and manner.

"Ah! you English people, you do not understand, you never will understand Ireland. In your imagination you have peopled our island with devils and conceive it to be your duty to exterminate the plague. 'The dirty Irish' is the way you think about us. Hunting down Irishmen is by some Englishmen regarded as legitimate sport. I am a native of Cork. I am not a Sinn Feiner. I do not want to see Ireland cut loose from the Empire. And I deplore as much as anybody the murders on both sides. But I understand my countrymen. I doubt if you do. I very much doubt if you can. The differences are too great. But whosoever goes to Ireland without clearly realizing that the English and the Irish are two distinct and separate nations will fail to understand the things he sees and hears when he gets there. I am constantly hearing talk on this side about the possibility of Ireland making terms with Germany, becoming even a German province if she secures self-government." Here his voice became louder and his manner more excited than ever; the newspaper he was holding dropped from his hand and fluttered away in the wind. "Surely if such people understood the racial differences between English and Irish they would realize that the same applies, though in a much greater degree, to the German and Irish?"

"Believe me," I said, holding out my hand, "there are many people in this country who do understand and who labour continuously to create understanding in others. They yearn to bring about peace between the two countries. Between peoples who speak the same language war is a crime. I am going to Ireland to get more knowledge about her, to talk to her people directly. And when I return I shall join the band of workers for peace and reconciliation."

He raised his hat, renewed his apologies for detaining me, and disappeared. Under the gas lamp I caught a glimpse of tears on his lashes — tears of a strong man for Ireland, his native land, a suffering thing he cannot help.

The Labour Party's delegation to Ireland had not included a woman. Several members of the Women's International League, and a few Quaker women on errands of mercy, had visited the country. This was some time before the Labour Party had decided upon an official visit. The secretary of the party had received from an Irishwoman a letter imploring him to include a woman amongst his investigators, but it was not thought wise to do this by the men on account of the danger and inconvenience. When one of the executive proposed my name as one of the delegates Mr. Henderson, with the most paternal solicitude, suggested that the Executive Committee ought not to take upon itself the responsibility of running any woman into such real danger as existed for travellers in general and investigators in particular in Ireland at that time. So the proposal fell to the ground.

No such objection was raised when the delegation to Russia was appointed. On the contrary, Mr. Henderson strongly pressed me to go to Russia. I cannot imagine that the concern of this genuinely kind-hearted man for the safety for his women colleagues was in abeyance on that occasion. Mr. Henderson had been to Russia and suffered considerable danger himself. I can only conclude that this serious-minded colleague of mine believed the danger to be greater in Ireland under British rule than in

Russia under the rule of the Bolsheviks! I agreed to go to Russia with some reluctance on my own account. Not because of any fear of going. Atrocity stories and wild tales of epidemics had no terrors for me. But the time of the proposed Russian visit was inopportune. I had received invitations to go to Poland, Spain, and Hungary. Preparations for the journey to Madrid had already been made and had to be cancelled.

But there were no obstacles to the Irish visit. I wanted to go. Irishwomen wanted me to go. I received one pressing letter after another. The Labour Party's objection was laughed to scorn. I must say the idea that women who have lived more summers than they care to confess cannot be allowed to take the responsibility for their own lives, but must be a burden and a charge, whether they like it or not, on the consciences of their men comrades is in these days vastly amusing; particularly to the women of the Labour Movement, whose conception of progress is of equality of effort, of danger, of suffering, and of reward for men and women.

None the less, I understood and valued at its very real worth the altogether gracious and kindly thought which lay at the root of the action of the Labour Executive.

It was impossible to resist the pleading of Irishwomen that as many women as could do so should go over there and see with their own eyes what the women and children of Ireland are called upon to endure.

On Saturday, January 15, 1921, I left Euston for Holyhead, alone, and without having in any way advertised my intention. I landed in Dublin in the evening and proceeded to friends in one of the suburbs. We drove from the station in a jaunting-car. In such a fashion did I get my first glimpse of Dublin under what the majority of Irishmen consider to be foreign occupation. Westland Row Station, as well as Kingstown Harbour, was full of soldiers and police. Passengers coming off the boat were heavily scrutinized. We were closely examined in the train. In the streets and public places of all sorts in every town I visited during the ten days of my visit, even in country villages and lanes, the atmosphere was tense with the expectation of the sudden assault, the quick firing of rifles, the rough arrest, the climbing of military lorries on to the footpaths, the humiliating search, the heart-breaking insult. Women and men alike feared these things. Here was an equality of treatment which nobody objected to so far as Irishwomen were concerned, least of all the Republican women themselves, who would think shame of themselves if they were unwilling to suffer what their men are called upon to endure. But the pity of it! Little children are often victims. Boys and girls have been shot dead.

On this night the streets of Dublin were lively with the clatter of armoured cars and lorry loads of singing soldiers not too sober. Occasionally a distant shot was heard. Now and then a side-car packed with merry little dare-devils flaunting their green flag provocatively for the sheer fun of the thing would rattle past. One trembled for the ignorant folly of madcap youth.

My host, who is one of the best-known and most highly respected citizens of Dublin, did everything in his power to bring me into touch with every shade of Irish opinion, so that I might judge of things for myself without bias or pressure from outside. I never was in any country where there were fewer attempts to make proselytes. He himself is a Quaker, and has a long record of devoted service to his country and to the less fortunate of his fellow-citizens to his credit, which inspired confidence and respect. His beautiful wife and lovely children gave me a warm Irish welcome, and, although an Englishwoman and, therefore, a justifiable object of suspicion, I was never permitted for a moment to feel myself an intruder.

From Saturday night till Tuesday morning the hours were packed with incident. I think it would have been difficult for anybody to see more people and hear more tales of woe than it was my lot to see and hear during these ten days in Ireland. Amongst my new acquaintances were Republicans of all sorts, Nationalist Home Rulers, Unionists, Labour Party officials, Trade Unionists, Quakers, humble citizens with no particular political affiliations, Catholic priests and Protestant ministers boys and girls from the country "on the run" in the city, newspaper men, writers of books and pamphlets, British officers, lawyers by the dozen, ex-soldiers, high-born ladies, the widows of men executed in the rebellion of 1916, suffragettes, women doctors, temperance folk, members of the Irish Republican Army, commercial travellers, and men and women suspected of being British agents and spies. I should like to disclose the names of all these interesting persons. In most cases I have full authority to do so. But when that permission is coupled with a declaration that they do not care two pins about the consequences to themselves, I am involved in too great a responsibility to be reckless in a matter where human life and liberty are so manifestly involved.

But because I believe even the present British Government, more profligate of its power than any Government of modern times in this country, would scarcely dare to mishandle a man so great in the esteem, not only of Ireland but of the whole world of culture, I feel I may write freely of that towering personality, Mr. G. W. Russell ("Æ"), whom I met several times in Dublin, always to my great spiritual profit.

Picture a face and figure not unlike those of William Morris in the prime of his life, with a tenderness joined to his strength which I imagine was less conspicuous in the English poet. Masses of wavy hair tossed back but occasionally falling over a fine square forehead, a full mouth, glorious eyes full of humour and gentleness, a soft musical voice; the frame of a Viking, the heart of a saint, the imagination of a poet, the vision of a prophet; a man to whom children would run with their troubles, whom women would trust unflinchingly, whom men would serve with utter loyalty; the embodiment of the real Ireland, the Ireland that is not known in England—this is the man whose devoted, lifelong work for the salvation of Ireland is being wantonly and savagely annihilated by British troops.

Mr. Russell spoke without a trace of bitterness, though I know he suffers keenly, when he told me of the destruction of Irish creameries and of the difficulties which co-operative enterprise is meeting with in every part of Ireland. He edits the *Irish Homestead*, and there he has voiced the complaints of Irish co-operators in language of the greatest beauty; but to hear him tell the story himself was a pleasure fraught with pain to his English auditor.

"It cannot be that the system of reprisals has become an integral part of the British nation's scheme of justice?" he asked, as we sat talking by the fire in the house of a friend. "It would be too terrible to think that that were true."

"The British people do not know all that is happening here," I replied. "Oh, I know they ought to. Enough has been said and written about it. The ignorance of affairs outside the little circle of their own interests of the average man and woman makes me almost despair of democracy at times. But there is this explanation of the inactivity of the British public about Irish matters. In the first place, very many people know nothing. Those who do read that part of their daily paper which is not devoted to the sporting news or the Divorce Court proceedings read a partial tale. The news is generally coloured in favour of Dublin Castle and the Black and Tans. I cannot believe that British co-operators would be content to tolerate the things which are being done to Irish co-operative enterprises if they knew the facts."

I was given a tiny yellow book containing the facts which I promised to help circulate in England. It is an amazing story. The statements would have appeared incredible to me had I not seen with my own eyes the blackened walls and twisted machinery of the gutted creameries in several parts of Ireland. Forty-two attacks by the Crown forces on these village and country town institutions had been made up to the time of my conversation with "Æ." In these attacks the factories were burned down, the machinery destroyed, the stores looted, the employés beaten and sometimes wounded and killed.

Questioned in Parliament, the Government has excused itself by declaring that the creameries were centres of propaganda and of Sinn

Fein activity. They alleged that in two cases shots were fired at the troops from the buildings. The most searching inquiries by responsible people, including Sir Horace Plunkett, failed to produce any evidence in support of the charges of the Government. But Mr. Russell is not concerned about the result of these inquiries. He wants a Government inquiry into the whole of the circumstances connected with this particularly lamentable form of reprisal, and this inquiry is steadily denied. Why?

Travellers in Ireland to-day see all over the country these new ruins, centres of village industry and culture utterly wrecked, and the peasant farmers and their families driven back to their lonely farms to live in poverty and isolation; driven back to feed not only upon their own scant produce but upon the black passions of hate and individualism from which the co-operative idea had begun so successfully to rescue them.

"Surely the English workmen begin to realize the connexion between our problem and theirs," said another distinguished co-operator. "If our economic life continues to be so seriously disturbed, or if it be destroyed, we cannot buy from England as we have been doing. Do you know that, with the single exception of India, Ireland is the best customer that England possesses within the British Empire?" The political views of this cultured gentleman are distinctly non-Republican, yet his house is not safe from the official intruder, and he is tormented hourly with the sense of outrage and injustice which the destruction of his life's labours must necessarily produce.

"To us it would be simply unbelievable but for the other follies we have seen perpetrated by your statesmen, that any Government with the least knowledge of the world-situation could willingly add to its dangers and difficulties. Yet I cannot believe that the members of the British Government are all ignorant and stupid." This third speaker was a man who had served with distinction in the British Army during the war. But the droop of his figure, the gloom in his eye, the bitter curl of his lips—everything about him spoke of a confidence lost and a faith killed.

"Two millions of adult people in Great Britain either wholly or partially unemployed; wives and children beginning to hunger; industrial strife on a scale hitherto unimagined clouding the horizon; men by the million trained to kill, ready to be used by one side or the other in a class war; hate and violence the fruit of it all, and appalling suffering for all classes before one side recognizes the right of the workers to an assured and abundant life and the other side realizes that Russia's way is not the way even for Russia. All this and more—and yet the British Government actually or tacitly encourages the troops to add Irish tens of thousands to the British millions of workless, starving, hating men and women, and is slowly but surely converting the only revolution in history which makes a point of preserving the rights of private property into something which will be akin to a class war for a Communist republic—an issue which I should deeply deplore."

I am bound to confess that I discovered no substantial evidence that the civil war in Ireland has either a Communist basis or a Communist ideal. The utter conservatism of the Irish is the most striking thing about them. Their determination to win self-government is based almost entirely upon that conservatism, the love of the Ireland of history, the passion for the Irish tongue, the devotion to the ancient faith, their love of the soil—these things and the memory of a thousand wrongs put upon them by the alien conqueror have much more to do with Irish discontent than any desire to hold the land in common and convert the industries from private to public ownership and control; which ideas would, indeed, be repugnant to the last degree to the peasant owners of the South and West of Ireland.

Speaking on this point with some of the workingmen leaders I asked how far, in their opinion, the Communist propaganda had captured the Irish workers. "Scarcely at all," was the quick reply. "There was fearful anger over the cruel death of Connolly. His execution did a great deal to unite the Labour Movement in Ireland with the Republican Party. It was the sheer brutality of it. The poor fellow hadn't more than forty-eight hours to live. He had been shot in the scrimmage in Dublin, and gangrene had set in. Yet they dragged him out of his bed groaning with pain, put him on a chair and shot him—the brutes! They think it's all in the day's work to shoot a 'dirty Irishman.' But our people will never forget Connolly and the way he died. No; the Irish workers are not Communists. They just hate England and want to be quit of her.

"Ay, and there's the case of Kevin Barry while you're on about the killing. Do you know they tortured that poor lad to get him to tell the names of his comrades? We have his affidavit. They bruised his flesh and twisted his limbs and then they hanged him—hanged him, mind you, when the poor lad begged that he might be shot as a prisoner of war! Your Prime Minister calls it war when he wants to excuse the murders of his own hired assassins. But if so, our men are prisoners of war when they are captured. Who ever heard of a civilized nation hanging prisoners of war? But praise be to God, every time you hang a boy like Kevin Barry you make hundreds of soldiers for the Republican Army. Eighteen hundred men in Dublin joined up the day Kevin was hanged."

The little man who thus broke in began to fill with tobacco the bowl of his small black pipe, and when he had lit it he turned on me, fiercely demanding: "Why have you come to Ireland now? Why didn't you come before? Why don't more of you come? How many thousands of our brave boys have got to be killed before you folks find out what your bloody troops are doing to Irish men, women, and children?" And he flung himself out of the room.

I felt sorry to have appeared indifferent for so long, and said so to the rest of the assembled company. "But to tell you the truth, I have lived all these years under the impression that Irish men and women preferred to win their own battles in their own way; that they regarded rather as an intrusion any effort of English people to help and advise them. From the first hour of my political life I have been a supporter of self-government for Ireland; but I never dreamt that you wanted me, or any of the rest of us, to come to Ireland to say so. I believed that you wanted to work out your own salvation."

"So far as *advice* is concerned you were right," said a young fellow with a large freckled face and fine eyes. "I reckon the English can't teach us much about politics."

"I'm not so sure," I said very softly. "After all, you have not got what you have been fighting for during more than a hundred years, and you have not got rid of the oppression that has tormented you for several hundreds of years. Perhaps it is possible that co-operation might have done it. We can all teach each other something. Ireland has glorious lessons for us English. Perhaps you could have learnt a little of something from us."

There was a long pause, and I continued: "It is of the first importance to carry the plain matter-of-fact people of England with you. Ordinary men and women in England have a strong sense of justice, but their imagination is weak. They find it difficult to understand what they do not endure themselves. They find it hard to believe in the wounds unless they can lay their fingers on the prints. You must admit that some of the things which are happening in Ireland are almost incredible. One thing which makes it difficult to open and keep open the minds of English people on the subject of Ireland's wrongs is what they regard as Ireland's wrongdoing, the killing of soldiers and police. Of course, a certain section of the newspaper press exploits this to the last degree. Why do you do it? Why use the methods so hateful in the others? Why put an argument in the mouths of the enemy? Why soil and stain a good cause?"

"Because we are at war," was the prompt reply. "You have just heard that your Prime Minister says so. He justifies the methods of the Government because it is war. We do not like killing people; but can we be expected to sit quietly whilst our own men and women are killed and their property looted? It isn't in human nature. Would Englishmen sit quiet under such provocation? We don't like it. And, remember, we don't kill innocent people like the other side. Every person executed by the Irish—executed, mark you, not murdered—is tried by the Republican Courts and found guilty on substantial evidence of traitorous conduct or brutal murder." He folded up the copy of the *Irish Bulletin* he had been reading, and then proceeded: "I'm glad you came over. I wish others would come. I'm sure you'll help Ireland. Tell your people that if it's war they want, war they will get till every young man in Ireland is dead. Then they can begin with the old men and the women—they've begun with the women—and after that they'll have to wait till the children grow up. But they'll find them every bit as keen as their fathers. It's in the blood of us. There are only two ways to peace, and God knows we want peace. You can either give Ireland her freedom, or you can sink the whole country in the sea. It's the peace of the dead you'll get if you won't have that of the living."

It is only fair to say that nine out of every ten of the Republicans to whom I spoke expressed sorrow and regret that the policy of violence had been adopted instead of that of passive resistance.

"But now that the fighting has been begun it is very difficult to stop it without laying ourselves open to the charge that we are weakening, or without giving the British Government the opportunity of saying that its policy of reprisals has succeeded. The very thought of these things is hateful to the sons and daughters of a brave fighting race." The distinguished old lady who said this drew herself up as she spoke with the dignity of a queen and flashed swords and daggers from her fine proud eyes.

Her house had been searched twice by Crown forces. They did some small damage to doors and windows, nothing serious, for she is a woman of property and social position, an outstanding example of the thing I found to be true, that the severity of the reprisals, the ruthlessness of the visitations, the length and discomforts of the imprisonments were generally in proportion to the means or in accordance with the religious beliefs of the suspects. Age and sex did not count.

During an official reprisal which I witnessed in Cork, the blowing-up of two excellent shops in one of the main thoroughfares, when armed troops kept the crowd moving, and armoured cars, fully manned, kept the roads, I heard an old woman tremblingly ask a good-natured Tommy carelessly swinging his rifle as he moved people along the pavement, what the matter was. "We're only going to send all you bloody Catholics to hell," was the cheerful reply.

To refer once more to the searchings of private houses and shops: I investigated three cases, the one to which I have referred, the house of the old lady and her secretary, and two others, both shops. The usual practice is to knock loudly and demand admittance, but to give no time for anyone to run to the door, which is frequently burst open. Sometimes shots are fired into the passage as a precaution, killing or wounding perchance the man who is descending the stairs to answer the summons, which often comes in the middle of the night. A soldier stands guard over each member of the family. If the house be big enough each is placed in a separate room. If it be small they are turned into the streets and guarded there. A rigorous search is made, beds stripped, mattresses sometimes bayoneted, drawers opened and their contents tossed out, pictures pulled off the walls, letters opened and read, cupboards emptied—the whole house turned topsy-turvy. A shop is usually looted of half its contents. Recently, in the attempt to restore discipline, the householder has been requested to sign a paper stating that the soldiers left all in order and stole nothing. But no opportunity of checking is allowed, and the dazed and frightened woman (it is generally a woman, for the men are "on the run") signs quickly, and would sign anything to get the soldiers and police out of the house and her terrified children into their beds.

In the case of the little sweet and tobacco shop the whole family, including two young children and an old woman, were turned into the street at midnight and made to stand there in the pouring rain for two hours. The gentle young Irish mother with the soft voice and seductive Irish drawl told me the story.

"It was me brother they wanted. He's in the arrmy. But it's weeks since Oi saw the face av him. Oi couldn't tell thim where he was, but they wouldn't belave me. It nearly broke me heart to see thim poke thurr bayonets thru the pickshure av the Blessed Virgin. An' all the swates was trampled on the flure. The bits av tobaccy wint into the pockets av the crathurs. An' the pore children was gittin' thurr deaths av cold in the rain outside. An' now the pore lambs will nut slape widout a light over thurr beds in the noight furr the fear av the cruel men that is on them. An' what have Oi done but keep moi house an' pay moi way like an honest woman? Shure," she said, with a droll look and a twinkle, "if Oi knew whurr moi brother was, would Oi be tellin' the soldiers? Oi would not, indade. Wolfe Tone is the name av him. An' wouldn't they be afther shootin' at sight a man wid a name loike that?"

The Irish sense of humour never forsakes them even in their deepest distress. Mrs. A. Stopford Green, the widow of the great historian and herself an historian of merit, told me of a Catholic priest who had his home invaded and sacked. Standing amongst the wreckage of his little home, he exclaimed, between tears and smiles: "Glory be to God! They've taken everything they could lay their hands on. But there's one thing they haven't taken, because they can't take it, and that is—the laugh!"

I came to one house in order to have an interview with a young Irish patriot who is "on the run." He came secretly and at great risk to himself. He was cheerful and jolly; but, like everybody else in Ireland, he showed clear signs of strain and of an imminent breakdown. Eight times his premises had been searched, and each time valuable things had been stolen. Even whilst we talked a telegram from a friend arrived to say that the night before they had raided him again and taken away a pair of much-prized army boots.

A splendid type of cultivated and idealistic young manhood, he was hunted hourly from pillar to post on suspicion of ill-doing; but his life's work had been humanitarian, designed by the slow but sure methods of education and co-operation to win the suspicious and illiterate peasant from his bondage to ignorance and intolerance.

He had been tried once and acquitted. He and his friend had been lodged in the guard-room. There was a struggle, and bombs, and the dead and mutilated body of his friend was carried out. The story was set about that the two of them had thrown the bombs at the troops. The bombs were lying loose in the guard-room. Nobody believed a story so thin. The pacific reputation of the two men was well known. Everybody asked why live bombs were left lying about in such a place. Were they put there to furnish an excuse for premeditated crime? Some believed this. Nothing is clear. In the subsequent inquiry before a Military Court composed of young and ignorant officers with a natural prepossession in favour of their profession and caste, it was denied that Clun's body was mutilated. But a reliable witness told me that he had counted thirteen bayonet wounds.

The first thing which impressed me about the Sinn Feiners I met was their culture, then their courage, finally their spirituality. I speak now of those I met in the city—probably two hundred. Many of them would have been shot at sight if they had been seen coming out of their hiding-places to meet me. At the moment of writing more than one of those with whom I talked lies in a dark and dismal prison cell, notably Desmond Fitzgerald, head of the Republican Propaganda Department.

What amazed me continually was the entire absence of bitterness in the speech of most of these people. Bitterness they must have felt, and yet so sure are they of the goodness of their cause and of its ultimate triumph, that they can talk with calmness and even humour of the tragic events of which so many of them are the central figures.

"They say in England that this is first and foremost and all the time a religious quarrel; that the domination of Irish politics by the Pope is to be greatly feared if Ireland gets self-government. What have you to say to that?" I asked the handsome youth whose effective propaganda has filtered through to every country in Europe. It is one of the important facts of the present situation that the conduct of England towards Ireland is breeding a cynical contempt for England throughout the world.

"I have to say of the first statement that it is not true, and of the question that the fear is groundless. The Irish priests have tried in vain to stop the ambush. They have denounced it from their pulpits. But they have protested in vain. This defiance is the symbol of a conviction that the place of the priest is at the altar. When he leaves that to meddle with matters which are not his concern, he is thrust aside. I am myself a devout Catholic. But I would not tolerate for a moment the interference of the priest with my politics. Young Ireland will not. Our movement is spiritual, deeply spiritual. But with the methods by which we shall, under God, win this battle with our foes neither priest nor pacifist must interfere."

Subsequent experience confirmed the impression that this is true; that the power of the priest in politics, if it ever seriously existed in Ireland, is rapidly on the wane. True also I found was the loathing of the priests for murder. I talked with several in different parts of the country. "Murder is murder by whomsoever committed," was the invariable comment on the killing by both sides.

CHAPTER XVI
MORE ABOUT IRELAND

It is, of course, as difficult as most such things to measure, but in the course of my travels and talks, I received the impression that there is less of religious intolerance amongst the Catholics than amongst the Protestants; at any rate in the South. The faith of the minority there appears to be treated with greater respect than the faith of the minority in Ulster. I came across numerous instances in the country between Dublin and Cork of a violent distaste for the provocative behaviour of bigoted religionists.

I spoke with a Tipperary man about the cruel treatment in the Belfast shipyards of the Catholic workmen by the Protestants. It will be remembered that the decline in shipbuilding necessitated a reduction in the staff in the shipyards, and that Catholic workmen were selected to be the victims of the labour depression, and were driven with violence from the yards. It was told me that they were forced into the sea and stoned as they struggled to regain the land.

"Serves them roight," said this Catholic workman of Tipperary unperturbed, "they be always trailin' thurr coats."

This good-natured fellow had had a brother killed in an ambush. He had lost his work through the firing of the shop where he worked. He had his own and his brother's family to maintain—"orr Oi would be wid the bhoys on the mountains, I would." He came to the hotel where I was staying to say that some unknown person had stopped him and asked him for the name of the lady to whom he was speaking.

"It's wan av thurr dhirty sphies afther ye. I just told him ye was me half-cousin, Mary Ann Watson, av Manchester, and ye'd called to see the pore childer an yurr way to Dublin. So now ye'd better be afther takin' yurr tickut for Corrk, forr Oi'm thinkin' the crathur isn't believin' me at all."

I had gone to Tipperary for a sentimental reason. Hundreds of thousands of gallant young Britons had marched out to meet the foreign foe, cheering one another and their own sad hearts with the refrain: "It's a long, long way to Tipperary." This song has become for all time associated with the British Army. On several social occasions in foreign lands I have asked the orchestra for an English song; or knowing my nationality the orchestra has volunteered the compliment. It was invariably "Tipperary." The very sound of it calls up visions of healthy, sturdy young British manhood marching out in its millions to engage its lives and fortunes in what it believed to be the most righteous war that ever was waged. Surely, I thought, if any place in Ireland should be sacred to Englishmen and to the memory of the 250,000 Irishmen who enlisted in England's battles, it should be Tipperary. But what did I see in Tipperary?

The whole of the principal street of this little market town was blackened and disfigured with burnt and burning buildings. A magnificent stone-fronted draper's shop was completely gutted. Such shops as remained were shuttered, for a murdered policeman was to be brought through the town for burial later in the day, and the authorities were afraid of a demonstration. The streets were full of "Black and Tans," the name derived from the nondescript clothing which these military police wear, black coats and khaki trousers, blue trousers and khaki coats, Scotch bonnets, and blue helmets—a mixture of garments as varied as their wearers' breeding. Officers on horseback dashed about furiously. Numerous groups of idle men lolled against the walls, regarding the ruins of their town with philosophy and curious about the stranger within their gates. Was she an English spy? was the query in their glances. Is she a Republican agent? the eye of the soldier on duty at the street-corner questioned. It was an awkward situation. I had no papers with me, nothing to identify me with one party or the other. And it was a lawless time.

One hundred and twenty-seven buildings in Tipperary (whether town or county was not quite clear) had been deliberately destroyed by fire. The damage was estimated by a lawyer in the district at £300,000. A girl had been taken to the barracks the day before, and not allowed any female attendance. A young draper's assistant had been bayoneted to death in the guard-room a little while previously. "Shot trying to escape," was the report from the authorities on a Tipperary lad brought into the barracks dead. But the wound was in the forehead, and men trying to escape do not usually run backwards.

The young women of the town rarely undress when they go to bed, so fearful are they of a midnight entry and search. The Irish girl has a delicacy all her own in matters of this sort. The nerves of the children are fearfully affected, and many of them scream in the dark. Ruin, misery, desolation and death in Tipperary—"It's a long, long way to Tipperary, but my heart's right there."

It was not very easy to go about Ireland's more remote districts. One day I walked for several miles into the country alone. On the way back I passed a country school. Through the open window came the sound of singing. Sweet children's voices sang of spring and the nightingale—an English nursery song. I stopped to listen. There followed two verses of "Men of Harlech," "The Bluebells of Scotland," was the next item on the programme. I waited for the Irish song. It never came. A face appeared at the window, a face with the strained look of every Irish eye. The first song was begun again. I walked away slowly, full of pity. The young voices shrilled forth:

"The awkward owl and the bashful jay
Wished each other a very good day,
Tra la la."

Within a hundred yards of this school, full of bright young creatures and their sad-eyed teacher, the smoke was still rising from a burning homestead, and the smell of scorched timber spoilt the freshness of the air.

A curious adventure befell me on this occasion. I sat on a low wall covered with moss. There had been a heavy shower of rain, and the country was very green and lovely. The sombre hills in the distance were relieved by the intense blue of the sky and white of the clouds. The long white lane wound coaxingly to the west calling for new adventures. Nobody passed me for full twenty minutes. There was much to think about: the stupid blunders of politicians and the many injustices of life. I was content to sit alone and muse on things in that loveliest bit of countryside. Suddenly the roar of a motor engine broke upon the stillness, and there flashed past me a large military lorry full of troops with grim faces and poised rifles. Ten seconds and they were gone; and I too rose to go. At my elbow, as if sprung out of the ground, was an old man who had come silently up during my musings.

"You are a stranger here, lady, and not an Irishwoman, and if you will take advice from an old man you will never sit on a wall in an Irish country lane. Not now, at any rate. I know a man who did that. He was found dead in the lane. He was picked off by a crack British rifleman who shot at the target from a distance to win a bet. Oh, it was an accident," he added hastily, noting my horrified expression. "It was not known that the chosen target was a human being. It might have been anything at a distance, a young tree, a large stone—anything. What happened once might happen again. And in that red cloak of yours what an excellent target you would be. You take great risks in Ireland during the foreign occupation. Good day to you, ma'am."

One day, having succeeded in hiring a car, I drove to some of the more remote farms in the hills I had seen and admired from the side of the road where I talked with the old man. The youth who drove me was a member of the Republican Army, but a discreet and quiet boy, who would not be drawn into conversation. We sped for an hour and a half along a bad road in a high wind. It was bitterly cold, but fine and sunny. We stopped at the cottage of an old widow to ask for some information, but she lived in hourly terror of the barracks two miles away, and would tell us nothing. On we went till we came to a farm at the crest of the hill standing back a little from the high road.

It was a poor farm, one of the poorest in the district. The farmer was a strong, thick-set type, not very easy to persuade to tell his story. His wife was a pale, delicate woman without the words to express all she felt and knew. Her ordinary speech was Irish. We sat down in the kitchen, and the wife worked the bellows till a bright blaze burst from the soft coal piled up on the old-fashioned huge hearthstone. The water in the large potato cauldron began to steam, and the tiny potatoes cooking for the pigs to stir in the pot. Three dogs of different breeds invited the stranger to caress them. A couple of cats lay curled up on the kitchen table. A white hen roosted on the top of a sack of grain, and chickens walked up and down the floor. An immense sow peeped in at the door just for friendliness, and turned away when she had satisfied her curiosity.

"It was midnight," began the farmer, "and the wife and Oi wurr in bed. All av a sudden a bullet flew through the window. Thin Oi knew that the Black and Tans was here. They broke in the door an' asked furr moi lads. The bhoys was slapin' in the barrn. They ran away, but they was caught, an' the soldiers made them kneel in the yard wid thurr hands above thurr heads whoile they surrched the house. They found nothin' at all. Thin they told the lads to run. They ran out av the gate an' the dirty blackguards shot at thim. But they got away, all but wan. He was shot in the arrm and leg, an' he's lyin' in the hospital now. We found him in the turnup field the next mornin' bleeding bad; for it was foive hours he was lying thurr before we found him, the pore lad." He spoke quietly and without emotion, but there was a gleam in his eye that spoke volumes of hate and fury. Later in the day I went to the hospital and saw the wounded son, a beautiful, modest boy with the sort of open face that invites perfect trust. He told me he neither smokes nor drinks, and passed the cigarettes I brought him to his comrades.

"It is the rule of the Republican Army," added the gentle Catholic sister who was nursing these wounded boys, "that no alcohol must be taken. Would to heaven it were the rule of the British Army too. But they tell me that Dublin Castle gives drink freely to the men it sends out upon its black errands." She stopped suddenly, and busied herself with one of her patients in some confusion for fear she had said too much. It reminded me of a pathetic school teacher in Petrograd who told me things about herself, thinking I was sympathetic, and then became overwhelmed with fear lest she had made a mistake and revealed her secrets to a Bolshevik spy. "You will not give me away, dear madame? I have said nothing wrong, have I? Only that we are all very hungry and very unhappy? Say you will not report what I have said. Swear it! Swear it!" And she pressed my hand in her fear of what might befall her till I could have shouted with pain.

The old peasant wife begged me to take tea, but there was much to do that day, so I begged to be excused, and drove away to a small farm still more remote from the broad highway. This farm was reached through two ploughed fields. In it lived an elderly farmer, his wife and daughter. I knocked loudly at the door, but there was no reply. I knocked again and again, but nobody appeared. A dog barked loudly, suggesting human habitation, so I persisted, and after a while the farmer appeared and roughly demanded my business. I told him who I was and what my errand—to hear his story and make it known.

"And what forr should Oi tell ye my sthory," he demanded fiercely. "Don't ye know, don't the people av England know that it was the English Crown that killed my bhoy? Don't the English people know widout my tellin' thim what thurr soldiers are doin' to Oireland? Av course they know; but they don't care. Oi'll not tell ye wan worrd av the tale."

His daughter came in, a buxom dark-haired girl, whose face was black with the smoke from the peat fire, and we two listened for ten minutes to the most terrible outpouring of hate and rage against England that it has ever been my lot to hear. I sat perfectly still, but the torrent of passionate words brought from an inner room the farmer's white-haired old wife, who greeted me with the grace of a queen and tried to stem the torrent of the old man's rage. "I understand, dear friend," I said to the old woman, "I understand. If I had lost a child in such a way I should probably have said much worse things than this, being a woman."

The old man's blue eyes softened a little at this, and after I had tried to make him understand that it was no idle curiosity that had brought me from England to his lonely farm, he said brokenly: "Well, ma'am, ye seem to have a koind heart, an' if it's really wantin' to help sthop this koind av thing ye're afther Oi'll thry to tell ye." And he tried. But he failed. He broke into awful weeping instead. And when she saw her old man broken down the old wife fell a-weeping too, and there was such a wailing and a sobbing in that little farm kitchen as almost drew the heart out of the body. I took the frail old woman in my arms and tried to soothe her. I begged her to cry on my shoulder. She said she couldn't cry, hadn't cried since they brought the boy home dead. Her eyes were wild and burning. Between dry sobs and moans I got the tale.

The men had come in the night, the same men who had shot the lad at the farm below, and the same night, and demanded the whereabouts of one of the sons. Neither man nor wife knew. They had not seen the boy for weeks. They pushed the old farmer against the wall and threatened to kill him if he didn't tell. A young and delicate boy, never allowed out at nights because of his lungs, hearing the noise and the scuffle dressed quickly and rushed into the room crying: "Don't shoot my old dad. Shoot me."

"Ah," said one of the intruders, "here's our man. I knew they had him somewhere."

"No," said another. "He's not the chap. It's his brother we're after."

"Never mind," was the retort. "This one will do." And they dragged him across the field to the waiting lorry and there they shot him dead. "Trying to escape," was the official story; but it was not true, and nobody believes it. If in Ireland you speak of this excuse in any company there are shouts of ironic laughter.

"And it was to save his father my poor bhoy went wid the murthering men," said the poor mother; "an' for that they shot him, the black-hearted scoundrels; an' no priest wid him wan he died. But if there's a God in 'ivin me pore bhoy will go straight to his arms, forr niver a word av wrong could be said against the lad. He was the best son Oi had, an' a good bhoy to his father."

A small black cross on the side of the road and the letters R.I.P. mark the spot where the young martyr was killed.

I left the farm sick with the sight of so much pain and sorrow. The old man accompanied me to the gate, choosing the path for me and offering his aid over the bad places with all the instinctive courtesy of his race. His eye lit up when he heard that "the President" had arrived in Ireland. He idealized De Valera with all the power of his native imagination. He told how, for miles around, men, women and little children were afraid to sleep in their beds at night, but took to the fields and hills, and slept in blankets under the hedges. The wind whistled past me as he spoke, and the rain began to fall, and I pulled my cloak more tightly around me, for I heard with the mind's ear small children in the night sobbing themselves to sleep under the dank hedgerows.

I had planned to visit other sufferers, but farther I could not go. The human spirit bruises itself to death in the perpetual contemplation at close quarters of misery and wrong, and relief in action becomes necessary for sanity. I would go to Cork and see the sacked city, and then return to England with the story of it all.

The train drew into Cork station an hour late, only twenty minutes before the hour of curfew. The jarvey who drove me to the hotel was determined that I should have a swift view of the ruins; or was it a laudable desire to earn more money made him take me by a circuitous route? It did not matter. I was glad of the view. And the ruins were softened by the moonlight into a poetry of aspect which the charred walls of daylight could never display. The whole of the town's business centre appeared to have been destroyed. It stood out in my mind as comparable with some of the newspaper pictures of Ypres after the great battle. Of course, there was nothing like the same amount of devastation; but the ruin of the particular section which met the eye on entering the city's centre was complete and very appalling.

The first thing I did at the hotel was to ask for the headquarters of the Society of Friends. My friend, Miss Edith Ellis, was doing relief work in the city, and I had mislaid her address. The Friends would know it. I also inquired for Mrs. Despard, for I had seen a picture of her in that day's newspaper standing in the ruins with Madame McBride, the beautiful widow of Major McBride, who was executed in the 1916 rebellion. I was told Mrs. Despard had left for Mallow two days before. This was disappointing. A tall evil-looking man leaning up against the hotel bureau scrutinized everybody who came into the hotel, and gave the impression of being there for that purpose. I have seen so many "Intelligence" men that I know them as well as I know a Lancashire weaver, a Yorkshire miner, or a school teacher from anywhere.

I asked if it were possible to have something to eat at that hour, for there was an ominous emptiness in the dining-room. This was 8.45 p.m.

"I hope, ma'am, that ye'll be comfortable here," said a kindly waiter. "I heard ye asking after Mrs. Despard. I hope ye'll have a better time than the pore lady herself had."

"Why, whatever was the matter with her?" I asked, with interest and alarm.

"Nothing was the matter wid Mrs. Despard, lady; but the pore lady was niver foive minutes widout somebody followin' her about, though she doesn't know ut."

"Mrs. Despard wouldn't be troubled about that. She is a gallant soul, and her only concern is the care of the poor and the oppressed. She is an Irishwoman, you know, and a true friend of your country."

"Indade an' she is, ma'am, an' if it's her friend ye are, ye'll be wishin' nothin' but good to the counthry too. But be vurry careful or wan side or the other'll be shootin' ye. The blood is up in Corrk."

There was much laughing and screaming in the streets outside, and my side-car had wormed its way through vast crowds of saunterers in the splendid moonlit evening. The hour for curfew struck, and in an instant an uncanny silence fell upon the city. Indoors, affected by the quiet outside, men crept about softly, or sought their beds early, afraid almost of the sudden and general noiselessness. The only sounds that were heard till the dawn of day were those of the racing lorries full of armed men and the armoured cars patrolling the city. Round the bend of Patrick Street they came, noisy and aggressive, to arrest or shoot at sight the unfortunate individual caught walking the streets after the hour of nine. On the second night a new sound struck upon the ear, cutting the perfect silence with its shrillness, the loud laughing and screaming of coarse women's voices, which suggested unspeakable things.

Apart from seeing the official reprisal to which reference has already been made and the awful ruins of the city, which included the Carnegie Library and the City Hall on the opposite side of the river, the short visit to Cork was fruitful of the conviction that the unhappy citizens of Cork are placed on the horns of a very terrible dilemma. General Strickland has made them responsible for the outrages on soldiers and police which are committed. He inflicts severe penalties on them for failing to stop them. This they would endeavour to do, but they do not know how and they are genuinely afraid to attempt. They believe that the shooting of police is done by people who do not live in Cork. As in all cities the citizens of Cork are for the most part not actively interested in politics. They vote when occasion comes, but this is the limit of their activity. And voting and not shooting is their chosen method of expressing their views. They do not know who shoots. If they did and informed they would be shot by the Republicans. As they don't know and cannot inform they are made to suffer reprisals by the British authorities. Their position calls for the utmost sympathy and understanding.

I cannot help feeling that the citizens of Cork who are against violence would be greatly strengthened if the findings in the official inquiry on the Cork burnings could be published and adequate punishment administered to the evildoers. This has not been done. British justice in Ireland is not evenhanded. Somebody is being sheltered. The Black and Tans would mutiny. The authorities themselves organized the looting. All sorts of things are being said, all sorts of things believed. The belief in British fair play is gone. Can it really be after all that we are living on our tradition in this matter as are the French on their reputation for good manners?

Back to Dublin from Cork and a final meeting with my good friends there. It was a splendid company, representative of the brilliant wit and intellect for which Ireland is so justly famed. I was going home, so it was entirely proper that these last hours should be devoted to question and answer on both sides.

I spoke again of the difficulty of winning and maintaining sympathy for Ireland in England so long as the killing of British soldiers continued. All deplored the necessity, but those who believed that the method could now be changed were in a small minority.

"Ask Englishmen who complain two questions," said a distinguished professor, whose name is known wherever scholarship is respected. "Who began it, and how they would behave in the same circumstances."

"Forgive the question," I said, "but who do you really think did begin it?"

"The Republicans certainly did not," said a young lawyer rather hotly. "I am not a Republican, but one must face facts. For two years after the killing of Irish civilians by British Crown forces no member of the forces lost his life. In the meantime unspeakable humiliations were put upon the Irish people. The miscreants who killed two Irish civilians in 1917 and five in 1918 were never brought to trial. No steps were taken to bring them to trial. In the meantime innocent men on the Irish side were arrested and imprisoned without trial; private houses were raided and their contents stolen, meetings and newspapers were violently suppressed, and deportations were very frequent. In 1918 alone 1,117 Irish men and women were arrested for political reasons; 77 Sinn Feiners were deported in one month; 260 private houses were raided by night, and 81 meetings were broken up with bayonets.

"The bottom fact of the whole trouble lies in this: The British Government is uneven in its administration of justice, and it breaks its pledges. It hangs the Casements and puts the Carsons in the Cabinet. What essential difference was there in their offences? The death of a British soldier or policeman is bitterly avenged even upon the innocent and out of all proportion to the crime. The death of a Republican is applauded, and that of a non-partisan is rarely even inquired into. Have you seen the kind of thing which is published and circulated broadcast with the approval of the authorities?" Here he handed to me a paper, an extract from which I quote. It was delivered to the Cork newspaper offices:—

Anti-Sinn Fein Society,
Cork Headquarters,
Grand P*arade, Cork.*

"In the event of a member of His Majesty's Forces being wounded or an attempt made to wound him, one member of the Sinn Fein Party will be killed; or if a member of the Sinn Fein Party is not available two sympathisers will be killed.

"(Signed) The Assistant Secretary."

"And you must agree," said a third speaker, "that Ireland has been very badly tricked by your Government. Witness the Convention and the use that was made of it to impose conscription upon Ireland; the conscription of a country which has been reviled by Englishmen for years, and which it was proposed even then to partition—conscription which was by very many disapproved of for England, accepted with extreme reluctance by Canada and rejected by Australia."

I recalled at this stage of the proceedings the humorous hall-porter at one of the hotels who had put his head round the corner of the writing-room when I was alone there and whispered: "John Redmond's the man who made all the trouble. He wasn't clever enough for your Lloyd George. Why the divil didn't he get the promise in writin'. There's no wrigglin' out av somethin' that's in black and white, wid a good strong name at the end av the paper. Shure," he continued with a roguish smile broadening his honest red face, "isn't it the Kingdom av 'Ivin Oi'd be afther promisin' if Oi was the Proime Minister an thurr was throuble brewin'?"

I am sure this must have been the man who tried to persuade one of the Labour delegates not to go into the street when the Black and Tans were busy shooting. "But I'm an Englishman, friend. They'll not shoot me."

"Shure, sorr, an' I wouldn't be trustin' thim divils. They'll shoot ye first, and thin find out ye're an Englishman afterwards."

"What about the rebellion of 1916? Talk to me a little about that," I said to a young fellow whose keenness was very attractive.

"It was a very small rising of extremists, a piece of insanity repudiated by nearly everybody in Ireland. A group of idealists, who believed they could imitate the Ulster Unionists and enjoy the same immunity, thought they would make a similar demonstration. The hideous severity with which the rebels were treated and the long-continued persecution of perfectly innocent people suspected of sympathy with the rebels were the causes of the rise of political Sinn Fein."

"And now?" I asked. "What is the exact situation now? What are the hopes for peace?"

"There is no hope unless the English people wake up, change this Government and Parliament for one more competent and humane, which will adopt a saner policy, the one for which they say they fought the war. Ireland must have the right to choose her own form of government."

"The Irish have chosen their government, and it is working very well," chimed in a determined-looking young woman wearing the uniform of the Irish Republican Army. "All we ask is to be let alone. We can keep order if the English will let us. *They* cannot do so."

I thought as these stern criticisms of England's Government stormed my ears, often expressed in stronger language than I have used here, that it is no use going into the enemy's country if one cannot stand fire. The person who has no facility for getting into the skin of another had better stay at home by his own fireside. The rôle of political pilgrim is not for him.

"The fact is there are two Governments in Ireland: the Republican Government representing roughly 75 per cent. of the population, and the British Government representing the remaining 25 per cent. The will of the majority should prevail in these democratic days. England says not. Very well. If we must die to establish the rights of democracy in Ireland we are ready."

"And we will fight and die with our men!" exclaimed a hitherto silent member of the company. She turned to me. "Do you know that the hate of England is so intense in my part of the country that a woman told me she scarcely knew how to bear the disgrace of having had a son who fought for England in the war? And the neighbours are so sorry for her they are breaking her heart with kindness and pity."

"There is an old man lives near here," said my hostess, "who is dying. He has eight children, and his wife is delicate. He is tortured with the fear of what will become of them when he goes. The priest came to administer the sacrament: 'I will get the boy a place in the munitions,' he said, speaking of the eldest son. 'He will help his mother.'

"'Thank you very kindly, Father. You mean it well, and you are very kind. But it cannot be. We are not of that way of thinking.'"

There was a long silence after this story. Memory took me back to the scene in London when the Irish Labour leaders came to explain their cause and solicit our co-operation. "You may remain indifferent or even refuse to help us," said Mr. Johnson, their spokesman. "Your Government may torture our women and kill our men by the thousand, but you will never break our spirit." It was a proud boast, but the reason was a revelation. "You will never defeat us, for we Irish have a *living faith in God.*"

I believe this to be profoundly true; and he will misread the Irish situation and misunderstand Irish men and women who fails to look beyond the picture drawn by partisan newspapers for their own ends to the vision in the souls of those to whom God and country are real and noble passions.

"But will you take nothing less than complete separation?" I pleaded.

"On grounds of economy, for reasons of efficiency, for our common safety, is not national self-government within the Commonwealth a happier issue for us all?"

"Ourselves alone," was murmured round the room; but from the general smile I felt a lighter heart.

"Give us the right to choose, free and unfettered, and — wait and see."

It is the least they can claim or that the British Government can give in its own interests as well as those of the Irish. It would be an act of faith such as few Governments in history have shown themselves capable of performing; but there are national and international situations where only a supreme act of faith will suffice.

And this is one of those.

CONCLUSION

And the fruits of these wanderings abroad are—what?

For two hours I sat in the old-world garden of an English manor house pondering the answer to that question. Old-fashioned and variegated flowers in every colour of the rainbow massed themselves around the moss-covered rocks, climbed the walls, and peeped out of the crevices and corners, throwing out strong, sweet scents of the wallflower and the jasmine. The shadow on the sundial crept slowly round its withered face. Tall elm trees sheltered the noisy crows. A bold cuckoo competed with the lark for our attention and regard. A typical English scene, suggestive of peace and plenty; so entirely different from any scene in the torn and stricken lands of Europe.

The twofold character of my work abroad has been told in these pages. The physical relief of suffering goes on through the American Relief agencies, the Society of Friends and the Save the Children Fund. The utmost that can be done is but a drop in the bucket of Europe's overwhelming needs. It is only the first dressing of wounds, which cannot be cured except by probing to the cause and clearing away the poison. This is not the business of philanthropy when the cause is political. An exaggerated sympathy, which is the very essence of charitable enterprise, could even hinder the work of political and economic recovery by an uninformed emphasis of the patient's suffering and a forgetfulness of his guilt. A stable internationalism can be built only upon a universal recognition of partnership in the guilt which has laid the world so low. But in such internationalism lies the hope of the future.

I returned from my travels reinforced a thousand-fold in the conviction of the necessity of internationalism if the world is to be saved; with this in addition, that the present problem for mankind is not to persuade the world to internationalism. It is rather to teach it the right kind of internationalism. Internationalism of one sort or another is as inevitable as the rising of the sun. The League of Nations is the second embodiment of an idea which held great masses of men and women before even the first, the Workers' International, was born. This idea can be safely trusted to persist and grow in spite of every menace, because it is in the direct line of political and economic evolution. It is the next inevitable step in the march of ordered progress.

In the realms of art, science, invention, commerce, industry, economics and finance nationalism is languishing towards its inevitable decay—if it is not already dead. Political internationalism is destined to crown the structure of the world society of the future as surely as the night follows the day.

But what kind of political internationalism is it to be? That is the question. Heaven forbid that it should be the anti-nationalism of Lenin, wrongly called internationalism, which will prevail over the earth. That would be to menace too alarmingly the truly valuable differences amongst men. The characteristic differences of nations should be, with very great reluctance and only for sufficient reason, sought to be obliterated. The variety in dress, manners, customs, speech of the various races and nations is the very spice of the world's life which gives it all its flavours. Difficulties of language, so fruitful of the misunderstandings which create wars, should be overcome by the provision of larger educational opportunities rather than by the establishment of one universal tongue. Esperanto is a wise and simple device to facilitate discussion between men and nations; but the compulsory study of French, German and English in the elementary schools would be of greater value to mankind than a knowledge of the most useful of languages manufactured for a purpose, and not born of a living nation's intellectual and spiritual growth. A knowledge of languages would add a richness and beauty to life which might well give place to the boasted utilitarianism of most British curricula.

But although Lenin's anti-nationalism is to be avoided like the plague, the militarist internationalism of a capitalist order of society should be shunned like the pestilence. The new "Balance of Power" would then be the balance of classes, the possessors in every country leagued against the possessed in every land. Victory would go to that side which controlled the fighting material. All the disorders of the old system would afflict the new, with the added terror which increased efficiency would produce.

To save the new international organization, the League of Nations, from such an evolution, is enlightened Labour's best reason for giving its support to the League. It is Labour's business to see that the organization of the League is on thoroughly democratic lines; that it admits at no distant date every country within its fold, and that the broad matters of its discussions be not conducted in secrecy nor its broad lines of policy be adopted without the knowledge and consent of the peoples of the world themselves.

And for the Workers' International, I know of no line of policy which they could adopt more advantageous to themselves than that of educating the public opinions of the various countries included therein to compel their respective Governments to disarm. The rationality of total disarmament has always been seriously questioned by those who have passed for wise. But *total disarmament by all the nations* is the only rational solution of the problems of peace and war. Such action may have to be gradual; it must certainly be taken in concert. But if the responsible statesmen of all lands would together lead the van and, scorning vested and professional interests, would declare for the ploughshare and the pruning-hook instead of the sword and the spear, the hosts of mankind would joyfully follow them in such a holy crusade.

It may be that men and women will have to wade through oceans of suffering before they recognize modern warfare for the organized filthiness it is. There was a certain personal dignity in physical strife when men met with bare hands, or with a stick or even a single sword, the human foe equally equipped. But the modern machine-gun, the tank, the poison gas, the fighting aeroplane—all the resources of science used against the innocent and guilty alike—women, old folks and babes—what single element of dignity or decency in such a conflict; honour, democracy, freedom, the pledged word setting the monstrous machine in motion, since men are too good in the mass to fight for anything less than these; and lurking in the shadow, anxious but safe, that insatiable dragon of greed, which for oil-wells and mining interests and timber concessions and goldfields will see millions of men welter in blood and millions of children and their mothers succumb to famine and disease.

Which brings me to my final word. That for the evils which afflict mankind there is no remedy save the elimination of selfishness, which is "the whole of the law and the prophets." Selfishness in the individual, selfishness in the State. When it is universally recognized that every child born is entitled to the "development of all the perfection of which it is capable"; when the equal rights of nations, great and small, are admitted by all the States in Council; when the power of law and not the rule of force is the governing factor in the relations of men and nations, then begins the new era.

On such a foundation only can the true International Order be securely built.

INDEX